THE THING

Towering cliffs of solid ice rose from the canyon they were exploring. They knew it was here. Fear rode the moaning wind on swirling razor-like flakes. On a muffled word from Bennings, Childs activated the nozzle. The tip of the flame-thrower sprang to life. Bennings was scanning the cliff's jagged crevices when something clutched his ankles. He looked down and barely had time to scream as his body was yanked below the surface of the ice. . . .

IT'S BACK.

A TURMAN-FOSTER COMPANY PRODUCTION

JOHN CARPENTER'S

"THE THING"

starring **KURT RUSSELL**

Screenplay by **BILL LANCASTER**

Special Visual Effects by **ALBERT WHITLOCK**

Special make-up Effects by **ROB BOTTIN**

Music by **ENNIO MORRICONE**

Director of Photography **DEAN CUNDEY**

Associate Producer **LARRY FRANCO**

Executive Producer **WILBUR STARK**

Co-Producer **STUART COHEN**

Produced by **DAVID FOSTER & LAWRENCE TURMAN**

Directed by **JOHN CARPENTER**

A UNIVERSAL PICTURE

Based on the story "Who Goes There?"
by JOHN W. CAMPBELL, JR.

THE THING

A Novel by
Alan Dean Foster

Based on a screenplay by
Bill Lancaster

BANTAM BOOKS
TORONTO · NEW YORK · LONDON · SYDNEY

THE THING

A Bantam Book / February 1982
2nd printing . . . . *July 1982*

ISBN 0-553-20477-7

Published simultaneously in the United States and Canada

Bantam Books are published by Bantam Books, Inc. Its trade-
mark, consisting of the words "Bantam Books" and the por-
trayal of a rooster, is Registered in U.S. Patent and Trademark
Office and in other countries. Marca Registrada. Bantam
Books, Inc., 666 Fifth Avenue, New York, New York 10103.

PRINTED IN THE UNITED STATES OF AMERICA

11 10 9 8 7 6 5 4 3 2

For my niece, Shannon,
With a great deal of love,
And so the kids at school will finally believe
you. . . .

THE
THING

1

The worst desert on Earth never gets hot. It boasts no towering sand dunes like the Sahara, no miles and miles of barren gravel as does the Gobi. The winds that torment this empty land make those that sweep over the Rub al Khali seem like spring breezes.

There are no venomous snakes or lizards here because there is nothing for them to poison. A bachelor wolf couldn't make a living on the slopes of its Vinson Massif. Even the insects shun the place. The birds who eke out a precarious life along its shores prefer to swim rather than fly, seeking sustenance from the sea rather than a hostile land. Here live seals that feed on other seals, microscopic krill that support the world's largest mammals. Yet it takes acres to support a single bug.

A mountain named Erebus stands cloaked in permanent ice, but burns with the fires of hell. Elsewhere the land itself lies crushed beneath the solid ice up to three miles thick. In this frozen waste, this gutted skeleton of a continent unlike any other, only one creature stands a chance of surviving through the winters. His name is Man, and like the diving spider he's forced to carry his sustenance on his back.

Sometimes Man imports other things to Antarctica along with his heat and food and shelter that would not have an immediate impact on an impartial observer. Some are benign, such as the desire to study and learn, which drives him down to this empty wasteland in the first place. Others can be more personal and dangerous. Paranoia, fear of open places, extreme loneliness; all can hitch free and unwelcome rides in the minds of the most stable of scientists and technicians.

Usually these feelings stay hidden, locked away behind the need to concentrate on surviving hundred-mile-an-hour winds and eighty-below-zero temperatures.

It takes an extraordinary set of circumstances to

transform paranoia into a necessary instrument for survival.

When the wind blows hard across the surface of Antarctica, the universe is reduced to simpler elements. Sky, land, horizon all cease to exist. Differences die as the world melts into blustery, homogeneous cream.

Out of that swirling, confused whiteness came a sound; the erratic buzzing of a giant bee. It cut through the insistent moan of the wind and it was too close to the ground.

The pilot let out an indecipherable oath as he fought the controls. The helicopter struggled to gain altitude. Whiskers fringed the man's cheeks and chin. His eyes were bloodshot and wild.

He should not have been walking, much less guiding a stubborn craft through wild air. Something unseen was compelling him, driving him. A recent horror. It overrode common sense and rational thought. There was no light of reason in the pilot's eyes. Only murder. Murder and desperation.

His companion was bigger, tending to fat. Normally he lived within the purview of a fine-grain microscope and composed lengthy dissertations on the nature of creatures too small to be seen by the naked eye.

But he was not hunting microbes now. His demeanor was anything but composed. There was nothing of scientific detachment in his voice as he shouted directions to the pilot while staring through a battered pair of Zeiss binoculars. Across his thighs rested a high-powered hunting rifle, the 4X scope mounted on it a clumsy parody of the elegant instruments he usually worked with.

He lowered the lenses and squinted into the blowing snow, then kicked open the door of the chopper and set the restraining brace to keep it open. The pilot growled something and his companion responded by raising the rifle. He checked to make sure there was a shell resting in the chamber. The two men argued madly, like children fighting over a plaything. But there was no note of play in their voices, no innocence in their eyes.

The wind caught the machine, throwing it sideways through the sky. The pilot cursed the weather and struggled to bring his craft back to an even keel.

Ahead and below, a dog turned to snarl at the pursuing helicopter. He was a husky and malamute mix, but still

2

looked as out of place on that cold white surface as any mammal. He turned and jumped forward just as a shell exploded at his heels. The sound of the shot was quickly swallowed by the constant, uncaring wind.

The chopper dipped crazily in the whirlpool of wild air. It continued to fly too close to the ground. An inspector would have recommended revocation of its pilot's license on the spot. The pilot didn't give a damn what anyone watching might think. He didn't care about things like licenses anymore, now his sole concern in life was murder.

A second shot went wild and hit nothing but sky. The pilot slammed a fist into his friend's shoulder and pleaded for better aim.

Panting heavily, the dog topped an icy rise. It found itself confronting an alien outcropping. The sign had been beaten up by the weather but still stood, its foundation imbedded in ice as solid as stone. It shifted only slightly in the wind. It read:

NATIONAL SCIENCE FOUNDATION - OUTPOST #31
UNITED STATIONS OF AMERICA

A blast from the rifle missed both sign and dog alike. The animal pulled itself together and galloped down the opposite slope, half-running, half-falling through the slick snow and compacted ice particles.

The plain, rectangular metal building lay nearly hidden beneath shifting snow, a structural corpse subject to regular winter burial and summer exhumation. Not far from it a tall tower thrust bravely into the wind, multiple guy wires keeping the unavoidable swaying to a minimum. Instruments poked out of its crown at various angles and for various purposes, sampling wind velocity, precipitation (which was rare), pressure, temperature, and a plethora of other meteorological phenomena without parallel anywhere else on Earth.

Lying at varying distances from the central building, which looked like a steel trap in the middle of the compound, were several sheds of varying permanence and composition. The solidity of their construction depended on the importance of their contents. Some were constructed of metal

3

welded or riveted together. Others were makeshifts cobbled together out of slats of corrugated steel, plastic, and scrap lumber. There was no evidence of that mainstay of modern construction, concrete. In the climate of Antarctica concrete quickly turned back into piles of sand and gravel. Wind and ice assaulted each edifice with a fine impartiality.

Walkways made of wooden planks regularly swept clear of blowing snow connected the hodgepodge of buildings, the wood starkly incongruous in a land where the only trees lay long buried and fossilized. Guide ropes stretched in pairs from structure to structure, marking the location of the walkways and singing steady songs to the wind with vocal cords of hemp.

Multicolored pennants snapped at the wind's whim, marking not only walkways and buildings but the often concealed locations of outdoor experiments; color-coding science.

Behind a slanted wind shield that pointed toward the nearby bottom of the world a pair of helicopters squatted idle, their blades rendered heavy and immobile with accumulations of ice, their transparent bubble cockpits turned opaque. A powerful bulldozer sat nearby, its protective tarpaulin flapping in the gale like the wings of a lumbering albatross.

A large red balloon bobbed and ducked at the end of its restraining cord. From the end of the cord hung a small metal box, ready to go wherever the balloon chose to carry it and already beeping efficiently to the automatic recorder safe inside the main building.

Norris held the middle of the line and stared at his watch. He looked something like the glacial outcroppings that occasionally broke the level monotony of the terrain surrounding the outpost. That was appropriate, since his interests were primarily concerned with rocks and the ways in which they moved and what moved below them. He was particularly interested in the black, viscous substance that filled the industrial bloodstream of the modern world. That interest was the principal reason for his presence at the outpost, though he often assisted in general study and research as well, hence his helping with the weather balloon.

He tried not to stay outside any longer than was

necessary. By rights he shouldn't be here at all because of his unstable heart, but his agile brain and repeated requests had overcome the resistance of those who made such assignments.

Bennings was glad of the help. The meteorologist had sent up dozens of red balloons and their beeping passengers by himself, but it was always easier with someone to hold the balloon while you made final adjustments. During his first tour he'd made the mistake of going outside alone in late fall, only to see his balloon soar gracefully off into the sky with its instrument package still sitting on the ground.

Twenty yards from them a much larger man was hunkered over a snowmobile. He'd pushed its shielding tarp aside and used a special plastic pick to chip ice from its flanks. This was necessary to gain access to the machine's guts, which were overdue for a checkup.

Childs had not been one for a long time, though he still knew how to enjoy himself like a youngster. He loved three things: machinery, singing groups who danced as much as they sang (and often better), and a woman far away. He'd grown up in Detroit, so Antarctica didn't seem as bleak and desolate to him as it did to most of the others.

A familiar but unexpected noise, a distant humming, made him turn and look curiously to his left. The fringe of fur lining his jacket hood tickled his mouth and made him spit. The sputum froze instantly.

Norris looked up from his watch and stared curiously in the same direction. So did Bennings, the weather balloon momentarily forgotten. A loud whine was coming rapidly toward them. He frowned, making the ice in his beard crack.

Out of the distant scrim of blowing ice particles came a helicopter. It shouldn't have been out in this kind of weather. It certainly had no business near the outpost, where aerial company wasn't due for months. Once it dipped so low that the landing skids flicked snow from the crest of the little hill it barely cleared.

A man was leaning out of the right side of the transparent cockpit, seemingly without thought for his own safety as the craft dipped and bobbed in the clutching wind. He was firing a rifle at a small, running object. A dog.

Norris looked to his right, and found Childs staring

5

incredulously back toward him. Neither man said anything. There were no words capable of explaining the insanity coming toward them, and no time to voice them if there were.

The complaining copter engine began to subside as its unseen pilot fought to bring it in for a landing. It was going much too fast. The skis bounced once off the hard ice, the force of the impact bending both. It bounced forward again, clearing the racing, dodging dog, which cut sharply to its right to avoid the plunging metal.

A third bounce and it seemed as if the craft would come to a safe halt. But the wind caught it, skewing it dangerously sideways. It flipped over on its side. Norris, Bennings, and Childs all dove for cover, trying to bury themselves in the snow as rotors snapped off like toothpicks. The fragments of steel blade went whizzing through the air in random directions like weapons thrown by some mad Chinese martial arts expert. One *whooed* dangerously close to Norris's head, coming within a yard of decapitating him.

The man with the rifle managed to jump clear and scramble to his feet. He was bleeding from the forehead and limped on one leg as he tried to aim the rifle.

Behind him, sudden warmth temporarily invaded the realm of cold as the fuel tanks ruptured and the copter vomited a fireball into the wind. Above it, an already forgotten red balloon was soaring toward the Ross Ice Shelf.

Norris and Bennings rose cautiously, then started toward the blazing ruin of the helicopter.

Less than a dozen men remained inside the compound. A few had been playing cards. Others were monitoring their respective instrumentation, preparing lunch, or relaxing in their sleeping cubicles. The sound of the exploding chopper shattered the daily routine.

The dog reached Norris and Bennings as they struggled through the snow toward the still flaming wreck. At the same time the copter's sole survivor spotted them and bellowed something in a foreign tongue. He was reloading his weapon as he raved on at them.

The two scientists exchanged a glance. "Recognize any markings?" Norris shouted above the wind.

Bennings shook his head, and yelled toward the bleed-

6

ing survivor. "Hey! What happened? What about your buddy?" He gestured toward the burning craft.

Showing no sign of comprehension the man with the rifle waved angrily at them. He was screaming steadily. Blood was beginning to freeze on his face, blocking one eye.

Norris stopped. The dog stood on its hind legs, pawing Bennings and licking his hand. It was whimpering, sounding confused and afraid.

"Say, boy," the meteorologist began, "what's the matter? Your master is—"

The man from the helicopter raised the hunting rifle and fired at them.

Bennings stumbled backward in shock, the husky going down in a pile with him. Norris stood as frozen as the land under his boots, gaping at the oncoming madman.

"What the fu—?"

The gun roared a second time. The man came stumbling toward them, trying to aim and yelling incomprehensibly. He was seeing, but not clearly. Blood continued to seep into his eyes. Blood, and something more.

Ice and snow flew skyward as one bullet after another whacked into the ground around the two stunned scientists. Another smacked wetly into the dog's hip, sending it spinning. It yelped in pain.

Childs stared at this windswept tableau in disbelief until the gun seemed to swerve in his direction. Then he dove behind the snowmobile's concealing bulk.

A fourth shot struck Bennings. Still gaping dumbly at their crazed assailant, he fell over on his side. Cursing, Norris reached down and got both hands on the shoulders of his friend's parka and began pulling him toward the main building. Trailing blood, the dog fought to crawl along beside them.

The stranger was very close now. The muzzle of his rifle looked as big as a train tunnel. But there was a sudden lull in the shooting.

Raving steadily to himself, the man stopped and frantically struggled to reload his weapon. Shells fell from his jacket pocket into the snow. He fell on them, scrabbling through the white powder and shoving them into the magazine one at a time.

7

Total confusion reigned inside the compound. Its inhabitants were used to coping with hurricane-force winds and abysmal cold, with power failures and short rations. They were not prepared to deal with an assassin.

Several of the men started throwing on outdoor clothing: parkas, down vests, insulated gloves. Their only plan was to get ouside and help Norris and Bennings. A few, mesmerized by the drama taking place out on the ice, simply stared through foggy windows as if blankly watching one of the several camp television sets.

From the recreation room came the sound of triple-paned glass shattering. It took several blows from the gun butt to break through the thick insulating panes. Then the muzzle of the .44 pointed through the sudden gap, steadied by two hands.

Outside, the intruder was gaining on Norris and Bennings. Having finally managed to reload the rifle its owner raised it and took shaky aim. A shot sounded, slightly deeper than any that had gone before. The man's head jerked backward, his rifle firing at a cloud. He dropped to his knees, then fell face down into the snow.

Norris halted his desperate backtracking, his chest pounding. He let go of Bennings's jacket. The meteorologist clutched at his wound and gazed in fascination at their suddenly motionless assailant. The injured dog lay close by, whining in pain. Across the veiled whiteness Childs cautiously rose to peer out over the top of the snowmobile.

Once again the only sound that could be heard was the wail of the constant wind.

Inside the rec room the rumble of confused voices had ceased. Men who'd been in the process of donning parkas stopped closing snaps and fighting zippers. Every eye had shifted from the scene outside to the station manager. Garry flipped open the cylinder of the Magnum and extracted the single spent shell, then closed it tight again, nudged the safety, and slipped the gun back into the holster riding his belt.

The station manager grew aware he was the new focus of attention. Ex-Army, he wore the gun more out of habit than necessity. Sometimes an old habit could prove useful.

"Quit gaping. Fuchs, Palmer, Clark . . ." he gestured

8

toward the outside with his head . . . "you're already half dressed. Do something useful. Get out there and put out that fire."

"Why bother?" Palmer was ever argumentative. He brushed long blond hair away from his face. "There's nothing else out there to burn. I've seen enough crashes to know that pilot didn't have a chance in hell."

"Do it." Garry's tone was curt. "Maybe we'll find something useful in the wreckage."

"Like what?" asked Palmer belligerently.

"Like an explanation. Now move it!" He turned his attention to the youngest man in the room. "Sanders, see if you can find a replacement pane for the window."

"That's Childs's job," came the quick reply. "I run communications, not repair."

"Childs is out there. Hurt, maybe."

"*Mierda del toro,*" Sanders grumbled, but moved out of the room to comply with the order.

The snowblower quickly subdued the flames, but they found no explanations in the seared cockpit of the chopper, and not much of the pilot, either. More of the men's attention was directed back toward the compound and the exterior digital readout, which provided a constant account of the temperature and windchill factor.

Back in the rec room the rest of the men were gathered around the body of the berserk man who'd wielded the indiscriminate rifle. There was a neat hole in the center of his forehead. One or two of the men muttered quietly that Garry might've aimed for something less lethal. Bennings and Norris wouldn't have thought much of such complaints.

Garry was going through the man's pockets, underneath the thick winter coveralls. He came up with a battered black wallet that contained pictures of a woman surrounded by three smiling children, of a house, some folding money, a couple of peculiar credit cards, other personal paraphernalia some of which was recognizable and some of which was not, and most importantly, an official-looking identification card.

Garry studied it. "Norwegian," he announced tersely. "Name's Jan Bolen. Don't ask me how you pronounce it."

Fuchs was standing next to the large relief map of

9

Antarctica that dominated the far wall. He was the youngest member of the crew, excepting Clark and Sanders. Sanders ran telecommunications and Clark ran the dogs, but sometimes Fuchs felt inferior to both of them despite all his advanced learning. This country was kinder to such men than to sensitive assistant biologists.

The body lay across a couple of card tables that had hastily been shoved together. Fuchs was the only one whose attention was on something else.

"Sanae's clear across the continent," he told the station manager. "They couldn't have flown all the way from there in that copter. But they have a base nearby. Recent setup, if I remember the bulletin correctly."

"How far is it?" asked Garry.

Fuchs studied the map, using his thumb to plot against the scale. "I'd guess about eighty kilometers southwest."

Garry didn't try to hide his surprise. "That far? That's a helluva distance to come in a chopper in this weather." Behind him Sanders was carefully fitting the heavy new glass into the gap the station manager had made.

Garry turned his attention to Childs. Norris was seated next to him. Both men had calmed down somewhat since the attack. Childs was still picking ice out of his beard.

"How you doing, Childs?"

The mechanic looked up at him. "Better than Bennings."

Garry grunted, glancing at Norris as he spoke. They all worried about Norris. "You catch anything he was saying out of all that raving?"

Childs gave him a twisted grin. "Am I starting to look Norwegian to you, bwana? You been out in the snow too many times. Sure I caught what he said. He said, '*Tru de menge, halt de foggen.*' That a help?"

Garry didn't smile, shifting his questioning to the geophysicist. "How about you?"

"Yeah, I caught something," Norris muttered angrily. "I caught that he wanted the better part of my ass to come apart. That was easy enough to understand."

The station manager just nodded, turning a concerned gaze back to the body on the table. It was past giving him the answers he wanted. . . .

Everybody liked Copper. The doctor seemed so out of

place at the station, with his ever present paternal grin and Midwestern twang. He didn't belong out here, serving the men who studied a frozen hades. He belonged back in Indiana somewhere, treating little girls for measles and boys for scratches caused by falling off fences. He ought to be posing for a Norman Rockwell type painting to adorn some middle-class periodical.

Instead, he plied his trade at the bottom of the Earth. He'd volunteered for the post, because beneath that Dr. Gillespie exterior lurked the heart of a mildly adventurous man. The others were glad he was around.

At the moment he was working on Bennings's outstretched leg. Off in a corner of the infirmary, Clark the handler was mending the hip of the wounded husky. The single facility had to serve the medical needs of both dogs and men. Neither resented the presence of the other, and Clark and Copper often helped each other during more complex procedures. The men didn't care, as long as the medications didn't get mixed up.

The meteorologist let out an "ouch" as the doctor moved the needle. Copper gave him a reproving look.

"Don't 'ouch' me, Bennings. At least be as brave as the dog. Two lousy stitches. Bullet just grazed you. Hardly broke your precious skin."

"Yeah, well, it didn't feel like it." The needle moved a last time and Bennings grimaced melodramatically.

Copper tied off the stitching and helped the shaken Bennings swing his legs off the table. The meteorologist was still trembling, and not from the effects of the wound.

"Jesus, what the hell were they doing?" he mumbled. "Flying that low, in this kind of weather. Shooting at a dog...at us...." He shook his head slowly, unable to make sense out of the madness that had intruded on an otherwise perfectly normal day.

Copper shrugged, unable to enlighten his friend. He put the needle back in the sterilizer and turned it on. It hummed softly. "Stir crazy, maybe."

"Is that a medical diagnosis?"

"Funny. I mean cabin fever, some kind of argument that exploded out of all proportion. We'll probably never find out exactly what caused it."

"Garry will." Bennings sounded assured. "If I know him,

11

he'll find out what the hell's going on or know the reason why. Give the man that. He's tenacious." He glanced down at his repaired leg, remembered staring down the barrel of the hunting rifle, and added quietly, "Also a helluva good shot."

A sharp yelp made both men turn to look. Clark tried to comfort the injured animal, while glancing apologetically toward the others. "I'll be here a while yet. The shell's in pretty tight. I'd rather work it out carefully and save the leg. Let me know what they find out, will you?"

Copper nodded, while helping Bennings limp out of the infirmary. Behind them the dog continued to whine in pain as Clark moved a light closer and continued probing for the bullet.

Blair leaned against the entryway to the telecom room and ran a hand across his naked forehead. Dirt and sweat came away against his palm. You were always dirty at the station, with showers restricted to two a week. It was funny, really. You trod over thirty percent of all the fresh water on Earth and had to ration your showers because of the energy requirements.

Damn the interruption, anyway. He had two papers to finish plus the regular weekly reports to file, not to mention a brace of ongoing outside experiments that needed constant checking. Ever since the funding cutback he'd been forced to manage with only Fuchs to help, though Bennings and Norris both had been good about trying to help out. But they had their own work to monitor.

He chewed on the unlit cigarette and stared as Sanders manipulated dials and buttons. Static hissed from an overhead speaker. Blair had been listening to it rise and fall for ten minutes. Faint reception never won fair lady, he thought sourly.

Finally Sanders turned to him, looking bored. "It's no go. Even if I could speak Norwegian. Even if I knew their damn frequencies."

"Well, get to somebody." Blair was as frustrated by the attack as everyone else. "Anybody. Try McMurdo again. We've got to report this mess before someone else beats us to it or we're liable to have an international incident on our hands. And you know what that would mean. Work interrupted while everyone troops off to file depositions and personal accounts."

"Wouldn't bother me." Sanders was a couple months over twenty-one. No one at the station seemed to know how he'd obtained his position, or why he'd bothered.

Probably the ads had made it sound romantic. Six months away from the sights and sounds (not to mention the warmth) of Los Angeles had changed the telecom operator's mind, and he made no effort to hide his unhappiness. He'd tell anyone who'd stop to listen how he'd been duped.

But he was stuck with the job for a year. No wine, no women, and not much song. Certainly no romance. The girl friend he'd taken the job to impress was probably lying on the beach at Santa Monica right now, drinking wine and nestling into somebody else's arms.

The coming winter would be harder on Sanders than most of them.

"Try McMurdo again."

Sanders sounded disgusted. "Who do you think I've been trying? Look, I haven't been able to reach shit in two weeks. I doubt if anybody's talking to anybody else on the whole continent. You ought to know what a storm like this does to communications."

Blair turned away from the younger man and looked toward the narrow window set high in the wall across the hallway. Beyond the damp glass he could see nothing but blowing snow. The lower half of the window was already buried. Another month would cover it completely.

"Yeah," he muttered resignedly, "I know. . . ."

2

The rumbling was subdued and steady, a sound not unlike the wind howling outside the station. But softer. It came from one of the many hallways that connected the multiple rooms and storage sections of the compound.

Slowly it moved toward the recreation room. Ears took

note of its approach, but none of the men assembled there bothered to turn toward it. The noise was well known to all of them and no cause for alarm.

Nauls skidded to a flashy stop in one of the doorways and braced himself against the jamb. His legs shifted alternately as he balanced himself on the roller skates and stared at the others.

"I heard." His eyes took in the body still lying on the card tables. "So what's it mean?"

"Nobody knows yet," Fuchs told him. "You got any ideas?"

"Sure." The cook grinned at the young biologist. "Maybe we at war with Norway."

Palmer wasn't much older than Nauls. He'd finally gotten control of his hair. It hung down his back in a single fall, secured with a single rubber band. He smiled at the cook's joke as he lit up a joint.

A funny smile, was Palmer's. He was something else with machinery and not a bad pilot, but from time to time he had a little trouble communicating with other human beings. Episodes from a slightly radical past (most during the sixties) occasionally rose up to haunt him, chemically as well as physically.

He inhaled crisply, turning the smile on Garry. The two were social opposites, but they got along okay. In a place like the station, you had to get along. Garry and Palmer did so because neither took the other too seriously.

"Was wondering when El Capitan was going to get a chance to use his pop gun."

Garry rebuked him with a stern look, and turned to face Fuchs. The biologist was still studying the large map.

"How long have they been stationed there? You said you didn't think they'd been set up for very long."

Fuchs walked away from the map and began rummaging through a box file. He pulled a card out of its middle. "Says here, about eight weeks."

Dr. Copper entered the room. Bennings was right behind him, limping rather more severely than the wound demanded.

Garry looked doubtful. "Relative newcomers. Eight weeks. That's not enough time for guys to go bonkers."

14

"Bullshit, sweetheart." Nauls kicked at the floor with his skates, making the wheels spin. "Five minutes is enough to put a man over the edge here, if he doesn't have his head set on straight when he arrives."

"Damn straight," agreed Palmer. He was beginning to look blissful. Garry didn't give a damn. Palmer did his work.

"I mean," Nauls continued, noticing the remnants of the tobaccoless cigarette and connecting it with the expression now slowly spreading over the mechanic's face, "Palmer's been the way *he* is since the first day."

Palmer's smile grew wider and he flipped a bird toward the cook.

"It depends on the individual." Copper's tone was more serious than the cook's, though the sentiment was the same. "Sometimes personality conflicts combined with related problems engendered by confinement and isolation can manifest themselves with surprising speed."

Garry considered this and spoke to Fuchs. "Does it say how many in their permanent party?"

Fuchs glanced back at the half-extracted card and pursed his lips. "If this is up-to-date, they apparently started with just six. So there'd be four back at their camp."

"That's not necessarily valid any longer," said Copper quietly. Everyone's attention shifted to the camp doctor.

"Meaning what, doc?" wondered Bennings.

"Meaning that we don't know when our two visitors went over the edge, or why, or if they had mental company. Even if they acted alone, guys as crazy as that," and he gestured meaningfully toward the motionless body on the card tables, "could have done a lot of damage in their own neighborhood before getting to us. Which might be another reason why Sanders can't raise their camp on the radio."

"They might only be monitoring their own transmissions," Norris pointed out.

Copper looked doubtful. "Every modern European speaks a little English. They'd at least acknowledge, I'd think."

Garry looked back at the tables. "*He* didn't speak any English."

"Stress of the moment," Copper suggested. "At such times, people usually can only think in their native tongue."

15

The station manager turned away, muttering unhappily. "If what you say is true about them doing damage to their own camp, there's not much we can do about it."

"Oh yes there is," the doctor countered. "I'd like to go over there. Maybe I can help someone. Maybe I can even find some answers."

"In this weather?"

The doctor turned to the man standing closest to him. "Bennings? What about the weather?"

The meteorologist considered. "I'd like to make a fresh check of the instruments, but according to the last readings I took the wind's supposed to let up a tad over the next few hours."

"A tad?" Garry gave him a hard look.

Bennings fidgeted. "Gimme a break, chief. Trying to predict the winter weather down here's like trying to find ice cubes in London. It's always a crap shoot. But that's my best guess, based on the most recent info."

"What's your opinion of the doc's idea?"

"I wouldn't care to do it myself." He moved to inspect the wall map. "But it should be a reasonable haul. Even taking the winds into account I figure less than an hour there, hour back."

Garry mulled the idea over, not liking it much. But he desperately wanted some explanations before both the weather and official inquiries started to come in. Besides which, as Copper had pointed out, there might be injured needing help at the Norwegian station. What would the official reaction be if he didn't make an effort to help them?

Palmer took the last hit off his joint. "Shit, doc. I'll give you a lift if—"

Garry interrupted him sharply. "Forget it, Palmer." He turned back to Copper, who was waiting patiently for a decision. "Doc, you're a pain in the ass."

"Only when I'm giving certain injections."

"Oh hell." The station manager turned away to hide his smile. "Norris, go get Macready."

A few easy laughs filled the room. Norris grinned at his superior. "Macready ain't going nowhere. Bunkered in 'til spring. Who says humans can't hibernate?"

"Neveready Macready," Bennings added.

16

Garry looked bored. "Just go and get him."

"You're the boss, boss." Norris headed toward the door. "Anyway, he's probably ripped. Palmer'll have to go anyhow."

Despite familiarity bred of constant repetition, it took Norris several minutes to prepare himself to go outside. Slogging along beneath sixty-five pounds of extra clothing, he made his way toward the outside door.

Wind hammered at his face as he pulled the door aside. Instinctively, he held his lips apart so the saliva in his mouth wouldn't freeze them together. Ice particles rattled on his snow goggles.

Maybe Bennings was right. It seemed as he started up the stairs that the wind *had* let up slightly. Windchill factor had fallen from the rapidly fatal to the merely intimidating. Of course they had yet to experience a real winter storm. They were still basking in comparatively mild autumn weather.

His destination was a shack one hundred yards from the main compound, connected to it by guide ropes and a wooden walkway. A hundred yards on foot in the Antarctic seems like a hundred miles, even when the hiker is blessed by the presence of a visible destination.

He emerged from the stairs leading down into the central building and started along the boardwalk, his gloved hands sliding easily on the familiar slickness of the guide rope. A few icicles drooped from it and broke off as his sliding fingers made contact with them. He used the rope not only to guide himself but to pull his way up the slight slope. Here arms had to compliment legs that had a tendency to go on strike after even brief exposure to the bitter cold.

It was comfortably warm inside the shack, which had double walls and radiant electric heat. Macready kept it as tropical as regulations would allow. He hated the cold, hated it even worse than Sanders. Isolation he didn't mind. The mitigating factor was the pay, which was astounding.

He took the ice cubes from the little refrigerator and dropped them into the glass. Amber liquid of impressive potency sloshed around the cubes.

"Bishop to knight four," said a calm voice that wasn't his.

17

He sipped at the whiskey and walked over to the table holding the game. A large, gaily colored Vera Cruz sombrero hung from his neck and bounced gently against his back. He bent to duck the naked light bulb hanging from the ceiling.

The shack was small, individualistic, and furnished in contemporary unkempt. Garry called it a pigsty. Macready preferred the description "lived-in". It was a point the station manager didn't press. Macready did his work. Usually.

Several large posters of warm places provided interior color. Naples, Rio, Jamaica, Acapulco, one blonde, and two redheads. It was hot enough in the shack to make you sweat.

The electronic chessboard on the table was larger than the average model. Macready sat down and chuckled over his opponent's bad move.

"Poor little son of a bitch. You're starting to lose it, aren't you?"

He thought a moment, then tapped in his move. The machine's response was immediate.

"Pawn takes queen at knight four." Electronically manipulated pieces quivered slightly as they shuffled across the board.

Macready's grin slowly faded as he examined the new alignment. Someone was pounding on his door. He ignored the noise while brooding over his next move, finally entering the instructions.

Again pieces shifted. "Rook to knight six," said the implacable voice from the board's internal speaker. "Check."

The pounding was getting insistent. Macready's teeth ground together as he glared at the board. He bent forward and opened a small flap on the side of the playing field. Colored circuitry stared back at him as he dumped the remnants of his drink over them. Snapping and popping burst from the machine, followed by a flash of sparks and very little smoke.

"Bishop to pawn three takes rook to queen five king to bishop two move pawn to pawn six to pawn seven to pawn eight to pawn nine to pawn to pawn to pawnnizzzz-fisssttt*ttt*. . . ."

Macready listened until the gibberish stopped, then

18

rose and stumbled toward the door, mumbling disgustedly to himself.

"... Cheating bastard ... damn aberrant programming ... better get my money back. ..."

Carefully he cracked open the door. Heat burst past him, sucked toward the South Pole. Norris pushed through and past him, a rush of snow following like a white remora.

"You jerking off or just pissed?" the geophysicist growled, slapping at his sides. "Why the hell didn't you open up?"

Macready said nothing but gestured toward the still smoking board. "We got any replacement modules for these chess things down in supply?"

"How the hell would I know? Get your gear on."

The chess game was suddenly forgotten. Macready regarded his visitor with sudden suspicion. "What for?"

"What d'you think for?"

"Oh no." He started backing away from Norris. "No way. Not a chance. Huh-uh. ..."

"Garry says—"

"I don't give a shit what Garry says." Outside, the wind howled. To Macready it sounded hungry.

Childs had one of the big torches out and was keeping it close to his body as he melted ice from the helicopter's rotors and engine cowling. Of all the outside jobs, melting off machinery was one of the most pleasurable. At least you could keep yourself defrosted along with the equipment.

The wind howled around him as he worked. He glanced skyward. Despite Bennings's assurances he didn't envy whoever had to take the chopper up. No one would, unless Copper insisted. Childs smiled to himself. Plump old Doc Copper usually got his way. Because once he proposed something, none of the other macho types could very well back out without looking silly.

He turned his attention back to the nearly de-iced copter and cut frozen water from its landing gear.

The little cluster of heavily dressed men resembled a group of migrating bears as they wound their way through the narrow corridor leading toward the helicopter pad. They were already starting to sweat, despite the special absorptive thermal underwear. The clothes they wore were designed to be comfortable at seventy below, not seventy above.

Dr. Copper carried a medical satchel. It was made of metal and formed high-impact plastic and could hold anything up to and including a portable surgery. Its standard color was yellow, but Copper had personally spray-painted it black. He was a bit of a traditionalist.

Macready was studying a flight chart printed on a plastic sheet and grumbling nonstop, his own mental engine already flying over their intended route.

"Craziness . . . this is goddamn insane . . . I don't know if I can even find this place in *clear* weather. . . ."

"Quit the griping, Macready," Garry ordered him. "The sooner you get out there, the sooner you're back."

"If we get there," the pilot snorted. "It's against regulations to go up this time of year! I'm not supposed to fly again 'til spring. I'll put in a protest. Regulations say I don't have to go up in this kind of weather."

"Screw regulations," Copper told him. "Records indicate there are six guys out at that Norwegian station. Two nuts from six guys leaves maybe four crawling around on their bellies praying for help. Antarctica's like the ocean, Mac. First law of the sea says you help a fellow mariner in trouble before you think of anything else."

"I don't mind helping 'em," Macready insisted. "I just don't want to end up crawling around with them when we go down."

Garry glared at him. "If you aren't ready to make an occasional risk flight in bad weather then why the hell did you volunteer for this post?"

Macready smiled, rubbing a thumb and finger together. "Same reason a lot of us did. But I can't spend it if I'm dead."

"Look, Macready, if you're going to keep on bitching, Palmer's already offered to take the doc up."

Macready gaped at the station manager, incredulous. "What are you talking about? *Palmer?* He's had maybe two months training in those choppers! Fair weather training."

"Four," Palmer corrected him defiantly from the rear of the pack. "A little blow doesn't bother *me*."

"'Little blow.'" Macready shook his head. "Hell, when you get stoked, Palmer, the end of the world can't bother

20

SADDLEBACK FORUM
CHERRY HILL MALL
CHERRY HILL, N.J.

- 5 OCT

$002.50   - 2
$002.75   2
$000.26   - X

$005.51 TOTL

you. But maybe the doc isn't as interested in dying happy as you are, pothead."

"So then you take him up and shut up," Palmer shot back.

"Ahhhhh!" Macready made a rude gesture and turned to face Bennings. "What's it like out there, anyway? Forty-five knots?"

"Sixteen," the meteorologist told him.

"Yeah, and the horse you rode in on," Macready snapped. "Sixteen for how long? You can't tell, this time of year. In five minutes it could be fifty."

Bennings nodded agreeably. "Possible."

"So what do we do?" Copper halted next to the outside doorway. The roar of the wind penetrated even the double-thick, insulated barrier.

"So you open the door," Macready growled, out of arguments, "unless you want to try and walk through it. . . ."

Childs was waiting for them, and gave Copper a hand up into the cockpit of the chopper. The doctor carefully secured his bag behind the seat. Outside the plexiglass bubble, blowing snow was already beginning to obscure their view.

Macready slid in next to him and began flipping switches and examining readouts on the console. The one readout he didn't bother to check gave the current exterior temperature. Once it fell below zero, he no longer cared what it said. And since it was always below zero it was the one instrument in the choppers he could usually ignore.

He tightened the sombrero's string beneath his chin. It hung outside his polar parka, incongruous against his back. Childs had thoughtfully activated the prewarm. Good mechanic, Childs. Macready trusted him. The engine had been heating up for thirty minutes. It ought to start.

He hit the ignition. For a moment the reluctant rotors strained against fresh ice. Then they began to spin. The engine revved with comforting steadiness.

"Hang on over there, doc," he told his passenger. "This isn't Disneyland."

He pulled back on the controls. The chopper lifted, swung sideways for an instant, then began a steady climb into the sky. Macready held it steady, then sent it charging

21

northeast over the white landscape. It slid into the wind, fighting the gale like a salmon returning upstream. Macready was too involved with the controls to consider throwing up. He couldn't. Not in front of the unruffled Copper.

The doctor relaxed back in his seat, rechecked his seat belt and shoulder harness, and studied the passing terrain. He appeared to be enjoying himself. Macready cursed him, but silently.

Several pairs of eyes watched through temporarily defogged windows from the rec room as the helicopter shrank into the distance. Clark rested his palms against the glass as he stared. Between his skin and the outside were three layers of special thick glass and two intervening layers of warmed air. The glass was still cold to his touch.

"Mac's really taken it up, huh?"

Bennings was feeling his leg, having to force himself not to scratch at the healing itch. "Copper volunteered to check the Norwegian camp for wounded, and Garry concurred."

"We could have used the dogs," Clark said, slightly hurt that he hadn't even been considered. "It would've been safer, in this wind."

"Safer, yeah," agreed Bennings, "but ten times as slow. We could get a major storm in here any day now. This way they'll be back in a few hours."

A thick bandage padding the hip where the bullet had entered, the husky trotted into the room. He padded happily between the tables and chairs, hobbling only a little on the damaged leg.

This is damned insane, Macready thought to himself as he lifted the copter over an ice ridge. The engine protested, but only for a second or two. A few boulders atop the ridge showed through the snow. Buried baldies, Macready mused. Funny how you could get lonely for something as common as grass. He grinned slightly. Except for Palmer and Childs's imports, of course.

The gale had lessened considerably since takeoff and he had to admit that flying had become almost pleasant. It was starting to look like they'd make it without any real trouble.

The chopper's cockpit heater whined loudly. Macready had it set on high. As far as he was concerned, that was the only setting it possessed. Copper was uncomfortably warm,

22

but said nothing. He'd stand the overheating to keep the pilot happy.

Macready glanced over at the plastic map set in the holder on the console. "We ought to be closing on it, Doc, if the coordinates Fuchs and Bennings gave us are right."

"This isn't the Arctic, Mac. Camps don't float around on ice floes down here. It'll be where it's supposed to be." He suddenly pointed down through the bubble. "There, what's that?"

Smoke was visible directly ahead, and it didn't come from somebody's chimney. There was one central, dense column and several smaller sudsidiary plumes. Too many. The wind made the smoke curl and dance in the Antarctic evening. Soon the sun would vanish altogether and the long South Polar night would settle over them.

Macready encircled the half-buried camp. Up close the smoke seemed unusually thick, almost tarlike. It billowed skyward from hidden sources. There was no sign of movement below. Only the wind moved here.

"Anyplace special, Doc?"

Copper was leaning to his right, staring solemnly through the bubble. "You pick it, Mac. From the looks of things I don't think it much matters."

The relaxed wind gave Macready no trouble as he carefully set the copter down. He cut the engine and switched over to the prewarm to keep it from icing up. The rotors slowed, their comforting whine fading to silence, blending into the mournful wind. Macready unlatched the cockpit door and stepped out. His first glance was for the sky. It showed cobalt blue, save for fast-moving clouds. There was no telling how long the break in the weather would last. They'd have to hurry.

They slogged toward the camp. A large, prefabricated metal building loomed directly ahead. It was full of gaping holes not part of the original design. Macready searched but couldn't locate an intact window. Broken glass shone like diamonds in the snow.

Smoke rose from the surface. Like their own camp, most of this one should be snuggled beneath the ice. It looked like the ground itself was on fire.

Individual pieces of equipment burned with their own personal fires, melting their way into the ice and eventual extinction. A flaming ember whizzed by and both men instinctively ducked, even though fire here was usually a welcome companion. But conditioning dies hard.

Copper said nothing, just stared. Macready's thoughts were a flabbergasted blank. The place looked like Carthage after the last Punic war.

This wasn't what they'd expected. Not this total devastation. Macready turned and went back to the helicopter and thoughtfully pocketed the ignition key.

Eventually they located the source of the main blaze and also the reason for the unusually thick column of smoke. It rose from what appeared to be a makeshift funeral pyre. Books, tires, furniture, scrap lumber; anything that would burn had been heaped together outside the main building and set on fire. Discernible among the rest of the inorganic kindling were the charred remains of several dogs and at least one man. Mounds of black goo that might have been asphalt or roofing sealant burned fragrantly among the rest of the debris.

A small gasoline drum lay on its end nearby, its cap missing. A larger fuel oil drum squatted off to one side. Macready checked the smaller container first, then the larger. Both were empty.

He glanced to his left. Was that only the wind whispering in his ears? He exchanged a look with Copper. The doctor's face was pale, and it wasn't from the cold.

Macready made another trip back to the copter and opened the door. The shotgun slid easily out of its brackets behind the pilot's seat. He made sure it was loaded, took a box of shells from the compartment beneath and shoved them into his pocket, then hurried to rejoin Copper.

The doctor glanced sharply at the gun, whose purpose was so different from the instruments he carried in his satchel. But he didn't object to its presence. It seemed small enough insurance in the face of the violence that had ripped this camp.

They started in toward the center structure, or rather what was left of it. Glowing embers continued to waft past them. One latched onto Macready's shirt-sleeve and he absently batted it out.

The door was unlocked. Macready turned the latch,

24

stepped back, and used the muzzle of the shotgun to shove it inward. It swung loosely and banged against the interior wall.

Ahead lay a long, pitch-black corridor. There was a switch just inside the doorway. Copper flipped it several times, without effect. He pulled a flashlight from his coat and aimed it down the corridor.

"Anybody here?"

No answer. The beam played off the walls and floor, revealing a tunnel little different in design and construction from those back at their own compound.

Only the wind talked to them, constant as it was uninformative. Copper looked to the pilot, who shrugged.

"This is your party, Doc."

Copper nodded, and started in. Macready followed and moved up beside the older man.

Their progress was slow because of the debris that filled the corridor. Overturned chairs, chests of equipment, loose wires, and cannisters of gas and liquid made for treacherous walking. Once Macready nearly went over on his face when his feet got tangled in an exploded television set. Copper winced, then gave the pilot a reproving look.

"Maybe I ought to carry the gun?" He extended a hand.

Macready was angry at himself. "I'll watch it. It won't happen again. Just watch where you point that flashlight."

Copper nodded, and tried to keep the beam focused equally on the floor and corridor ahead. It was as cold in the hallway as it was outside.

"Heat's been off in here for quite a while," he said.

Macready nodded, his eyes trying to pierce the darkness in front of them. "Anybody left alive would've frozen to death days ago."

"Not necessarily. Just because this one section is exposed and heatless doesn't mean the whole camp's the same way. Your shack has its own heat, for example."

"Yeah, but if the generator went out I'd be a popsicle in a couple of hours."

"Well, they might have portable propane heaters, then."

Macready threw him a sour look. "I love you, Doc. You're such a damn optimist."

25

Copper didn't reply; he continued to play his flashlight beam over floor and walls. The wind wailed overhead.

Macready stopped. "You hear something?"

Copper strained, listened. "Yes. I think so." He shifted the light. "Mechanical."

They followed the faint noise, which soon turned to an audible hissing. As they continued down the corridor the hiss became recognizable as static.

There was a door blocking the end of the corridor. The steady sputtering came from the other side.

Copper moved the light over the remnant of a door. Something had taken it apart. An axe protruded from the center, its head buried deeply in the wood.

Macready put the gun aside, grabbed hold with both hands, and yanked until it came loose. The cutting edge was stained dark. He studied it briefly, looking to Copper for confirmation.

The doctor said nothing, which was confirmation enough for Macready. There wasn't much blood on the axe, and what remained was frozen to a maroon crust.

Putting down the axe he retrieved the gun, holding it a little tighter now as he tried the doorknob. It rotated and the door opened inward, but halted after moving only a few inches. The pilot put his shoulder against it and shoved, but it refused to budge further.

"Blocked from the other side," he said quietly to Copper. He put his face to the slight opening. "Anybody in there?"

There was no reply. Copper moved up against Macready's side and shouted past him. "We're Americans!"

"Come to help you!" Macready added. His tongue moved against the inside of his mouth and he added, "We're alone!" Still no response. He steadied himself and leaned harder against the door.

There was a creak. "I think it moved a little," he told the doctor. "Give me a hand."

Copper added his own bulk to Macready's and pushed. The frozen floor of the passageway gave poor purchase to their boots. But by alternately hammering and pressing hard they managed to edge the door inward an inch at a time.

Eventually they'd widened it enough for Macready to stick his head inside.

"Give me the light." Copper handed it over and the pilot directed its beam inward. The static was loud now.

"See anything, Mac?"

"Yeah." The flashlight revealed banks of electronic instrumentation, most of it shattered. One console appeared to be the source of the steady humming. "Communications," he told the doctor. "Looks a lot like Sanders's bailiwick, anyway." He gave the light back to Copper, wedged himself into the opening, and pushed. The door gave another couple of inches.

Copper followed him through, shining the light around the little room. Wind kissed their faces, unexpectedly brisk. He leaned back and picked out the holes in the ceiling.

A Ganz lantern rested on a corner table. Macready dug out a match, struck it carefully and applied the flame to the lantern as he turned the control knob. The butane caught with a rush, forming a little circle of light.

Lifting the lantern, he turned in a slow circle. The soft light picked out the top of a man's head, showing just above the back of a swivel chair.

"Hey, Sweden," he called to the figure, "you okay?"

The chair rocked slightly in the breeze from the ceiling. Both men moved slowly toward it. Macready put out an arm and halted the doctor a yard short of the chair, then poked at it with the shotgun.

"Sweden?"

Copper's gaze moved to the arm resting on one arm of the chair. A thin red line fell from it, a frozen crimson thread that ended in a pool of coagulated blood on the wooden floor.

Macready poked the chair again, stepping around it. Copper moved around the other side.

The man in the chair was lightly dressed, too lightly for the subfreezing temperature in the room. His eyes were open, fixed on something beyond their range of vision. His mouth was frozen agape. He seemed to have been petrified in the act of screaming.

Macready's gaze traveled down the stiff body. The throat had been slit from ear to ear; both wrists were also slit. An old-fashioned straight razor lay in the man's lap. It was stained the same color as the axe that had been buried in the door. The razor seemed out of place in the communications room, an antique among solid-state technology. It had done its job, however.

Macready reached past the wide-eyed corpse and flicked a switch. The radio's steady hiss died.

There was a door in the far wall, which also turned out to be blocked from the opposite side. Macready rammed his shoulder angrily against it, banging it inward. He paused to catch his breath, and saw his companion gazing in fascination at the corpse and its multiple slashes.

"My God," the doctor was muttering half to himself, "what in hell happened here?"

"Come on, Copper," Macready growled at him impatient. "This one's blocked, too."

"What?" The doctor stared blankly at the pilot, then snapped out of his daze and moved to help. Together they battered at the new obstacle until it moved enough to let them through.

A metal storage cabinet had been used to brace the door. Beyond lay more blackness. The wind was stronger.

Copper switched off the flashlight and took the lantern from Macready, freeing the latter to hold the gun with both hands. He held the lantern high, revealing a series of wooden steps leading downward.

"Hey, Sweden!" Macready shouted into the blackness as he started downward.

"They're not Swedish, goddamn it," Copper corrected him irritably. "They're Norwegian, Macre—"

Something swished out of the darkness and smacked into his face. . . .

3

The lantern fell from his startled grasp and went bouncing down the stairs like a runaway jack o'lantern. Copper stumbled and felt himself falling as he flailed at something whipping around his head. Macready leaned back against a solid wall and extricated his own flashlight, olding it in one hand and the shotgun in the other as he tried o locate their assailant.

But Copper had recovered his equilibrium and subdued is attacker. He held it up, letting the wrinkled paper flap in he breeze that carried it down the stairwell.

Macready walked over and took the paper. The notations at its bottom were in Norwegian, but it wouldn't have made any real difference if they'd been Chinese ideographs.

"Norwegian-of-the-Month, Doc. Harmless." He started to toss the centerfold away, thought better of it and pocketed it for detailed inspection later on.

An embarrassed Copper self-consciously adjusted his clothing and descended the last couple of steps to recover the still burning lantern. He waited there until Macready had rejoined him. Together they started down the subterranean corridor.

The support beams holding up the ceiling were wood. They were twisted and buckled from the steady pressure of the ice around them. This was a more glacially active area than the plateau where the American outpost was located.

The recent conflagration that had seared the camp further strained the strength of the woodwork. They could hear it creaking and complaining around them as they made their way up the tunnel. Bits of ice and silt trickled down, landing in their hair and tickling their cheeks.

A broken beam lay crossways ahead of them, blocking the tunnel. It still smouldered. Macready ducked to slip gingerly underneath, brushing it gently. A shower of fine debris rained from the arched ceiling.

"Easy here, Doc. This one belongs in the roof, not on the floor."

Copper crouched and passed under the beam. It groaned but held steady. They continued onward.

"Hey!"

"Mac? Something wrong?" Copper whirled, shining the light toward his companion.

Macready was searching the wall behind him. "Bumped into something. Didn't feel like wood. I thought it moved when I hit it. Holy shit." He grimaced.

The arm was sticking out of the edge of a steel door set into the corridor wall. The elbow was about three feet off the ground. The door was shut tight. Fingers clutched a small welding torch.

Copper leaned close, examining the trapped limb.

"Watch it, Doc," Macready warned him. "Might still be gas running to that sucker."

"I don't think so." Copper indicated the torch controls. "The switch is in the on position, I think. I don't smell anything." He licked a finger, held it under the nozzle of the torch. "Nothing. Fuel burned or leaked out long ago."

Macready tried the door. It was unlocked and unlike the previous two they'd had to wrestle with, this one opened easily. The arm dropped loosely to the floor. It wasn't attached to anything anymore, having been severed as well as held in place by the door. There was no sign of its former owner.

That was about enough as far as Macready was concerned. He turned away and coughed, feeling his stomach play ferris wheel inside his belly. The dips and bobs of a wind-tossed helicopter didn't bother him, but this. . . .

"Christ," Copper mumbled. He peered into the new passageway, raising the lantern high. "Let's see where this one goes."

A short walk brought them to another door. Norwegian lettering ran across the wood at eye level. Macready readied the shotgun and gave the door a kick.

At least the doors were becoming more cooperative. This one swung obediently inward, creaking to a stop. Dozens of papers were flying around the room beyond the door, fat white moths shoved around by the wind pouring through gaping holes in the roof. It was difficult to determine the purpose of the room because it was a total wreck.

Macready played his flashlight over the carnage.

"Laboratory," Copper announced as the beam traveled across broken beakers and fragmented test tubes. A fine microscope lay on its side on the floor, near a cracked workbench. Other equipment was scattered as if by a tornado. An expensive oscilloscope sat undamaged on a shelf, save for the fact that something had punched out its single cyclopean eye.

"Hey, look at this, Doc." Copper turned. Macready's flashlight had picked out a gray metal box attached to a

30

carby wall. A single unbroken lens pointed toward the oor. "Portable video camera."

Copper glanced up at it, then started working his way rough the mess toward a tipped-over filing cabinet. Its rawers had been pulled out, mute testimony to the casual estruction that had invaded this room as well as to the ource of all the paper fluttering around their heads.

Other papers lay beneath weights or overturned equip-ent on the main work table. He shuffled through them, earching hopefully rather than realistically for the clue that ight explain how catastrophe had overwhelmed this ation.

Macready continued to examine the video camera, ishing Sanders was with them. "Anything?" he asked ithout turning.

Copper shook his head regretfully. "All in Norwegian, 'm afraid." He pulled out a couple of sheets, squinting at hem in the weak light. "No, here's a couple in German."

"So what?"

"I can read a little German."

Macready turned to him and spoke eagerly. "Yeah? Vhat's it say?"

The doctor continued to inspect the papers, his lips noving as he followed the long words. ". . . allgegenwertig laci. . . ." He broke off and looked up, disappointed. "It's a ract on the movement of pressure ridges, I'm afraid."

"Wonderful," said Macready sarcastically. "That's a reat help." Copper carefully aligned the sheets and began dding selected reams of additional material. The pilot rowned.

"Now what are you doing? Nobody back at base can ead that stuff, either."

"I know." He bent to retrieve a packet of paper bound in ed plastic. "But this could be important work. It looks like ix people have died for it. Might as well bring it back before t blows away. If the positions were reversed I'd want some other scientist to do the same for me."

Macready forbore from mentioning that Copper was only a GP, not a scientist. "Okay," he said impatiently, "but t's getting late. Hurry it up. I'm going to check out the last few rooms." He turned and exited.

Copper continued to gather the papers, stacking them neatly in one arm. Perhaps some Norwegian bureau or university would be able to make sense of them.

Scattered among the rubble was a pocket tape recorder. Several cassettes lay strewn across the floor nearby. He picked one up. It was hand-marked. Unless it was part of somebody's private collection, that meant it probably contained scientific notes and not prerecorded music.

Something behind him . . . he whirled. No. Nothing. Easy, Copper, he told himself. This place is too cold even for ghosts. He popped one of the tapes into the recorder and tried fiddling with the controls.

Macready bulled his way into another room and was greeted with a shower of splinters and cracked ice. Grumbling, he brushed the debris from his parka as he angled the flashlight upward. Here too, the ceiling was a mess. He lowered the light and started inspecting the interior.

Copper found the playback switch. A casual Norwegian voice droned away in pedantic, unemotional tones. He fast-forwarded the instrument. The voice was the same and so was the pattern.

A distant shout broke his concentration: Macready.

"Copper, come here! "

Now what, he wondered? Found the owner of the arm they'd encountered in the other hall, maybe. He shut off the recorder and rushed out of the room.

Macready hadn't gone far. Copper had to squeeze his greater bulk through the narrow opening leading to the next room and drew more of the dirty little avalanche that had greeted the pilot's initial entrance.

"Careful," Macready warned him with a gesture toward the ceiling. "This one's ready to go."

The doctor flicked debris from his arms and walked over to join his companion. Macready was standing next to a huge block of ice. A glance showed that it hadn't fallen from the ceiling. Copper was no geologist, but he'd helped Norris often enough to know that this mass was composed of old ice, not newly formed surface material.

Automatically his orderly mind made approximations. The block was about fifteen feet long and six wide, maybe four high. It lay on the floor, too massive to rest on any table.

The edges showed signs of recent melting, a process halted by the freezing temperatures that had invaded the camp.

Other than its size, it was unremarkable. "Block of ice," he said to Macready. "So what?"

Macready leaned over the block, shining his flashlight downward. "Check this out."

Copper moved nearer. The center of the block had been thawed or scraped out. It looked as if someone had tried to make the block into a huge frozen bathtub.

"What d'you make of this?"

Copper shook his head, thoroughly puzzled. "Beats the hell out of me, Mac. Glaciology's not my department. Anything else here?"

"Don't know yet. This caught my eye right off." He turned away from the block, searching with the light until it caught a large metal cabinet standing against a wall. Closer inspection revealed several Polaroid prints taped to its front. They walked over to it. The pictures showed men at work and play around the compound.

"At least something's intact," he murmured. He put the shotgun carefully aside and held the flashlight in his mouth as he used both hands to try to open the cabinet.

The latch gave slightly, but the doors refused to come apart. Stuck, he decided. Perhaps frozen. He pulled again. Dust trickled down from the top of the cabinet. The partially collapsed ceiling was slightly blocking the tops of the doors. He yanked again. Something groaned overhead.

Copper took a step back, eyeing the roof warily. "Watch it, Mac."

Macready readied himself, shot a cursory glance at the unstable ceiling, and pulled hard. Too hard. The doors flew open and he stumbled backward, fighting for balance.

Large chunks of insulation and wood tumbled from the roof. Macready coughed and waved at the dust as he made his way back toward the cabinet.

The contents were a disappointment, not that he'd expected to find much. His struggle with the doors produced no revelations. Some of the shelves were empty. Others supported small scientific instruments, several programmable calculators, racks of slides, a few unbroken beakers, and some glass tubing.

33

His flashlight focused on a large photograph taped to the inside of one door.

Five men filled the picture. They stood arm in arm, all smiles, holding glasses raised in a mutual toast. It was an exterior shot, taken somewhere outside the camp.

In front of them on the snow lay the block of ice. The photo made it appear larger. Perhaps some of it had melted in transit, Macready decided. It was obviously set out for the benefit of the camera, though he couldn't decide from looking at the photo whether the men were toasting it or each other.

He looked over his shoulder at the block of ice, back at the photo, then at the ice again. There was no doubt in his mind that the block in the picture and the one resting five feet away were one and the same. The dimensions of the one in the picture might be slightly greater but the proportions were identical.

He carefully untaped the photo and slipped it into a coat pocket, then reclosed the cabinet doors.

As he did so more debris tumbled from the ceiling; wood, plaster, fiberglass insulation, and something else. Something cold but still soft. Macready screamed; Copper gaped.

The corpse was missing an arm, but was still heavy enough to knock Macready down. . . .

The howling was sharp and melodic. It penetrated much of the American compound, reaching the rec room via connecting corridors and the few speakers inside.

Beneath one of the card tables, the injured husky perked up his ears. The howling degenerated into lyrics, something having to do with werewolves in London. Once the howling had metamorphosed into human speech, the dog shifted its attention elsewhere.

Nearby, a ball of light danced across a video screen, beckoning would-be players to manipulate it. There were no takers in the room just then and the dog could only trot disinterestedly past.

The howling was loudest in the kitchen, blasting from a cassette deck vibrating on a shelf above a multiburner stove. Nauls skated past, kicking the door of the massive walk-in freezer shut with spinning steel wheels. The large chunk of corned beef he'd extracted from the freezer was slam-dunked onto the big butcher block. Pots and pans steamed up the air and the aroma filling the room was thick with pepper and bay leaf.

Nauls rolled easily from one station to another, keeping time to the music. He used a spoon to sample the contents of one cauldron, frowned, added something from a couple of large shakers, then tasted it again. This time he smiled.

He took pride in his work. The station could function without any of the scientists, without the chopper pilots or mechanics, without Garry, but it wouldn't run for very long without Nauls's talents. No sir. Nauls could insult everyone in camp with impunity. His cooking more than made up for the offenses committed by his mouth.

Still, there were occasional objections to his irreverence. Garry peered through an open doorway, grimacing. "Turn that crap down, Nauls! You can hear it all over the camp."

"Disconnect the hall and rec room speakers."

"More trouble than its worth," the station manager argued. "Play that junk if you must, but lower it."

Nauls sniffed disdainfully. "Some folks have no appreciation for culture."

Garry's fingernails tapped on the doorjamb. "Warren Zevon isn't culture, Nauls. Beethoven is culture. Janácek is culture. Vaughan Williams is culture."

"Yeah? I hear that 'Antarctica' symphony blaring from your room one more time, I think I'll go nuts. You want to hear stuff like that all you got to do is open your window. Culture just depends on your point of view."

"Well, deafness doesn't. So turn it down."

"*Oui, mon sewer.* Can do." He skated over to the stereo and lowered the volume. Slightly.

Garry shook his head and gave up, continuing on his way.

The communications room was next on his agenda. To no surprise, he found Sanders at his station. Also to no surprise, the operator was leaning back in his chair, sound asleep. His headphones were still in place.

Garry tiptoed around the chair and studied the console briefly before selecting a dial from the mass of controls. He pushed it all the way to the right.

Violent static jolted the radio operator awake. He

35

clutched at his ears, ripping the headphones off.

"Hey, man. . .!" When he saw it was the station manager his outrage subsided somewhat. "You could deafen somebody that way."

"It's not any louder than Nauls's stereo. Your sensitivity could use some tuning."

"I'm sensitive as hell, chief."

"Yeah? You reach anybody yet?"

Sanders explained as if he were talking to a child. "We're a thousand miles from anybody else, man. You can't pick out anything through that crap outside." He waved his arms. "If Bennings is right, it's going to get a helluva lot worse before it gets better. Now, if we had a geostationary satellite in range, it'd be easy."

"Well we don't," Garry reminded him. There wasn't much call for a communications satellite stationed in the spatial vicinity of the South Pole. He sighed resignedly. "Stick to it. Keep trying. And let me know the minute you get through to McMurdo or anywhere else."

"Yeah? Even the Russkies?"

"*Any*body. We've got to get the word out about what's going on here."

The individual living cubicles all fronted on the same corridor, a passage wider than most in the compound. The husky trotted curiously down the empty hall, his tongue hanging lazily from his mouth.

A single door stood open on his left. The dog halted and peered inside. The light was dim and there were rustling sounds.

Casually the animal glanced back up the corridor. It was still empty. Same for the walkway ahead. He turned and padded into the room. An indistinct voice greeted him, surprised.

"Hello, boy."

There was a pause, then the unexpected sound of breaking glass. Muffled sounds issued from the room, as though someone were scuffling. The door was slammed shut.

Then it was quiet in the corridor again.

* * *

Fuchs was certifiable. Most of the others would have attested to that. The assistant biologist was sensitive, concerned, friendly, and unassuming. But certifiable.

Because nobody goes jogging in the Antarctic evening. You jog in Los Angeles despite the smog, in the mountains around Denver despite the altitude, along the beach south of Miami, even in New York's Central Park. But you don't jog in Antarctica.

Well, Fuchs had jogged all his adult life and he was damned if a little inclement weather was going to make him break the routine of a lifetime.

So every morning before beginning work he'd bundle up, put on snow goggles, and jog around the camp, using the guide ropes where available, keeping sight of a familiar landmark where they weren't.

Garry had thought of forbidding the practice, but Fuchs was adamant. And the station manager was forced to admit there was nothing in the regulations forbidding it.

"It wakes me up," Fuchs continued to insist despite the derisive hoots of his companions. "Gets the blood flowing."

"Everywhere but to the brain," Palmer had quipped.

Garry couldn't find it in his heart to order the biologist to quit. There was little enough entertainment in the camp. If Fuchs wanted to amuse himself by trying to freeze to death every morning, well, that was his prerogative.

The only concession to reality the assistant biologist made was the substitution of winter boots for his jogging shoes. It slowed his pace if not his enthusiasm.

He came to a halt, panting, his breath freezing in front of his face. Warm air rose from a vent pipe nearby. He was standing on top of the kitchen.

Most of the camp's permanent structures were buried beneath the shifting snow, cut into the frozen ground and out of the heat-sucking reach of the constant wind. Stairways led down to home.

Fuchs unlatched a roof entrance, looked around and then down past the ladder. The corridor was empty, no one was watching. He assumed a commanding pose.

"Dive, dive!" he muttered, making hornlike sounds,

37

and started quickly down the ladder, pulling the hatch shut behind him.

He jogged down the corridor toward the central complex. Off to his right he saw Clark coming out of one of the supply rooms, rolling a wheelbarrow filled with what looked like brown pebbles. The dog handler waved cheerfully at the biologist, trailing dry food in his wake.

The underground kennel was close by. As Fuchs receded into the distance Clark unlatched the kennel door. As he rolled the barrow inside, seven sled dogs began jumping at his legs and onto the load, kicking dry food in all directions. They yelped and barked eagerly.

Sled dogs had lousy table manners, he mused. They snapped at each other's flanks and legs, not to injure but to reestablish dominance roles prior to gorging themselves. Sometimes Nauls would give Clark kitchen scraps to mix in with the dry food. Then things really got noisy in the kennel.

"Take it easy, take it easy!" he shouted at them. "Lord, what a bunch of chowhounds!" He inspected them as they settled down to eat, making sure there were no signs of infection or disease, checking their teeth for breaks or accumulated plaque.

The men he worked with were okay, but his dogs were better. They were ever affectionate, did their jobs unhesitatingly when required, and rarely argued with him. In return, the sled dogs had conveyed their highest honor on Clark. They thought of him as one of their own. He was the lead dog.

Besides which he brought the food.

The storage section, which held the fuel tanks, was older than the rest of the compound, having been put in place first. The wood-and-metal supports that held up the roof there were starting to look rickety. Antarctica put pressure on metal and wood as steadily as it did on the men who had to survive there.

Piping and concrete blocks were stacked neatly nearby. The concrete was special, designed to withstand the cold without cracking. The blocks were tongue and grooved so they could be fitted together without mortar.

Doors sealed off other smaller rooms filled with duplicate electronic gear, duplicate plumbing supplies, duplicate everything. There was no hardware store a block or two from Outpost #31. The men had six months of polar winter ahead of them. They had to be ready to replace anything that broke down without outside help.

Childs was humming to himself as he entered the main storage area. He stopped in front of a door that was close to the massive horizontal fuel tanks. There were six locks of varying types attached to the door. A couple were combination jobs, several required keys, and one a magnetic bar. He opened each one carefully.

The little room behind the door was unusually warm. Heat flowed from a small radiant heater that looked like a painting of the American Southwest. Bright fluorescent lights of slightly purplish hue beamed down from the ceiling. The room smelled of Wisconsin farmland and Mendocino coast.

Childs grinned paternally as he inspected the rows of healthy plants rising from the hydroponic tanks. They had narrow green leaves with serrated edges. Some of them were nearly as tall as the mechanic.

He chatted with them as he added nutrients to the metal tanks, pouring the stuff from a plastic jug. "How my brothers and sisters doing today? Looks like everyone's doing fine."

He knelt to check the gauges that monitored soil moisture and pH, checked the thermometer on the wall and adjusted the heat control slightly. A hum rose from the radiant heater, warming the mechanic's face. Little light came through the small skylight overhead.

Turning to a tape deck he selected a well-worn cassette from the pile next to it and switched the machine on.

"What say to some nice Al Green for my babies, huh?" He pushed the "on" button.

A high, wailing voice softly filled the little room.

". . . IIIIII cried *out*. . . ," the voice sang agonizingly.

What a waste, that man going and turning to preaching, Childs thought sadly. He remembered seeing him in L.A. at the Music Center, in the Dorothy Chandler Pavilion, singing on the same stage usually occupied by the Philharmonic. Oh well. I guess when you get the call, you got to answer.

But how that man could sing. Damn shame.

A new sound reached him above the music, a steady panting. He whirled. It was only their new visitor, the dog the crazy Norwegians had been trying to kill.

A thought made the mechanic frown at the animal, who cocked its head to one side and regarded him querulously. The bandage was gone from its hip. Probably scraped off against a wall or piece of furniture, Childs mused. Dogs had a tendency to do things like that.

They also had a tendency to do something else, which is why the mechanic was frowning. He moved toward the dog, making shooing motions with both hands.

"G'wan, beat it, mutt! You get the hell on out of here! Scram!" He took a swing at the wet nose.

The dog eyed him reproachfully, then turned and trotted off. Childs turned back to his garden, grumbling under his breath.

"Comin' in here . . . goin' to pee on my babies. Damn dogs, you can't even get away from their dirty at the bottom of the world." He shut the door carefully behind him and bent over the burgeoning plants.

"That's my babies." Al Green shifted to another song. "Be all grown pretty soon. All nice and green and healthy. And then me and my babies going to have a nice, long smoke. . . ."

Blair's gaze was fixed on the chart he was carrying as he strolled down the corridor. Preoccupied, he nearly fell as his feet got tangled in something unseen.

"What the . . .?" He bent, picked up a torn, shredded piece of stained bandage. "Well shit," he muttered, looking around for its owner. But the husky was nowhere to be seen.

Have to mention it to Clark, he thought as he resumed his walk. Dog'll bleed all over the place. Shouldn't worry too much, though. The exposed wound was unlikely to draw infection. Germs didn't last very long inside the compound, and those that attached themselves to the men died quickly once exposed to the outside. Antarctica was a difficult place to get sick, so long as you were careful not to catch cold.

The generator whined steadily down in the lower level, keeping men and equipment in working order, fighting back the constant cold with light and warmth.

Palmer was probing its driving mechanisms, trying to

locate possible failure points ahead of time. Normal maintenance. A rising whine made him frown, until he pulled his head away from the interior and recognized the sound as coming from outside. Helicopter blades fighting with the wind.

A loud crash sounded close by. Screwdrivers and probes spilled across the floor as the tool box banged against the planks. The husky had jumped onto Palmer's work table and knocked the box over. The dog stood panting atop the table, trying to peer out the narrow window just below the ceiling, its forepaws resting on the little ledge there.

Palmer cursed softly and got to his feet, and started to gather up his tools, replacing them carefully in the box. He yelled toward the open doorway.

"Hey, Clark! Will you kennel this goddamn dog? If he's healthy enough to jump up on tables he's sure as hell healthy enough to join his cousins!" When no reply was forthcoming he picked up a wrench and started banging against a pipe running toward the kennel. "Hey, Clark!"

The dog ignored him, pawing at the window as it stared out at the arriving chopper.

The helicopter jiggled unsteadily in the wind, finally settling on the pad near its mate and the bulldozer. Childs and Sanders were waiting for it.

As soon as the steady *whup-whup* of the rotors had slowed sufficiently they came running toward the craft, bent over against the wind, hauling guy wires behind them. Childs snapped one hook onto the link welded to the copter's tail while Sanders did the same near the cockpit. Macready was out quickly, assisting them.

"What'd you find?" Childs bellowed at him through the gale. The wind was picking up again. It bit at the mechanic's exposed cheeks.

Macready appeared not to hear him. Childs snapped on another guy wire, attaching it to the side of the copter. It sang in the wind as he moved closer to the pilot.

"Hey, Mac. I asked you what—" He broke off as Macready turned to face him. The pilot's anguished expression was eloquence enough for Childs.

"Later," Macready mumbled. Childs stared into his friend's face and just nodded.

4

The science staff had crowded into Garry's quarters. The station manager's room was somewhat larger than the others, but the atmosphere was still claustrophobic.

There was initial concern that the Norwegian videotape wouldn't play back on the camp monitors because of the difference in broadcast signals used by U.S. and European stations. The concern had turned out to be well founded.

At first try the screen had displayed only intense visual static and aural mush. But Sanders was able to transfer the tape via the station's own elaborate video equipment and come up with one that put out a signal the camp monitors could read.

The result wasn't perfect, but at least it was viewable. The picture was grainy and faint and there was no sound. No one commented on the video as it unspooled.

Whoever had operated the video camera was no Victor Seastrom. The picture weaved and tilted, occasionally blurred by overexposure, darkened by under. Not that they seemed to be missing anything of importance.

There were numerous, matter-of-fact shots of the Norwegian team at work, a long sequence of them playing soccer out on the ice, shots of the cook preparing meals, of men playing chess, of day-to-day life. Which was to say, long stretches of tape boring to look at.

Norris was barely paying attention to the monitor. He was devoting his attention instead to the thick bundle of notes Dr. Copper had hauled back to camp.

"Seems they were spending a lot of time at a place four miles northeast of their compound."

Blair looked questioningly at him. "And when did you start reading Norwegian?"

Norris threw him a thin smile. "About the same time I mastered Xhosa." He tapped the uppermost sheet of paper. "There are maps in here. The notations are in Norwegian,

42

but the topographic features are the same. A contour line's a contour line in any language. And of course the math is the same, once you convert the metrics."

"Oh. Right," said Blair subsiding.

"Any indication of what they were involved in?" asked the station manager.

Macready was fiddling with the video monitor, trying to improve the picture and failing miserably.

"Lots of manuals and pictures scattered around the place," Norris told Garry. "Indications of ice-core drilling, seismology, glaciology, microbial biology. Same old shit we do."

Snatches of a rowdy song burst suddenly from the monitor's speaker as the scene on screen shifted from someone at work by a laboratory bench to an unsteady shot of a bunch of naked Norwegians holding a sign in front of their waists as they stood outside their camp in super-freezing weather. Several held artifacts common to every contemporary culture, though the brand of beer was unknown to the disgusted watchers. The sign itself was incomprehensible. In all likelihood it contained nothing of enduring scientific value.

Bennings turned away from the TV, muttering disgustedly. "How much more of this down-on-the-farm crap is there?"

"If Sanders's timing is right," Macready told him, "about nine more hours."

The meteorologist shook his head. It was hot and crowded in the room and he had important work to do. "We can't learn anything from this."

Copper nodded reluctant agreement. "You're probably right. Maniacs don't usually think to turn video cameras on themselves while they're in the process of going crackers." He glanced over at the station manager.

"All right. Mac, kill it." The pilot shut off the video deck and the television, and disconnected the patch cord linking them. Garry looked back over at the doctor. "You two find anything else?"

"Maybe," Copper replied. He nodded to Macready, who took a small, battered tape deck from his pocket and handed it over to the doctor.

"Macready and I were listening to some of these

43

cassettes on the flight back from the Norwegian camp. I'd like the rest of you gentlemen to hear this particular one." He gave the "play" switch a nudge.

A Scandinavian voice filled the room. It was flat, calm, methodical; the boredom apparent despite distance, time and even a different language.

Norris let out a bored sigh. "Sounds like the verbal equivalent of the tape we've been mooning over. Hours of notes and nonsense."

"What do you want from us?" Bennings wanted to know.

Macready gestured for them to be patient. "Just listen. We thought the same way you do . . . at first."

Copper played with the fast-forward control, eyeing the built-in tape counter as the machine squealed. At five-oh-one he stopped the racing cassette and depressed "play" a second time. The calm voice was heard again.

Then something sounded dull, loud, and ugly, as though a distant explosion had taken place. The little machine's omnidirectional internal microphone wasn't large, but there was no mistaking that sharp *cruuumppp* from the speaker.

A pounding noise followed the explosion. There were shouts, some near, some far away. Then echoes of confusion, of equipment being tipped over, of glass shattering. Running feet grew loud, fading as their owners moved away from the recorder.

Something went *thunk* and the volume intensified, as if the recorder had been hit or thrown against something hard. Feet sounded close by, banging wooden planks.

A violent gurgling rose above the general cacophony, then a loud hiss like a steam boiler shutting down. Men screamed and raged in Norwegian.

Then a piercing screech that made the hair on Norris's neck stand erect. Several explosions next, like cannon firing in the distance. The execrable screeching again, louder now, mixed with the howls of distraught, panicky men.

Copper noted the grim expressions on the faces of those gathered around him. He derived no satisfaction from the effect the tape had on them. Soon all sound stopped. The tape had come to its end. He switched the machine off and regarded his companions in silence.

"That's it?" Fuchs asked softly.

Copper shook his head. "No. It's a split tape with automatic rewind. It goes on like that from the beginning of the second half for quite a while." He let that sink in before asking, "What do you gentlemen make of it? Neither Macready nor I could make any sense out of it."

"Could be anything," Garry suggested. "Men in isolation are subject to pressures the psych boys don't always plan for. Could be the result of some beef that snowballed, got out of hand. Some little thing; an argument over a soccer score, ownership of a magazine . . . we've no way of knowing.

"Something else, too," he added speculatively. "These guys weren't here very long. Usually serious psychological differences among crews show up in the first couple of months or wait until the end of a year's stay."

"Yeah," agreed Copper, "but the differences usually don't end in homicide."

"Maybe it wasn't just mental," Norris ventured. "Maybe their whole camp got bent out of shape from some other cause. Something they ate, maybe." He looked over at Copper. "What about it, Doc? Could some kind of food poisoning make 'em go crazy like that?"

The physician mulled over Norris's theory. "It's not impossible." His eyes went back to the now quiescent tape deck. He recalled the screams, the sense of panic it had recorded. "Many men play around with mild hallucinogens during their duty tours. It's a good time to experiment. There's not really anyone around to arrest them. We do it ourselves. Take Palmer, for example."

Fuchs defended the absent pilot. "Palmer's still flaky from all the acid he dropped back in the sixties. These days he doesn't touch anything stronger than sensimilla. At least, as far as I know he doesn't."

"I know he doesn't," said the doctor soothingly. "His monthly checkups show that. None of us fiddle with dangerous stuff. But just because we don't doesn't mean these Norwegians didn't get into something heavy. If you've the time and inclination and a little chemical know-how you can whip up all kinds of cute goodies in the simplest of labs."

"Yeah, like what?" asked Norris, with mock enthusiasm. It drew forth a few long-absent chuckles from his neighbors.

45

Copper smiled with them, but only for a moment. His mien quickly turned somber again. "There's something else we want you to see." He exited Garry's quarters, the others trailing curiously behind him.

The portable surgical table gleamed in the middle of the infirmary. Macready and Copper went to a corner and lifted a heavy-duty plastic sack between them. The contents were dumped unceremoniously onto the table.

"Besides the papers, the videotapes, and the cassettes, we also found this," Copper told them.

The mess on the table had once been a man. It was badly charred and broken, but that wasn't what drew the instant attention of the onlookers.

What remained of the trousers and shoes were ripped lengthwise and split into long shreds, as though the legs and feet they normally concealed had suddenly grown five sizes too large for them and had burst the seams from within. The upper torso was an almost unrecognizable gnarly mass of indistinctly formed protoplasmic mush.

There were no visible arms; just lumps of dark goo and flesh flanking the chest region. The head was oddly disfigured and looked larger than normal. Its location was far more disconcerting than its appearance. It seemed to be growing out of the stomach. There was nothing atop the shoulders, or where the shoulders ought to have been.

Peculiar appendages that resembled loose tendons were wrapped around the carcass like white rope. The ends stuck out to the sides at odd angles, stiff and hard as plastic. They'd reminded Copper of vines climbing the walls of a hothouse, save for their color. One circled repeatedly around the body's left leg like the striping on a barber pole. Another was wrapped securely around the misplaced skull.

Scattered colorfully amid the goo-like morass of the chest area were torn fragments of a shirt, like feathers protruding from tar.

Fuchs turned away for a moment, but no one threw up. None of them, not even the usually unflappable Garry, was unaffected by the viscous grotesquerie, but the corpse was too far removed from humankind to affect them intimately. It was a specimen, like Norris's rock samples or Blair's tubes full of aerial bacteria. It was too bizarre, too distorted to connect with any of the grinning, beer-guzzling figures hey'd seen in the salvaged photographs from the Norwegian amp.

"I know it's pretty badly burned," Copper finally uttered into the aghast silence, "but could a fire have done ll this? At high temperatures human bodies burn. They on't . . . melt."

Sickened but fascinated, Blair poked at the tendonlike rowths and the asphaltic goo. Some of the liquid came way on his fingers and he hastily wiped it off on his pants g.

"Curious, isn't it?" Copper asked him.

Blair grimaced. "I don't know what to say. Never seen nything like it. Hope I never do again."

"I'd like for you and Fuchs to help me with the autopsies n this one and the man Garry had to shoot this morning."

"If you insist, Doc." The senior biologist looked nhappy. "But I'm not volunteering."

"You don't have to volunteer," Garry informed him urtly. "I'll make it official." He nodded toward the carcass. This is your department."

"I'm not sure this is anybody's department," the iologist replied, still wiping his fingers on his trousers. The amn stuff had the tenacity of a black glue. He turned to egin the necessary preparations. He'd assisted Copper efore, Outpost #31 not being large enough to rate a nurse, ut this time he felt like going on sick call himself.

"If it's any consolation, Blair," said the doctor, "I'm not ooking forward to this either. But it's got to be done."

"Yeah, I know." Blair was removing pans from a locker. 'So let's quit talking about it and do it. The sooner we start, he sooner we'll be done with it."

Fuchs was the only one who might have volunteered to help. He was examining the body with care, growing interest having replaced his initial queasiness.

The rec room was always the busiest in the compound. Unlike the scientists, the maintenance personnel had a considerable amount of free time. Their expertise was only required during emergencies, normal checkout procedures usually taking only four or five hours a day. They spent the remainder of their days relaxing with a ferocity only the truly isolated can appreciate.

Tiny wooden figures spun on metal poles, furiously manipulated by Nauls and Clark. The football game they were playing was badly battered, the paint scratched, the legs bent by frustrated kicks, the rubber grips missing from several of the control bars. Dog handler and cook were going at it hot and heavy.

Sanders relaxed in a corner on one of the old, beat-up, thoroughly comfortable couches. He was thumbing through an old issue of *Playboy,* whistling to himself and wishing, as usual, that he was somewhere else. Anywhere else. A table and chairs were occupied by Bennings, Norris, the station manager, and a deck of dirty cards.

"Take two," said Garry, placing a pair face down on the table. Bennings obediently dealt him a couple, then gave one to Norris and three to himself. Garry studied the new cards, found that he now held an ace, a four, a deuce, one king, and one queen. Terrific.

Something nudged him under the table, then moved off to irritate Bennings. Judging from the meteorologist's tone as he responded to the interruption, he hadn't done any better on the draw than Garry.

He looked over toward the frenetic football game. "Clark, will you put this mutt with the others where he belongs! We're trying to play poker here!"

Clark exchanged a knowing look with Nauls, walked over and bent to look under the table.

"That's all right, boy," he said coaxingly to the husky, "it's all right. Nobody's going to hurt you. Come on now." He reached under and grasped the animal by the ruff around its neck. It submitted docilely to the grip.

Clark gently tugged the dog out from beneath the table and started walking it toward the door. As they passed the irritated Bennings, the handler glanced over his shoulder.

"Trying to play poker is right . . . drawing to an inside straight."

Bennings made a rude noise and threw his cards at Clark, who ducked and hurried out the door, the dog trotting easily alongside him.

The lab was larger than most of the nonstorage rooms at the outpost and was well equipped, in contrast to the

48

regularly abused contents of the recreation room. Glass tubes and beakers gleamed beneath bright fluorescents. The steel sink shone argent. Even the floor was relatively clean.

Copper was working at the center table. His gloves were stained dark red. The other body lay nearby, draped with a white sheet and awaiting its turn. The corpse Copper was working on, or rather in, was that of the berserk gunman who'd invaded the compound earlier that morning and attacked Bennings and Norris.

Blair hunched over a microscope, studying one slide while Fuchs carefully prepared a fresh one. The assistant biologist utilized scalpel and tweezers and stain with all the skill of someone repairing a fine watch.

Copper wiped sweat from his forehead with the back of a forearm as he turned away from the body, which was already beginning to ripen in the warm air of the lab. He pulled off the stained gloves and tossed them into the nearly laundry bin.

"Nothing wrong with this one," he announced to his two co-workers. "Physiologically, anyway." He let out a tired breath and glanced at Blair. "Have any luck?"

"Not so far."

"Nothing toxic?"

Blair stood away from the eyepiece he'd been staring through and blinked at the doctor. "No drugs, no alcohol, no inimical intestinal bacteria. Nothing. Everything you've excavated checks out as normal."

Copper pursed his lips and nodded. He opened a drawer and took out a clean pair of the disposable surgical gloves. His gaze shifted to the strangely distorted humanoid mess lying beneath the white sheet.

"Fuchs, leave the slides for a minute and give me a hand here. Let's switch these around."

"You're getting healthy enough to make a nuisance of yourself, boy," Clark told the husky as he led it through the long, cold tunnel leading to the kennel. After removing him from the rec room the handler had carefully placed a new bandage and dressing on the animal's injured hip.

"You've got to understand, to most of the guys you're just another piece of camp machinery. Machinery ain't

49

allowed to intervene in camp activity, especially card playing." He ruffled the dog's head between the ears. It licked his hand appreciatively.

"You're okay in my book, though. Maybe we can get you assigned here permanently. I don't think the Norwegian government would object. You'll have to learn to stick with your buddies, though." He unlatched the kennel door and walked the husky inside.

The kennel was a metal box some twenty feet long and five wide. It was not well lit and smelled powerfully despite the presence of the dog door at the far end, which gave access to a ramp leading outside. The dogs used it, but the box still smelled. The canine miasma didn't trouble the handler, however. He was used to it.

Some of the sled dogs were sleeping, curled up against each other for extra warmth. The kennel was heated, but not to the extent the rest of the outpost was. Too much heat would have been unhealthy for the animals.

Two of them lapped at the section of metal drum that served as a watering trough. Another was nibbling at the pile of dried food the handler had dumped into the kennel earlier. Others rose at his entrance, stretched lazily and rubbed against his legs. Two sniffed curiously at their new companion.

Clark patted the husky, and greeted several of the other dogs. "Nanook, Archangel, meet . . . well, we'll find a name for you one of these days, fella." He urged the new dog forward. "Now you make friends." He addressed the others as they all slowly began to gather around.

"Lobo, Buck . . . the rest of you make our visitor feel at home, you hear?"

He gave the newcomer a last, reassuring pat, then turned and left, latching the door behind him. He stood there, listening. No growls or snarls sounded from the other side of the door. Then he left, satisfied that the new animal would adapt successfully to his new surroundings and they to him. Sled dogs were very adaptable.

Childs lay in bed in his room, staring at the color portable screwed to the wall. On the screen a housewife was trying to guess the price of a new washer/dryer combo. The announcer and audience combined to make it seem like a matter of life and death instead of ring-around-the-collar.

Childs didn't give a damn for game shows, but this one was different. Each man could put in requests for videotapes, going down the list that the regular supply flights could bring down from the States. Most of the men requested football games, new movies, situation comedies. Childs always asked for this particular game show, to the consternation of the supply clerk at Wellington. But he got his tapes.

Everyone at the base assumed this preference had something to do with nostalgia and, in truth, Childs had religiously watched this particular game show back in Detroit. He watched because whoever selected the contestants from the audience always managed to choose a steady stream of dynamite-looking ladies.

Childs got more pleasure from watching them win stereos and cameras and trips to Bermuda than he did the tired actresses who populated the porn tapes that were also available. These were real women, and they weren't acting. He enjoyed watching the pretty women from Phoenix and New York and Muncie bounce gleefully around the stage in genuine delight far more than he did the moans and groans of thirty-year-old blondes trying to act eighteen.

The lady currently on screen won the washer/dryer, and jiggled delightedly across the stage to claim her prize. Childs raised himself up and leaned over to switch off the VCR. He'd already seen this particular tape.

Time to go on to something new. He ran his eyes down the tape box, selected another tape and inserted it into the player, thumbing the "play" control.

This time the object of the game was to roll oversized dice on a crap table to win money and a chance at merchandise. The lissome dark lady currently gambling happily with the network's money was built like a hot night in August. Childs leaned back against the headboard and wondered why all the fine fillies were already married.

Palmer was stretched out on the cot opposite the mechanic, reading. The sound from the television didn't bother him. Not much could bother him when he was smoking. He alternated cultivating duties with Childs at their semisecret little "farm." Last season's harvest had been particularly fine. Pungent smoke drifted through the room.

Childs beckoned to him and Palmer handed the joint across. The big mechanic took a couple of hits and mentally

51

urged the game show director to go to an overhead shot, while Palmer returned to the cerebral stimulation afforded by the collected works of that renowned philosopher, Gilbert Shelton.

Macready sat alone in the pub, staring at the television monitor there. He was sipping the drink he'd mixed for himself.

The pub was actually a large metal storage crate. One side had been cut away and the interior decorated with shelves and bottle holders. The elegant wine list, a product of Norris's talented calligraphy, listed twelve different kinds of beer from Foster's Lager (Australian) to Dos Equis (Mexican) to the rare Hinano, brewed in Tahiti. There were also bottles containing darker and more potent liquids.

A Hamms beer sign hung at a crooked angle from the back wall of the pub, its sky-blue waters running downhill from a never-ending mechanical lake. Macready wiped his lips and took another slug of his drink.

He was forcing himself to run through every foot of videotape he and Copper had salvaged from the Norwegian camp. Thus far their contents had been unalterably boring. There were endless scenes of men at work, horseplay, the taking of ice samples, the recording of information. In other words, scenes of all the usual day-to-day activities you'd expect to see at such a station.

Worse, the cameraman was no Abel Gance, Macready told himself ruefully. The picture tended to be out of focus much of the time, and bobbed and weaved so that his eyes throbbed and his head ached as he forced himself to watch.

It was the very sameness of those tapes that troubled him and kept him at it. There was nothing on any of them to hint that any of the men depicted at work or play stood on the verge of a mental breakdown. They all appeared perfectly normal, and the fact that he couldn't understand a word they were saying did nothing to alter that evaluation.

Of course, a violent breakdown could occur suddenly and without any outward manifestation of internal trouble on the part of the disturbed. Copper had reiterated that point when the pilot had queried him about it.

Also previously discussed was the unlikelihood of a candidate for treatment displaying his symptoms for the benefit of the probing camera. But Macready continued to stare blearily at the tapes in the faint hope of discovering something revealing, some clue to what might have disrupted the placid daily routine of the Norwegian camp. It was hard going. Already he was on his third drink.

Blair hovered over the microscope. He put a new slide under the clips, examined it carefully, and frowned. Pulling away, he rubbed his eyes, then pressed the right one to the eyepiece for a second look.

"Doc. Come here a second."

Copper walked over and took the biologist's place at the instrument as Blair stepped aside. The doctor gazed at the slide for a long time, then stood back and shrugged.

"I don't understand. What's that supposed to be?" he said, gesturing at the microscope and its contents.

By way of reply Blair stepped around him and walked over to the badly disfigured corpse, which now lay on the center table. As Copper followed him, Fuchs took the opportunity to look into the microscope.

Blair indicated one of the stiff, tendonlike growths that protruded from the central mass of dark, viscous material and partially dissolved flesh, then pointed back toward the microscope.

"It's tissue from one of these sinewy rods."

Copper accepted that. "What did you stain it with?"

"Nothing." He looked over to his assistant.

Fuchs glanced back at them, as thoroughly befuddled by what he saw through the eyepiece as his associates were. "What in the world kind of cell structure is this?"

"Precisely my point," Blair said grimly.

"You posed a question, not a point."

"Can't they be the same?"

Copper interrupted the two scientists. "I don't follow you, Blair. What are you trying to say?"

"That I'm not sure it's *any* kind of cell structure. Biologically speaking."

"If it's a tissue sample, there has to be cell structure," said Copper.

"Does there?"

"If there isn't, then the material is inorganic."

"Is it?"

"You can't have organic material devoid of cell structure," the doctor added exasperatedly.

"Can't you?"

Copper gave up. "Look, this really isn't my field, Blair. I'm a simple GP. I do my best to repair the known, not decipher the exotic. Let's wrap it up for the day. I'm tired of cutting."

"So am I," added Fuchs wholeheartedly.

Copper unbuttoned his coat, which was no longer clean and white but instead resembled a Jackson Pollock canvas. He tossed it into the laundry bin on his way out the door. Fuchs followed him, disposing of his gloves. His lab coat was still relatively clean.

Blair held back, returning to his desk to take one last look through the microscope. The peculiar pattern under the eyepiece hadn't changed, hadn't in the absence of attention metamorphosed into something comfortably familiar. Copper's confusion was understandable.

The biologist was badly mixed up himself.

The weather had warmed slightly and the blowing snow melted a little faster when it struck something warm. It battered the outpost and spanged off the corrugated metal walls of the shed.

Inside the main compound, monitors kept the hallways and rooms pleasantly warm and moist. The humidifier was a necessity. It was a paradox that, despite the presence of frozen water everywhere, the air of Antarctica was bitingly dry. Chapped skin was a constant problem and Copper was always prescribing something for it.

After every shower the men oiled themselves as thoroughly as they did their machines, because the cascading hot water washed away body oils that were only slowly replaced. Dandruff was an irritatingly persistent, if not serious problem.

The wall clocks in the complex read four-thirty. Only night-lights illuminated the corridors and storage areas, the empty rec room, and the deserted kitchen. Snoring issued softly from behind closed doors. Sleep came easily in the white land.

Only one section was still occupied. As dazed as he was determined, Macready sat in the little pub and continued staring at the television screen. He was on the last of the Norwegian videotapes.

54

At the moment he was keeping one eye on the screen while inflating a roughly irregular flesh-toned balloon. This mysterious object soon took on the crude outline of a life-sized woman. Macready's wind was weak and he was having a hard time of it. His polyethylene paramour's proportions fluctuated with his unsteady breathing.

Something on the tape caught his attention and he stopped suddenly. Holding the filler tube clamped shut with one hand he reached up and hit the reverse. Pictures streaked the wrong way like a bad movie until he touched "play" again. He squinted at the screen.

There were the Norwegians again, working against a pale sky. No blowing snow obscured the picture. They were dressed for heavy outdoor work.

As he watched they separated and spread out. The picture momentarily showed waving sky as the cameraman changed his position without turning off the camera. When it steadied again it showed the team of foreign researchers standing on flat, wind-scoured ice. Their arms were outstretched toward one another as if they were trying to measure something.

Within the circumference of their outstretched arms was a huge, dark stain on the ice. The perimeter they'd formed with their bodies encompassed only one small section of a sweeping curve.

That was what had attracted Macready's faltering attention. The dark stain seemed to lie beneath the surface rather than on top of it.

The picture went to black, then came to life again. He could hear the Norwegians mumbling in the background.

The location hadn't changed but time had passed. In the background the sky showed blue rather than white. The Norwegians could be seen moving around the dark, roughly oval shape. They had its boundaries clearly marked off with little flags set on ice probes.

Again the scene faded. When the picture returned Macready found himself watching three men with ice drills boring holes in a little triangle above the center of the dark oval. The camera swayed as its operator moved in close to shoot downward.

Black, then picture again. The camera was shooting down into a large hole in the ice. Something dark and metallic showed at the bottom. Macready leaned closer, now more than slightly curious.

The next sequence showed the men using the drills to sink small, widely scattered holes into the ice at various points above the oval, using new flags as positioning marks. Others moved around the drill sites, working on their hands and knees with small boxes.

Macready frowned, mumbling to himself. "Too much to drill out. Decanite, maybe? Or thermite charges?"

The next time the picture cleared the little flags were hanging limply from their staffs. The view was from far away and there wasn't a Norwegian in sight. Several small explosions kicked up clouds of powdered ice, confirming the pilot's guess as to what the men on their knees had been doing while temporarily obscuring the view of the oval.

Suddenly the view yawed wildly. Something rumbled over the monitor. Then the camera seemed to be thrown through the air as a tremendous explosion strained the bass range of the television's tiny speaker. A startled Macready jumped out of the chair. Suddenly he was awake.

"What in . . .?"

The tape continued to play, the picture now badly distorted, showing only white ground. A jagged dark line ran the length of the picture. It took Macready a couple of seconds to realize that the line represented a crack in the camera lens.

Forgetting his airy companion, Macready jabbed the rewind button. The rejected mannequin went sputtering around the pub until it ran out of air and crumpled limply on the floor.

It was as quiet in the kennel as in the rest of the outpost. Perhaps quieter, for none of the sled dogs snored.

Not all of them were asleep. A few lounged lazily in corners and against companions—licking paws, yawning, scratching their backs against the hard floor, or simply gazing out of half-lidded eyes at nothing in particular.

Only one of them was fully awake. The bandage was missing from the husky's hip again. It studied its somnolent companions with quiet intensity.

After several minutes of this it trotted over to a cluster

of five dogs, sat down in front of them and continued its uncharacteristically intense watch, more catlike than canine. Gradually the five dogs became aware . . . of something. One moaned. They began to awaken, aware that something peculiar was in their midst. An uncertain whine came from a second animal as it rolled to its feet.

None of this activity altered the posture of the kennel's most recent arrival. It continued to sit motionless and stare at the others. Its back was abnormally rigid. It did not pant.

And there was something else, something more. The other dogs were aware of it only as a barely sensed unpleasantness in the stranger's stare, a not-rightness. A man would have noticed it immediately.

The new dog no longer possessed pupils. The eyes had become solid, lusterless black spheres.

Bewildered, several of those subjected to this unflinching gaze started to pace the kennel floor. As yet, they were still more confused than frightened. Several began to growl at the newcomer.

Still the new dog remained frozen in place. The growling around it began to get louder. Several of the other dogs awoke and started to join in the pacing and grumbling. They instinctively began circling the stranger. Growls turned to angry, frustrated snarls. This newcomer was not reacting as a proper dog should. The lack of any kind of response was beginning to infuriate the other inhabitants of the kennel.

One barked at the husky, then a second. The circling became faster, the growling more frenzied. With one mind, three of the pacing animals stopped circling and turned to face the stranger. They jumped it simultaneously.

A fascinated and thoroughly absorbed Macready was running through the footage immediately preceding the violent explosion and subsequent shattering of the camera lens when the far-off clamor from the kennel reached him. Reluctantly he dragged himself away from the monitor, after shutting it down with the freeze-frame control, and stalked out of the pub.

It was silent in the deserted corridor as he made his way toward the sleeping rooms, silent save for the constant din the dogs were raising. He stopped outside one of the cubicles. The door was unlocked and he let himself in.

57

Clark lay beneath light blankets on his back, snoring Macready hesitated, listening. If anything the dogs sounded more upset now than when he'd left the pub.

"Clark. Hey, Clark."

There was no response. Macready moved close to the bed and reached down to nudge the handler's arm. Annoyed Clark turned onto his side and pulled the blankets higher around his shoulders.

Macready reached over and pinched the handler's nostrils, cutting off his air. That made Clark sit up quickly He blinked at the intruder, too groggy to be really mad.

"What's the idea, Mac? What's up?"

"Can't you hear?" Macready jabbed a finger toward the doorway. The cacophony from the kennel was clearly audible. "Dogtown's going nuts. I was up and it didn't bother me, but if you let those mutts wake everybody, the rest of the guys will make dog food out of you. Take care of it."

"Well, hell." Clark swung his legs out of the bed, bent over and rubbed his eyes as Macready disappeared into the corridor. Having discharged his responsibility, the pilot was anxious to get back to the videotape.

Clark fumbled for his pants. He liked his animals, but sometimes even the best sled teams could be a pain. High-strung creatures, the slightest argument was enough to set the whole bunch of them off. A fight over who was going to be lead dog, over a particular morsel of food, over anything except mating privileges (all the females were spayed) was enough to send them into mindless frenzy.

He didn't mind that and wasn't surprised when it happened. It was the nature of sled dogs. But did they have to prove it at five in the morning? He had to break it up of course, and not just because the noise might interrupt someone's beauty sleep. The dogs were valuable. Childs and Palmer and Macready took care of their machines. It was up to Clark to take care of his four-legged ones.

The heat in the corridor was automatically turned down during sleeping periods. His bed-warmed body protested at being dragged out so early. You could hear the wind whistling hungrily overhead.

Sleepy and annoyed, he turned a corridor corner that faced the kennel. The noise from within was louder now,

58

much louder than he'd expected. He hurried toward the door. It sounded like tapes he'd heard of sled dogs attacking a bear.

Confused, he fumbled tiredly with the door, slipping the latch. "Now what's got into—"

Just as the door opened something hit him in the chest hard enough to send him staggering backward, his arms flailing for balance. He felt the same way he had one summer afternoon when Childs had accidentally blind-sided him during a game of touch iceball. The breath was knocked out of him as his diaphragm was compressed.

The two dogs who'd struck him got to their feet slowly and dragged themselves back into the kennel, whimpering. From within there came a roaring straight from hell, a grotesque symphony of barks and snarls, growls and frantic whining.

And an unearthly screeching . . . .

5

Macready was in the kitchen, having made a detour prior to returning to the pub and the waiting videotape. He had the big refrigerator open and was taking out a couple of beers to replenish the bar's stock when the far-off wailing reached him.

For an instant he stood there, frozen by the eerie sound, shocked into listening. Then he turned and sprinted out of the kitchen, forgetting to close the refrigerator door.

He used a beer can to smash the glass exterior of the fire alarm out in the hall, reached inside heedless of the broken glass still adhering to the box and pulled hard on the lever. Bells began to ring throughout the camp, startlingly loud in the silent, insulated corridors.

Macready and Norris followed the station manager and Clark toward the kennel. Macready carried a shotgun from the small armory while Garry hefted his Magnum. None of them were fully dressed. Clark carried a fire axe.

"I don't know what the hell's in there," he was telling them as they moved forward, "but it's weird and loud and pissed off, whatever it is. Sure as hell ain't no dog."

"What makes you so sure of that?" Garry asked him.

Clark's voice was solemn. "I've worked with animals most of my life, chief. No dog ever made a sound like that."

Far behind them, the hallway outside the sleeping cubicles was rapidly filling up with the rest of the outpost's personnel. Men stumbled half-naked into each other, into doors, hopping on one foot as they tried to shove the other hastily into pants' legs. Feet were jammed into shoes, heedless of possible damage to heels. The peaceful night had turned into a violent morning of confusion.

Childs was fighting with his belt buckle, which refused to tighten. He still wasn't fully awake. Bennings shouted at him from a nearby doorway.

"Mac wants *what?*" The camp's chief mechanic sought clarification.

"That's what he said. And he wants it *now.*" Bennings whirled and vanished up the corridor before Childs could think to question him further.

Clark and his armed companions approached the kennel door. After the two dogs had come flying out at him the handler had reflexively thrown himself against the half-opened door and relocked it. Garry eyed him questioningly.

"I couldn't think of anything else to do," the handler told him. "And in any case, I didn't want to try anything by myself."

The two dogs who'd been locked out were barking hysterically as they clawed at the steel door in frantic attempts to get back into the fight. One of them was badly bloodied, and not from the collision with Clark.

The melee continued unabated inside, the noise giving the shivers to the men standing outside.

Garry reached for the handle, then hesitated. "How do you want to handle this? This is your department."

"I'm not sure it's anybody's department anymore," Clark replied. "You and Norris hang onto these two." He indicated the impatient dogs. "Macready and I will flank the opening. If nothing comes out, we'll go in."

Garry mulled it over briefly, then nodded agreement. He and Norris each grabbed a dog by the collar and wrestled

60

them away from the door. Macready took up a position to the right of the doorway, readied the shotgun and looked tense. Where the hell was Childs?

Clark moved to the other side and put a hand on the latch. He looked over at the pilot. "Ready?" Mac thought of a sarcastic reply, bit it back and nodded affirmatively. The handler gave the other two a glance, saw that they were too busy trying to control the raging dogs to comment.

Clark took a deep breath and flipped open the latch. The heavy door swung outward. The noise inside the kennel was deafening. When nothing showed itself he nodded to Macready. The two men entered side by side.

The interior light had burnt out or been broken. It was coldly, unexpectedly dark. Macready cradled the shotgun and snapped on a flashlight, but before he could shine it around the chamber something hit him from behind and knocked him sprawling.

The moment the two men disappeared inside, the two dogs had broken free of Norris and Garry. Unused to handling anything as powerful as a sled dog, Norris had gone flat on his face. One of the dogs had raced up against Macready's legs and upended him.

"Mac, where are you!" Clark was shouting. If anything, the decibel level of the snarling and screeching and howling they'd stepped into had doubled.

"Here, dammit!" The pilot lay on the floor, groping for his flashlight. It had rolled from his grasp when he'd fallen but rested on the floor nearby, still glowing brightly thanks to the tough housing of aircraft aluminum.

Righting himself, Macready raised the end of the shotgun and hunted with the light. Clark quickly came up to stand next to him. Very little light entered from the dimly illuminated corridor outside. Macready moved the light around, trying to get his bearings in the unfamiliar chamber.

The far corner of the kennel was a seething mass of flashing teeth and ferocious snarls. The latter alternated with that high-pitched, bone-chilling screech. Something periodically threw dogs out of the pile with considerable force, but each time they were tossed aside they struggled back to their feet and rushed back in to rejoin the battle.

The light moved and illuminated something else. Something that wasn't a dog. Some thing. Or . . . was it a dog? It

61

was impossible to tell because it seemed to have some of the aspects of a dog one moment and when the light revealed it the next, something entirely different. Its very shape seemed to alter as they watched.

Macready blinked. The weak light was playing nasty tricks on his eyes. He tried hard to focus on what was a dog one second and wasn't the next.

A voice sounded imperatively from behind him.

"What's going on, dammit!" Garry roared.

"There's something in here with the dogs! Some kind of animal." He lifted the shotgun and aimed it toward the pile in the corner. "I'm going to shoot."

"No, wait, you'll hit our animals!" Clark warned him. Macready hesitated.

"Do something else, then!"

Clark waded into the heaving tangle of fur and fangs and began grabbing at necks and bodies, tossing them aside. As soon as he'd cleared several away he started swinging the fire axe, chopping and hacking at the gurgling, hissing silhouette that the dogs were attacking.

From out of the darkness came a thick, bristly dark leg. It looked like something borrowed from a spider, or maybe a crab. It wrapped itself tightly around the axe and jerked spasmodically, sending Clark smashing into the wall. The handler somehow retained his grip on the weapon.

The rest of the station team was arriving in ones and twos. They tried to squeeze into the kennel entrance behind Garry for a look at the chaos inside.

Macready thought he could see the thing clearly now. He was damned if he was going to wait on Clark any longer. The shotgun went off several times, an ear-splitting thunder in the enclosed kennel. A furry missile, one of the still-fighting huskies, was flung at him and sent him stumbling to the floor. The flashlight rolled free again.

As soon as Macready went down Garry moved toward him, holding the Magnum with both hands and firing steadily in the direction of the screeching and moaning. A dog yelped, struck by a round. Macready was crawling past the station manager's ankles, trying to recover the flashlight.

"Clark! Where are you? Clark!" There was no reply from the dog handler. He'd hit the wall hard. In any case, it was difficult to hear anything in the kennel now, between the issing, the frenzied barking of the dogs, and the regular ruption of Garry's pistol.

Childs came loping down a side corridor. He was owing a large tank on a two-wheeled dolly. Dual hoses ran rom the top of the tank to a heavy industrial torch.

He halted outside the kennel and shouted to the men nside.

"What's happening in there?"

"Childs, is that you?" Macready's voice.

"Yeah, it's me, Mac. What the hell's going on?"

"You bring that torch? You get your ass in here with it!"

Childs didn't hesitate. He opened valves on the top of the tank, then switched on the gunlike device itself and rushed nto the kennel trailing hoses behind him. The other men made a path for him.

It was still crowded inside and he bumped into Garry, throwing him off balance.

"Sorry, chief. Can't see clearly yet."

"Never mind me!" the station manager snapped at him, trying to reload in the near blackness.

"Childs!" Macready howled.

"I'm coming, dammit. Where are you?"

"Here!" Macready signaled with his flashlight, then directed the beam toward the reduced cluster of battling sled dogs. "It's over there in the corner. Torch it."

"What about the dogs?" the mechanic hesitated.

"Screw the dogs! Torch it!"

Childs touched a switch. Blue flame spurted from the tip of the device. He aimed it grimly toward the tangled mass and opened a valve wide.

Flame shot across the floor and struck the center of the mass. The dogs broke away immediately, a more elemental terror temporarily overwhelming their fear and anger at whatever they'd attacked. They scattered and broke instinctively for the open kennel door.

Part of the wooden kennel floor began to burn crisply. Something mewed and screeched and clawed at the back wall, too big to fit through the dog door.

"We're on fire!" Childs shouted worriedly.

"Don't let up," Macready ordered him. He was firing the shotgun repeatedly into the flames.

Garry joined the firing and emptied his Magnum into

the back of the kennel, then spoke calmly as he reloaded a third time. "Extinguishers," he told the men gathered behind him.

Macready had run out of shells. He stood next to Childs, keeping the twin hoses from getting underfoot. His expression bordered on the demonic.

"That's it, that's it! Don't let up, Childs. Burn the sucker, burn it!"

The mechanic held the stream of flame steady as he moved slowly toward the back wall. The hissing continued to fill the kennel, more distinct now since the surviving dogs had fled.

Outside in the corridor the rest of the crew was chasing smoldering dogs, spraying them with chemical fire retardant. The smell of burning fur filled the air. Dogs and men choked on smoke and chemicals. Norris led a couple of the crew into the kennel, where they began spraying the floor to keep the flames from spreading.

After a brief eternity the screeching and howling began to fade. There was a last lingering hiss. Then it was silent, except for the steady roar of the torch.

Macready was standing next to the mechanic, hammering on his shoulder with a fist, his eyes wild. "That's it, man. Burn it back to hell, burn it . . .!"

Childs turned off the torch. His voice was subdued. "That's it, man. It's done. It's over."

Macready stared up at him, breathing hard, his fist still poised to strike. Childs grabbed the pilot's arm and squeezed. "It's *over*, Mac." He put the torch down and walked around the pilot. A body was sitting there, leaning up against the wall of the kennel.

"Hey, Clark." Childs stared into the handler's face. Clark's eyes were open, staring, but the man did nothing to acknowledge Childs's presence. The mechanic turned and shouted anxiously toward the corridor. "Hey, somebody go get Doc Copper. Fast!"

Garry was standing alongside him. He bent over, shining a flashlight into that handler's face. "Shock, looks like."

Childs rose, then turned to gaze back to the corner where he'd played the torch. "He's got company . . ."

* * *

That morning the recreation room slowly filled with exhausted men. Their faces showed the effects of worry and little sleep. There wasn't much conversation, none of it the usual light bantering, and none of it very loud. They conversed in urgent whispers and pointed toward the middle of the room.

Blair stared silently at the badly burned corpses on the central table. There were two unfortunate dogs there, and something else.

The bodies were connected together like Siamese twins, bound in an inextricable embrace that had nothing to do with love. One animal wore the remnant of Clark's bandage and was otherwise easily identifiable as their Norwegian visitor. It was much larger than its companion, bigger than any husky had a right to be, and there were aspects of it that were anything but doglike.

From hips to chest the main torso was cracked like old plaster and peeling back at the edges. It looked as though something had blown up inside the animal's gut and was trying to force itself outward.

Odd appendages, a peculiar kind of organic cording, were wrapped around both bodies and connected to the flesh of each. They were uncomfortably like those protruding from the body of the deformed Norwegian that Copper, Blair, and Fuchs had been dissecting.

Clark sat in a chair against the far wall. His eyes were still glassy, but Copper had administered a relaxant and the dog handler was beginning to emerge from shock. Nauls stood next to him, talking slowly and patiently, trying to comfort his friend.

Childs stood nearby and sucked on a joint, trying to relax and failing. There was no pleasure in the smoke, not this morning. His eyes were fixed on the floor. When he'd torched the thing that lay on the table back there in the kennel it had let out a terrible scream, and he couldn't get that inhuman wail out of his head.

The burned and battered corpses of two other dogs lay on the floor in the middle of the room, close to the table with its gruesome burden. At least, they looked like dogs. Blair turned his attention from them back to the travesty of life on the table. His face showed growing concern.

He turned and walked over to a wall intercom, and pushed the button connecting the rec room to the infirmary. "Fuchs?"

The reply was slow in coming. "Yeah. That you, Blair?"

"Yes. How's it coming?"

The assistant biologist turned and looked over toward the surgery table. Three more dogs lay on it. All were sedated and badly cut up. But they were still alive.

"Slowly. I'm no vet."

"Neither's Clark." Blair looked across the room to where the handler was still sitting dazedly in his chair. "He's still not in any shape to help."

"I know." The younger man chewed on his lower lip. "I'm doing the best I can for them."

"Okay. See you."

"Yeah. Hey, you figure anything out yet?"

"Not yet. Bye."

"Bye yourself." Fuchs moved away from the intercom and started unwrapping new bandages. One of the dogs on the table whined at him.

"Easy, boy. We'll get you fixed up as fast as we can. I'll do your leg in a minute." He started toward the table.

Nauls was patting Clark on the shoulder and smiling, trying to raise the other man's spirits. "Hey, it's okay now, man. It's dead. It's over." He gestured toward the card table. "You see? There's nothing to worry about any more."

Clark's head turned slowly and he bestowed a dreamy grin on the cook. "I know. Childs killed it. I saw. Last night, wasn't it?"

Nauls let out a relieved breath. "That's right, man. You got it." If Clark's time sense had returned that was a sure sign he was going to be okay. At least, that's what Copper had said. He fervently hoped so. He liked the handler. He wasn't snobbish, like some of the scientists.

Nauls looked over at the senior biologist. "What happened to those dogs, Blair?" He indicated the card table and its distorted shapes.

The scientist looked back at him, then at the table again. "You tell me, Nauls. You tell me."

The little work cubicle was filled with filing boxes full of three-by-five cards, tapes, small tools, and open plastic crates filled with pieces of rock. Norris sat at the single small desk. A light hung over him, its flexible metal neck bent at a convenient angle, giving it the look of a steel cobra. It shone brightly on the maps the geophysicist was sorting through. Some of the notations on the maps were in Norwegian, some in English.

Eventually he found the chart he was hunting for and placed it above one of the Norwegian maps. He used a black marking pen to make identical notations on both.

"Here," he announced confidentially. "This is where they were spending most of their time. I cross-checked with their notes. You can figure out the months where they've been written out. They used numeric notation most of the time, though." He continued to make little arrowheads and dots on the maps."

Macready stopped looking over Norris's shoulder and turned at a sound. Bennings poked his head into the room.

"Well?" Macready asked him.

"Pretty nasty out, Mac. Thirty-five knots."

"Any chance it'll let up?"

"Hard to say. I wouldn't count on it. There's one good thing, though."

"What's that?"

"Not much snow in suspension right now. It's pretty clear, and you shouldn't have any icing problems. But it's not what I'd call recreational flying weather."

Macready turned to glance over Norris's shoulder again. "Screw it. I'm going up anyway. I'll take Palmer as a backup, just in case we run into any trouble." His eyes were concentrated on the lower of the two maps, the one with the English markings.

"You sure we can find that place, Norris?"

The geophysicist nodded reassuringly and rose from his chair. "The coordinates are the same on both maps. We'll find it, all right." He started rolling the maps together, and turned out the cobra light.

Garry entered the rec room, glanced momentarily at the still stunned Clark and the attentive Nauls, then walked over to join Blair in gazing down at the interlocked animal forms. The station manager wore a clean shirt and had just shaved. The Magnum rested in the holster at his belt, cleaned and reloaded.

"What have you figured out, Blair?"

"Other than a slow way of going nuts, not much." He picked at the fragments of bandage still attached to one bulging leg. "It sure as hell wasn't anything new that got in from outside." He looked over toward Clark. "I'm sure the kennel was locked when Clark found it. We checked the outside dog door. It was still latched from the inside.

"It had to be the new dog. The Norwegian dog."

Garry looked doubtful, and angry. "I just can't comprehend any of this. It was *just* a dog."

A sharp, derisive laugh sounded from the other side of the room. There was no humor in Childs's voice. "Wasn't no dog, chief. I don't have to have no degree to figure that out."

"That tape Macready showed us earlier this morning," Blair murmured softly.

"Couldn't make much out of it myself."

"I've asked him to try and locate the site where they were working," the biologist went on. "Where that peculiar oval in the ice was, where the explosion broke their video camera. He's taking Palmer with him. Norris volunteered to go along. Okay with you?"

"Sure, if you think it's advisable."

"I'm damned if I can think of anything else to advise."

"You think there's a connection?"

"Maybe." He turned to stare back down at the table and the enigma it held. "Anyhow, like I said, I don't have any other bright ideas. You?"

The station manager tried to make sense of the insane happenings, but could only shake his head dolefully.

The wind flailed the white desert. The chopper bounced and dipped and only experience and determination kept the men inside her from doing the same.

Macready fought the controls as they rode the currents, trying to stay as close to the ground as possible so that they wouldn't miss anything, while still leaving enough leeway for evasive action in the event the craft was caught by a downdraft. It was hard work and you couldn't relax for a minute.

The storm had passed quickly, but the crystal-clear air

68

was deceptive. The only difference so far as Macready was concerned was that when there was no blowing snow or ice you could have the pleasure of seeing where you were most likely to crash.

Palmer occupied the copilot's seat while Norris peered over their shoulders from behind. The geophysicist was pointing at the plastic map taped to the flight console.

"One of their sites should be directly over here. The one we're after is a few hundred yards farther south."

"I know." Macready leaned on the controls and the copter heeled over to starboard. A high, even-topped white wall loomed directly ahead.

Norris regarded it professionally. The symmetry of the formation hinted that more than normal mountain-building activity might be responsible for its formation. The wall might mark the location of a minor fault line, or a lava tunnel. Or there might not be any stone present at all if it was a fossil pressure ridge of pure ice.

The copter rose and they soared over the wall. On the other side a flat glacial plain stretched toward distant high mountains.

Instantly visible as soon as they cleared the ridge and marking the center of the white plain like a giant ink spot was an enormous blackened crater.

The lab was full of dead dogs. They lay in a macabre row, each carefully tagged on one leg. Clark had eventually recovered his senses sufficiently to assist in the unpleasant work, but the pain finally became too much for him and he had to flee the room. Each of the dead animals had a name, each had been a close friend.

Fuchs was preparing new slides, which Blair studied under the microscope. Two cells were visible through the eyepiece. They were active, neither quiescent nor dead. One looked quite normal. Its companion looked anything but.

At the moment the two were joined together by a thin stream of protoplasm. Material from the larger cell, which was long and thin, flowed into the smaller, spherical cell. As it did so the smaller cell swelled visibly, until the cell wall fractured in three places. Immediately the smaller cell assumed a flattened shape like the other and three new streams of material began to flow outward from its interior. Neither cell appeared to have lost any mass.

Blair pulled away from the eyepiece and frowned as he checked his watch. It was running in stopwatch mode. He turned it off. The resulting readout was very puzzling.

Macready bounced the copter a couple of times as he set it down, but neither ship nor passengers showed ill effects. The steady hum of the rotors slowed to a stop. He pulled down his snow goggles and stepped out onto the ice. Norris and Palmer were right behind him.

It was a short walk to the fringe of the crater. Macready paused to kick aside a gnarled chunk of gray metal. The impact reduced it to splintery fragments. Another piece was so big they had to walk around it.

The massive hole was more than fifteen feet deep. Considerably more. The bottom of the crater was lined with charred, blackened metal. Everything was gray or black. The metal fragments were lusterless, dull as antimony but smooth all the same. Macready didn't know what to make of a polished surface that was nonreflective.

The ice around the rim was as smooth as glass and only recently rouged over with freshly blown snow. What hadn't been blasted away or vaporized had melted.

The outline of the hole suggested that it had contained a large sphere. Macready met Norris's eyes and said nothing. Only Palmer made no pretense of concealing his awe.

"Wow. Whatever it was, it was *big*."

"Look at this." Macready moved to his left and picked something off the ice. His companions gathered around.

"Recognize it?" he asked them. Palmer shook his head, but Norris nodded quickly.

"Looks like the remains of a medium-charge thermite cannister. Standard military ordinance. NATO uses the same stuff we do."

"Yeah." Macready heaved it toward the helicopter, the beginning of a growing collection. They spread out slightly and began to circle the crater.

There wasn't much solid debris. Much of what remained was too large to be carried. A fine gray ash lay on the ice and radiated outward from the center of the hole. Norris knelt and took a couple of small plastic tubes from a pocket.

Using a small pick he started taking ice and powder samples from the crater's perimeter.

There wasn't much for the two pilots to do except wait for the scientist. Palmer continued to marvel at the size of the crater. Glacial ice this far south was solid as rock. No thermite charge had ripped that wound in the surface.

Macready got tired of walking, retraced his steps and bent over alongside Norris. The geophysicist was examining a small piece of metal. He had a small box out and open. It held tiny vials of reagents and catalysts. A chart full of fine print was glued to the inside of the cover. A few of the words were in English, the rest in rarified words of many syllables. The symbols were completely alien to him.

While he watched, Norris dribbled a little red fluid from one of the vials onto the specimen of debris. Nothing happened and the fluid ran off into the snow. The contents of a second vial were tried, with the same result. A powerful smell rose from the liquid and Macready's nose twitched.

Norris looked up at him. "At first I thought it was some alloy of magnesium. It's light enough. More than light enough." He carefully wiped the gray splinter against the ice, then the side of his boot.

"I never saw metal with such a low specific gravity. It has some of the characteristics of metallic lithium, but that's crazy. Stuff like that can't be worked like normal metal. At least, that's what I've been told." He carefully put the last vial he'd utilized back into its slot in the box.

"That was concentrated sulfuric acid. Might as well have been water for all the effect it had on this." He tapped the fragment with a gloved finger. "Yet some it turns to powder if you so much as blow on it."

"So you don't know what it is?" Macready asked.

Norris shook his head. "Haven't the foggiest. Some kind of alloy. Wish I'd taken more metallurgy. But I'd bet a two-year sabbatical that this stuff is unique." He turned to give the empty hole a look of disgust.

"And those poor dumb bastards had to go and blow the hell out of it."

"Give 'em a break, Norris," Macready said. "I'm sure they planted their charges carefully. They were probably just trying to break up enough ice to make digging easy."

"I guess." Norris didn't sound very understanding.

Macready picked up the splinter and gazed at it. "Some of it powders, but some, like this piece, resists strong acid. Then how the hell did they blow it up?"

"Something in the metal, or in something that vaporized during the explosion, must have reacted chemically with the thermite. Or maybe it was the heat that did it, I don't know." He took the specimen back from Macready, slipped it into a plastic sample tube and began writing on it.

Macready rose and studied the horizon.

"There've been a lot of temporary camps set up in this area. Could some outfit, the Soviets or the Australians or somebody, have dug in a short-term station here and then pulled up stakes without taking everything with them?"

"Like what, for instance?"

"You know the big tanks we use to store the fuel for the choppers and the tractor?" He gestured toward the crater. "Could some group have left one here? The thermite could've set off any remaining gas."

Macready was reaching. He knew it, and so did Norris.

"Sorry, Mac," the geophysicist countered. "In the first place, the shape of the crater's all wrong. Next, this ice is glacial, not recent. You don't bury a temporary storage tank under twenty feet of solid ice. Also, propane and gasoline, any kind of fuel, is strictly rationed at any outpost. Nobody would take off and leave a lot of valuable fuel behind. Costs too much to get it down here."

"Maybe they intended to return."

"Maybe, but I wouldn't think so." Norris held up a gloveful of chipped ice. "This doesn't show any of the telltale signs of having been disturbed. It would if somebody'd had a base here. There'd be skid marks at least, even if all they put up were surface quonsets." He rose.

"Of course we can check on it when we make contact with McMurdo again. They'd have records of anything that's put down hereabouts."

"What if the Soviets or one of the Eastern European consortiums like the East German-Rumanian team were running a clandestine operation here?"

"C'mon, Mac," Norris chided him. "There's plenty of ice cover just as interesting as this a helluva lot closer to their permanent installations."

"Yeah." The pilot kicked at the surface, sending particles flying. "But maybe there isn't any oil there."

Norris considered a moment. "Now *that's* a possibility." He stared evenly at Macready.

After a moment the pilot grinned sheepishly back at him. "Okay, I give in, I don't believe any of that either." His expression turned serious once more. "So what do you make of it?"

"You know damn well what we both make of it."

"No chance it could have been some new kind of test craft?"

Norris shook his head. "No, and for a lot of the same reasons. This ice is too old and too undisturbed. Seismic activity has been shoving this region upward for a long time, not the other way round." He held up another ice sample.

"It's tough to be certain in the field, but I'd say this ice the thing was buried in is over a hundred thousand years old. Pleistocene at least."

There was a shout from behind them and both men looked around. Palmer was waving to them.

"Now, what's he found?" wondered Norris. He and Macready walked over to stand alongside the younger man.

Palmer was standing some fifty yards from the rim of the crater. A large, rectangular chunk of ice had been cut from the surface near his feet. The excavation was some fifteen feet long, six wide and about eight deep, according to Norris's eyeball estimation. All three men stared silently at the hole.

There was nothing down there except more ice. Snow whirled around their boots like white laces. . . .

6

This time of year night came quickly to the bottom of the world. Several of the men in the rec room were gathered around the large TV monitor. It was playing back the sequence showing the Norwegians finding the mysterious buried object that Norris and Macready, at least, were ready to believe was a vessel of unknown type and origin.

Suddenly the landscape on the screen, the movements of the members of the Norwegian team, no longer seemed so matter-of-fact. The tape was no longer a dull record of ordinary, everyday events. It had acquired something more than mere historical interest. Something intangible and yet very real to the men in the room who stared at the flickering, badly focused pictures.

It contained a presence.

Macready was sitting quietly across from a new chess set, though his attention was split elsewhere, between private thoughts and the glass of Scotch resting on the edge of the table.

Clark had recovered from the previous day's shock. He was sitting by himself in a corner chair, flipping through a magazine salvaged from the Norwegian camp. The contents were not of a scientific nature, but the handler found the succession of glossy photos edifying nonetheless. They took his mind off other, less pleasurable things recently observed.

He turned another page, his free hand toying with a piece of the peculiar metal the exploration team had brought back from the site of the explosion.

Childs finally turned away from the group studying the videotape and walked over to confront Macready. The pilot looked up absently.

"Hi, Childs." He waved indifferently at the board. "Want to play?"

The mechanic shook his head. "Don't know how."

"I'll teach you. I get tired of playing the machine."

"Not now," Childs said impatiently. "Okay, Mac, now run this by me again. Thousands of years ago this rocket ship crashes, right?"

"It probably didn't have rockets, according to what Norris tells me."

"Yeah, well, I don't give a damn if it used oars. This ship crashes here on the ice and the. . . ."

Macready's mind was elsewhere.

"Macready!"

The pilot blinked, sat up straighter in his chair. "Look, we're just guessing about this stuff. It could've been part of some Soviet installation or something. Some secret experiment they were running."

"That's not what you told Garry."

"He wanted my opinion. That's all it is at this point. Norris's too."

"Yeah. Go on."

Macready sighed as he started to reiterate the theory he and the geophysicist had concocted on the flight back from the site of the crater.

It was hard to participate fully in the daily life of the camp when you were required to spend most of your waking time in one room. Nauls didn't mind the isolation, though. It left him alone with his music.

At the moment the Gossamers were cooking in the background while he prepared to do so literally at the stove. He hunted through the large storage cabinet.

"Where's that big ol' steel pot of mine? Damn! Never can find anything the day you need it."

He slammed the door of the cabinet shut and turned in frustration to several of the overhead storage shelves. That's when he spotted something in the nearby trash bin. Curious, he walked over to check it out. When he recognized what it was his curiosity turned to disgust.

Somebody was always playing jokes on him. Good old Nauls, always the easy target. Everybody in camp knew how fastidious he was about his kitchen.

He reached into the trash bin and pulled out the dirty, torn pair of long johns. Somebody was going to own up to this outrage. Practical jokes were one thing, sanitation something else.

". . . and so it crashes," Macready was telling Childs, "and this guy, the pilot or whatever he was, gets thrown out, or walks out, and ends up freezing. Then a hundred thousand years down the line the Norwegians come moseying along, find him and dig him up, and then accidentally blow up his ship while they're trying to excavate it."

Childs made a face. "I just can't believe this bullshit." He looked across the room. "You believe this bullshit, Blair?"

Lost in thought, the biologist failed to reply. Cell structure and alloy structure were all jumbled together in his mind, confusing him worse than ever.

"I'll stick with your Soviet camp theory," Childs told Macready confidentially. "As for that big block of ice they cut out, it might've held corroborating evidence. Something with Cyrillic markings or stuff. That's why they were trying so hard to get at the bigger stuff. Maybe it blew because it was booby-trapped."

Macready eyed the mechanic challengingly. "Sure, and then they buried it under twenty feet of glacial ice. Anyway, we'll know soon enough. Garry's checking the station records to see if the Russkies have been operating in that region in the past. We'll double-check with McMurdo as soon as Sanders can get through to them.

"But don't hold your breath. Norris says it's impossible to bury anything in ice that old and that solid without leaving some indication that you've been digging. And we didn't find so much as a shovel scratch, except for what the Norwegians left behind."

The joint dangled loosely from Palmer's mouth. It was unlit, but its presence comforted him. He was already pleasantly high anyway, a nice condition to be in when you had to deal with the possibility that an ancient alien spaceship might've just blown itself to powder barely a few miles from your bedside.

The relaxed state of mind also facilitated Palmer's personal research. Norris and Blair weren't the only ones at the station who could perform serious research, no sir! Palmer still had several months of back issues of the *National Enquirer* and *The Star* to catch up on.

He looked up at the scoffing mechanic. "Happens all

the time, man. They're falling out of the skies like flies. Government knows all about it. Chariots of the Gods, man. They practically *own* South America. I mean, they taught the Incas everything they knew. How do you think those skinny little Indians built Sacsayhuaman, man? You think they hauled those ten-ton boulders around on their backs?"

Childs gave him a disdainful look. "Somebody ought to hit you with a ten-ton boulder, man. Shake out the cobwebs." He indicated the stack of scandal sheets. "That shit you're reading ain't exactly *Scientific American,* you know."

Palmer waved a handful of garish headlines at the mechanic.

"It's all suppressed in the slick magazines. The government doesn't want anyone to know. Read von Däniken! Have you ever read von Däniken, huh? Get your facts straight. They've been watching us for years." He rolled his eyes skyward, his voice full of mock fear. "They're probably up there, watching us right now."

"If they're looking for specimens I sure as hell hope they take you," Childs shot back. "They'll never bother us again." A few guffaws sounded from some of the other men.

Clark slid lower in his chair and turned the magazine he was looking at sideways. A bottom page flipped down. "Jesus," he breathed reverently, "why would those guys ever want to leave Norway?"

A snicking noise grew steadily louder out in the corridor. Nauls grabbed a door and swung himself into the room, his skates skidding to a sharp stop. He shook the crumpled-up long johns at the befuddled crew like a declaration of war.

"Which one of you ugly muthers has been tossing his dirty underwear into my clean garbage bin?" He threw the offending garment across the room. It settled like a blanket over Macready's wooden chessmen.

"I want my kitchen *clean,*" the cook railed at them. "Germ free. You schmucks better knock it off. Next time I find something like that in my kitchen I'll bake it into your next supper!"

Without giving anyone a chance to reply he whirled and skated off down the hall. Macready leaned forward and gingerly plucked the oddly torn underwear off his chessboard, rolling it up into a ball. Childs ignored the brief, noisy intrusion and resumed his pacing, uninterested either in the long johns or Nauls's complaint. It had been a poor joke at best and it wasn't *his* underwear.

"So come on now, Macready. Let's try it one more time. These Norwegian dudes come by, find him and dig him up. . . ."

Macready threw the ball of cloth across the room. It landed cleanly in a small trash can. He smiled inwardly. He preferred basketball to chess, but it's tough to set up a court in Antarctica.

Not that he hadn't tried. If you could move your arms at all in summer weather, you discovered that the ball didn't dribble too well on snow. Beneath the thin layer of snow was ice, which made for a more exciting but far more lethal game. Chess was safer. He rubbed his leg where he'd broken it last year while trying to make a simple layup.

"Yeah," he absently told the attentive Childs, "they dig him up and cart him back to their base. He gets thawed out, wakes up, and scares the shit out of them. And they get into one hell of a brawl."

"Okay, okay, right!" Childs jumped enthusiastically on the last part of the pilot's explanation. He wore an expression of triumph. "Now you just tell me one thing, Mac. One thing. How's this mutherfucker wake up after thousands of years of making like a side of frozen beef, huh? Tell me that."

The mechanic's intensity annoyed Macready almost as much as the persistent inconsistencies in his theory. "I don't know how. What am I, Einstein? He does it because he's different than we are. Because he's a space guy. Because he likes being frozen for a hundred thousand years. Maybe he'd just finished piloting for a couple of hundred thousand and he stopped to take a little nap. What do you want from me, anyway? Go ask Blair. He's got the brains. Me, I'm just a flyboy."

Childs turned and spoke brusquely to the senior biologist. "Okay, Blair, what about it? You buy any of this?"

Blair was staring straight ahead, but he was seeing something other than the far wall. Something insubstantial. He was talking to himself, but just loud enough so that everyone else could understand his words.

"It was here . . . got to that dog . . . it was here in this camp. That's why they were chasing it . . . that's why they were acting nuts. Not shooting at Macready and Norris . . . just trying to hit the dog. . . . didn't care whether they hit anyone else or not . . . just the dog, just get the dog. . . ."

It was suddenly very quiet in the rec room. Blair's monologue had quietly overwhelmed all other conversation. Even Clark had looked up from his magazine.

"So," Garry finally said from his seat near the pub, "so what? It's over with, done."

Blair turned to him, said nothing. He didn't have to. His expression was eloquent enough.

"Well," Bennings said edgily, "isn't it?"

Blair rose from his seat. His eyes seemed to come back to the room, but his voice was still subdued. "All of you come with me. Everybody. I've got something to show you, and a few things to say."

They filed slowly out of the recreation room, talking softly among themselves.

"And I mean everybody," Blair announced from the doorway. "Somebody get ahold of Nauls. Dinner can wait."

As they entered the lab the biologist methodically flipped on each of the several light switches. Then he moved to the center study table and pulled away the sheet covering its contents. Some of the men crowded around. A few took chairs. They'd already seen the two bodies on the table.

The two intertwined dogs were no prettier the second time around then they'd been the first. Cold radiated from them. They'd been kept in the lab freezer until only a few minutes ago. Despite the cold and Blair's treatments they were already beginning to smell.

"Whatever that Norwegian dog was, it . . . it was capable of duplicating itself," Blair told them solemnly. "Not to mention changing its form. Our visitor," and he pointed at the larger mass resting on the left side of the table, "wasn't a dog anymore.

"When it attacked our animal, whatever had taken possession of it began to try and link up." He indicated the tendon-like structures wrapped tightly around both corpses. "I believe those structures to be part of the duplicating-takeover process.

"When I speak of 'taking possession' of another dog I

mean in the biological sense. Technically, there's nothing mysterious or supernatural about the process. The methodology is purely mechanical.

"We can only theorize at this point as to the details. I don't have nearly the facilities to do more than that. What I believe happens during the takeover process is that the original thing injects a certain quantity of its own DNA into the cells of the animal it wishes to control." He held up a gooey dog leg that had been part of the Norwegian animal.

"For instance, this isn't dog at all. It *looks* like dog, but the cell structure bears no resemblance to normal canine cellular architecture. The cell walls, as in the original creature," and he waved with the leg, a gruesome baton, "are incredibly flexible. Controlled by the patterns in the DNA, they can conform to any pattern the creature wishes, provided it can obtain a DNA 'blueprint' to copy. In this case, dog DNA. Get me a good electron miscroscope and in a few hours I won't be guessing at that, I'll be proving it.

"The critical requirement is DNA to copy. Apparently the thing's incapable of duplicating a living creature out of nothing. It needs the control information contained in a subject's nuclear material to merge with. Fortunately, we got to it before it had time to finish."

"Finish what?" Nauls muttered.

Blair indicated the remains of the camp's sled dog. "Finish taking control of our animal." His hand rested on the furry skull. "The merging activity which occurs among the cells of the brain is particularly rapid and insidious. Like I said, I don't really have the right equipment here for this kind of work, but from what I've seen so far, brain tissue from that animal," and he indicated the bloated corpse of the Norwegian dog, "contains some of the damnedest synaptic connections any biologist ever imagined. Combinations and linkages that haven't got shit to do with canine evolution.

"So you see, in addition to taking control of existing cell structures and patterns, the original creature is also able to create new ones to its own requirements."

Copper frowned down at the table. "A body is only designed to support so much cellular material. If the invasion by this creature creates new matter in addition to taking over existing structures, how does the body's life-support system cope with the extra load?"

80

Blair's voice remained even, tutorial. "As you say, the body is only designed to keep so much organic material alive and functioning. Portions of this dog's brain, for example, have been blocked off by new structures. The flow of oxygenated blood has been redirected."

"In other words," Copper said quietly, "part of its brain has been turned off?"

Blair nodded. "Certain cerebral regions were dead before this animal died, having been supplanted in importance by new activity elsewhere."

"What regions were kill . . . were turned off?"

"Difficult to say. There was massive parasitic invasion. Some of those which control portions of the memory, intelligence, and in particular individuality. Hard to tell with a dog, of course, be it dead or alive." He turned his gaze back to the interlocked bodies.

"I think the whole process would have taken about an hour. Maybe more. I've no way of knowing for certain, of course. There's nothing comparable in the literature. I'm extrapolating as best I can from what little we've been able to find out."

"And when that hour was up?" Garry asked pointedly.

The biologist looked over at him. "The conduits supplying connective material . . . these tendon things . . . would vanish and you'd have two normal-looking dogs again. Only they wouldn't be normal anymore, and they'd be dogs only in appearance."

"I'll buy that," agreed Palmer fervently. "That thing in the ice the Norwegians dug up sure weren't no dog."

"Of course not." Blair tried to control his impatience. These men are not scientists, he reminded himself, except for Bennings, Norris, and Fuchs. "If nothing else, the size of the missing portion of the excavated ice block points to a much larger creature.

"How much larger we've no way of knowing. As I've said, the altered cell structure is remarkably flexible. It's capable of a good deal of expansion or contraction."

"What do you think happened?" Garry asked him.

The biologist considered the question carefully. "Whenever the original thing was thawed out, revived . . . well, it was certainly disoriented. If its memory was intact, it must have realized it couldn't survive for long in our

81

atmosphere in its orginal state. Being the incredibly adaptive creature that it is, it tried to become something that could."

Once again he indicated the recumbent mass on the table.

"Before the Norwegians killed it, it somehow got to this dog."

"What do you mean, 'got' to the dog?" Clark asked.

Blair tried to be patient. "I've tried to make this simple. That may be impossible. This thing was a life form that was able to take control of any creature it got ahold of, cell for cell, neuron for neuron. The concept is staggering. The closest terrestrial analog I can think of is the lichen, which is not really an individual creature but an association of two very different kinds of life, algae and fungi.

"But this is much more complex and complete, and it's certainly not in the least symbiotic. The invading thing acts like a true parasite, taking complete control of the host for its own advantage. There's no mutual assistance, insofar as I've been able to determine. I . . . I don't pretend to completely understand all the ramifications myself."

"You're saying," Childs broke in, pointing skeptically at the Norwegian intruder on the table, "that big mother in the ice those guys chipped out became that dog?"

Blair nodded. "And there was no reason for it to stop there. As we can see here, it tried to take control of one of our dogs as well. I don't see what its limits would be. It could have become as many dogs as it wanted to, without surrendering control of its original host body. It doesn't take much organic material to alter DNA, though I'm not sure about the other large-scale changes.

"One cell is enough. The DNA pattern of the new host is irrevocably altered. And so on and so on, each animal it takes over becoming a duplicate of the original thing."

"You been into Childs's weed, Blair?" Norris muttered.

Blair's fist slammed onto the table. "Look, I know it's hard to accept! I know it's difficult to picture an enemy you can't see. But if that stuff gets into your system, in about an hour—"

"It takes you over," Fuchs finished for him.

"It's more than that, more than you becoming a part of it. The 'you' is gone, wiped out, shunted aside permanently by a new set of cellular instructions. It retains only what it needs of the original, the way it used the memory patterns of the Norwegian dog to make certain it acted in a recognizably doglike manner."

"It licked my hand," Norris murmured, "as it was being chased by those guys in the helicopter. It came right up to me and licked my hand and whined for help."

Blair nodded. "Sure it did. It keeps anything useful. This organism is highly efficient, not wasteful. And it's clever. Much too clever for my liking."

"So what's the problem?" Garry wanted to know. He indicated the two bodies lying unthreateningly on the table. "The torch crisped it pretty good."

The biologist turned to stare down at the canine forms. "There's still some cell activity. Clinically speaking, it's not entirely dead yet. . . ."

Clark jumped backward and stumbled over a waste can. The reaction from the rest of the men was similar if not as extreme.

"Take it easy," Blair told them, hiding the glimmerings of a smile.

"You said one cell was enough to take control," Norris murmured, his eyes on the suddenly malignant corpses.

"To imprint a pattern, yes," Blair admitted, "but not to initiate the takeover procedure. That requires a much greater quantity of protoplasmic material. The tendon structures which seem so important to the process, for one thing. They're composed of millions of cells." But the men shuffled uneasily, still uncertain, still fearful.

"Look." Blair tried to reassure them. "If there were any kind of danger d'you think I'd be standing here running my hands over the thing?" The men relaxed slightly. Blair looked down at the two bodies. "As far as I'm concerned, however, any cell activity, however minimal, is too much."

"What do you recommend?" Garry asked him.

Blair glanced at his assistant. They'd discussed the possibilities previously, when Blair had detected the minimal remaining cell activity. Still, Fuchs's eyes widened when he saw in his superior's expression which choice had been made.

* * *

83

"You can't. You can't do this!" Fuchs was screaming into the night.

It was very dark outside. The wind had let up and there was no snow in the air to obscure the vision of the heavily bundled-up men trudging out of the compound. Their purpose was equally clear.

Macready and Copper dumped the two dog corpses onto a cleared patch of ground. Childs upended the big can he was carrying and soaked the two bodies. The smell of gasoline was sharp in the perfectly clean air. He used the entire contents of the can, shaking the last few drops onto the rigid bodies.

"You can't do it," Fuchs was arguing violently with his companions. "You can't burn these last remains!" He was beside himself with a mixture of frustration and fury. But he didn't know what to do about it.

Childs put the gas can aside and picked up the big industrial torch while Macready emptied the contents of a second can onto the bodies. They were going to be as thorough as their orders allowed.

"And the horse you rode in on, Fuchs." The pilot stepped back and tossed the can after its mate. The empty containers rang loudly in the darkness when they struck. "Light it up," he told Childs.

The mechanic activated the torch. Fuchs started toward him, suddenly determined.

"Well, I'm not going to let this happen."

Childs struggled with him for a moment, then tossed him aside. Copper intercepted the angry Fuchs and sat astride the younger man's chest.

"Take it easy, Fuchs. Doctor's orders," he added gently. "This is necessary."

There was a roar in the dim light as the torch sprang to life. Unhesitatingly, Childs turned the jet of flame toward the corpses. They exploded impressively when the fire touched them. Snow melted around the bodies, which burned furiously. The mechanic kept the torch on them even after the gasoline caught.

Fuchs lay on the snow and turned his head away in disgust. "I just can't believe this. The greatest biological discovery in hundreds of years, and we incinerate it down to

84

the last cell. We're going to go down in the books as the biggest bunch of assholes in scientific history."

"Fuck history," said Macready tersely, watching the corpses burn. "I'd rather go down as an ignorant old asshole than an enlightened zombie." He looked over his shoulder at the assistant biologist, his expression grim.

"I don't suppose I should have expected anything like a scientific attitude from you, Macready. But to get that from Mr. Blair, and Norris." He looked up at the man sitting on his chest, a hurt look on his face. "And from you too, Doc. And you call yourself a scientist."

"No, I call myself a physician, though I have a few research projects of my own. My primary concern, however, has to be the health of the men at this station. That's why I agreed with Blair's decision to destroy every last remnant of this thing." He rose, moved to one side and gave the younger man a hand up. Fuchs brushed ice particles from his back and pants legs, saying nothing.

"I'm sorry, Fuchs," the doctor continued. "Sometimes you have to be satisfied just to know that cobra venom is deadly. Its not always efficacious to study the snake face to face. You have to balance what you might learn against the known chance of getting bit."

Childs had finally switched off the torch. The corpses continued to blaze away for several more minutes.

When they started back toward the compound there was nothing left on the ground but some fine powder and a few fragments of carbonized bone. . . .

7

Blair was taking blood samples from the three healthy dogs who remained in the kennel. He'd already checked out those caged in the infirmary. Nearby, Clark was dishing out the evening meal. The kennel seemed empty with only three inhabitants and the handler's melancholy was palpable.

Blair's face had been reflecting conflicting thoughts ever since he'd entered the kennel. Something had been bothering him for quite a while now.

"Say, Clark, did you notice anything strange about that Norwegian dog? I know it was a perfect imitation of dog reality, but wasn't there anything at all that piqued your curiosity about it? Any little thing?"

Clark finished dishing out the food, wiping his hands as he considered the biologist's questions. The three surviving animals swarmed around the food trough, tussling and fighting for position with their usual enthusiasm. The absence of their companions seemed not to concern them.

"No. Just that he recovered real quick. That night when I found him in the recreation room, he'd already scraped off his bandage. I redressed the wound before I put him back in with the others. Noticed that it had healed up real good, but I didn't think it was anything extraordinary. Not at the time, anyway."

Blair was suddenly attentive. "You said, when you found him in the rec room 'that night'?"

The handler moved toward the trough and affectionately scratched the ears of one of the dogs. "Yeah."

"What was he doing in the rec room?"

"After I worked on him, I thought I'd let him rest a while. Be traumatic enough to shove him in with a whole kennelful of new mates if he'd been healthy. I left the room for a bit, and when I came back he was gone."

"Well, where was he?" The biologist sounded funny, as though each word was a strain. "Where did he go?"

Clark shrugged. "Hell, I don't know. I looked around for him a couple of minutes and couldn't find him. I figured he'd be okay by himself. He couldn't get outside, and Nauls keeps the food locked up. So I didn't worry about him."

Blair hesitated a moment, then asked, "You're saying that he wasn't put into the kennel until late that night?"

Something in the biologist's expression made Clark suddenly uneasy. "Well . . . yeah, that's right."

Blair seemed to have forgotten his instruments, the testing, the two little vials full of fresh red dog blood. He seemed to have forgotten everything except Clark.

"How long were you with the dog? Alone, I mean?"

"Ah . . . he was hurt bad. Bullet nicked the artery in the hip. I can't say for sure. An hour, hour and a half." Blair kept staring at him, moon-eyed. "What the hell are you looking at me like that for?"

"No reason," the biologist muttered, "no reason at all." He was backing out of the kennel.

When he'd vanished down the corridor the puzzled Clark turned back to his feeding animals, shaking his head in wonder. "Now what d'you suppose got into him?" The irony of his words didn't register on the dog handler.

Blair finally located the station manager walking down the hallway near the south main entrance. He had to hurry to match strides with Garry as he headed purposefully toward communications. The biologist's face was pale, his expression filled with worry.

"I'm telling you," he was saying urgently, "that in the time it was wandering around the station all by itself it could have gotten to somebody. And I'm not talking about one of the surviving dogs."

"Anybody sick?"

"No, no, I don't mean that kind of infection. You know damn well what I mean."

Garry stopped outside the door to the communications room. For a change, every piece of equipment inside was on line, including the operator.

"Any luck yet?"

Sanders shrugged, glancing back at the two men in the hallway. "Nothing from McMurdo, if that's what you mean. Couple seconds of an Argentine disco station."

Garry tried to hide his disappointment. "Well, stick with it. I want you at it round the clock. Get Copper to prescribe something for you if you need it. We've got to get some help in here."

"No, no!" Blair was suddenly alarmed. "You can't bring anyone in here. That dog was all over the camp."

Garry frowned at him. "You said yourself you don't understand what's been happening here, that you need better equipment and experienced advice. We need to get some experts in here. Nothing personal, but . . ."

"Hell with that, I don't give a damn about that," Blair shouted. "I'm telling you we can't. . . ."

Bennings turned a corner, interrupting them. As he

talked he referred to a complex plastic chart filled with hastily scrawled meteorological symbols. Arrows and X's and readings in millibars covered the continent as thoroughly as ice.

"What'd you come up with?" Garry asked him.

"Travelwise, tomorrow may be okay," the weatherman told him. "But after that some pretty nasty northeasterly shit's supposed to be coming in. It *is* becoming winter down here, after all. We could be socked in for several days at least."

"Goddamn fools . . ." A new voice joined them, accompanied by a blast of icy air as the door at the far end of the corridor opened and Fuchs came stomping into the hall. "The discovery of the ages, papers in every journal, maybe even a Nobel . . ." He glanced accusingly over a shoulder. "All thrown away in a moment of panic."

Garry looked past him. Childs was removing his heavy outside gloves. He'd already stowed the torch. Macready and Copper moved past him. The chopper pilot noticed Garry staring expectantly at him and nodded once.

"You sure?"

Macready unbuttoned his outer coat. "Nothing left but residue, chief. And damn little of that."

Garry nodded his approval. Blair was tugging at his arm. "Listen to me, Garry. Please, you've got to—"

But the station manager was talking with Macready. "If the weather clears enough before Sanders can contact anybody, I'm sending you and the doc over to McMurdo."

"No!" Blair was horrified. "You can't let anybody leave the camp!"

"I ain't going anywhere in anything over forty knots, Garry. No matter how 'clear' it is. Especially not all the way down to McMurdo."

"The hell you won't, Macready!"

Blair stepped between them, desperately trying to gain the station manager's attention. "Don't you understand? Didn't anything I said earlier make any impression on you? That thing became a dog because it had to. Because there wasn't anything else available at the time. It didn't want to become a *dog*."

Garry whirled on him, his iron self-control finally cracking slightly. "Damn you, Blair! You've already got

88

everybody half hysterical around here. Why don't you shut up for a while?

"I remember what you said and I think I understand the ramifications as well as anyone else. But I'm station manager and I've got to make the hard decisions. And it's my decision that we need some expert help in here, and the sooner the better.

"I'm sorry if that doesn't square with your personal theories, but kindly keep in mind that I have to do what I think is best for everyone involved, and that's just what I'm going to do."

"But you can't let anybody leave!" Blair insisted emphatically. "You can't . . ."

"Look, I'm just about fed up with this whole business, Blair." The station manager was restraining himself with an effort. "I've got six dead Norwegians on my hands, a destroyed research station belonging to a friendly nation, a burned-up flying saucer, and according to Fuchs I've just ordered the scientific find of the century cremated. How do you think *I* feel. Now fuck off!"

He turned deliberately away from the biologist and resumed his conversation with the phlegmatic Macready. Blair went silent, ashen-faced and suddenly suspicious. And more than that.

He was terrified.

It was deep night outside the station, the sky obscured by the racing clouds that were the harbingers of the storm Bennings had forecast. No stars shone through the gathering clouds, no eerily beautifuly aurora decorated the heavens with its delicate pastel strokes.

There was no sound save the wind and the pattering of ice particles against corrugated metal siding. A faint flare of lightning, wild and distant, momentarily threw the camp buildings into ghostly silhouette.

It was toasty warm inside Macready's shack. The glare from the single naked light bulb fell equally on unclad pinups and garish travel posters.

At the moment, the pilot was leaning over the one table, carefully setting a tiny screw in place on the side of his recently mended, oversized chessboard.

Across the table his busty, inflatable companion occupied the other chair. She was the ideal chess partner—quiet, not argumentative, and she didn't guzzle his secret stock of booze. His sombrero hung down her back, keeping her in place. Hawaiian music, as authentically Polynesian as the Volkswagens choking Waikiki, rose melodiously from the stereo.

"All set," he informed his companion. "About time, too. I was getting sick of that little board they have in the rec room." He put the screwdriver aside, lifted his glass and offered a toast, a wide grin on his face.

"To us, my dear." The inflatable figure moved slightly in the warm air blowing from Macready's wall heater. He clinked his glass against the one he'd prepared for her, then took a long slug from his own.

Settling down in his chair he turned the renovated machine on. A red "ready" light winked to life in one corner and he let out a grunt of satisfaction.

"Now go easy on me, Esperanza," he told the figure across the table. "Remember, I'm just a beginner. And remember what happened last time." He entered his first move.

The set answered for Esperanza, whose bloated plastic lips could not move. "Rook takes bishop at queen four, rook takes pawn at queen two, rook takes queen at queen one. Check-mate-mate-mate."

"Aw shit." Macready turned the machine off and flipped up the panel concealing the intricate programming circuitry. A screwdriver and several printed circuits got tossed onto the board, without consideration for the pieces they dislodged. Macready grabbed his drink and summarily downed the rest of the shot glass' amber contents.

"Sorry, hon," he apologized to the plastic diva. "I know you did your best. You've got to lay off the hard stuff. It blows your game all to hell." He looked around. "We'll try again in a few minutes. First we lubricate your opponent, then the board." He reached inside the nearby ice bucket and brought his fingers out, dripping.

"Never any damn ice around here," he muttered disconsolately. He pushed back in his chair, rose resignedly and headed for the door. A small ice pick of the kind favored by Norris for more important excavations hung from a hook nailed into the wall.

The pilot removed the instrument and unlatched the door. He let the wind blow it inward about a foot before kicking the wedge into position at its base.

Five minutes outside in the Antarctic night, dressed in light clothes as he was, and you'd freeze to death. But he would only be outside for a minute. A large bank of ice crested against the side of the cabin. He started chipping at it with the pick, holding the ice bucket underneath. He grumbled as he worked, the skin on the back of his neck already turning numb.

"Now in Mexico, in Tahiti, they got ice. They got ice coming out of their ears." He hammered away with the pick. The ice was being stubborn.

Ah, Tahiti, he thought to himself as he worked, trying to warm himself with memories. Now *there* was a place to run a chopper. Which he had, for a year, until a falling out with the owner of the scenic flight service had shattered that relationship and sent him packing in search of another job.

Green and warm, that was Tahiti. No snakes, no scorpions, lots of good food, plenty of happy tourist ladies wanting company and consoling (tourist ladies only because the local vahines were all married or engaged, despite what the travel brochures implied). Flowers and warmth all year round. Now if they could only do something about the French . . .

A clanking sound interrrupted his reverie. He frowned, turning away from the ice bank. His fingers were slightly numb at the tips, but that didn't bother him. He hadn't been outside long enough to be damaged. He pushed his ice into the bucket and took a step toward the open door.

There it was again: metal rubbing against metal. That was funny. It would take a real idiot to be working outside this late at night.

Sometimes the door catches in the main building failed, their special lubricating oil having frozen up or a leak having deceptively sapped the protective fluid. In that case a door could freeze shut, trapping someone outside.

Macready hesitated. Probably something had gone bust in the electrical system. That happened a lot. But that kind of damage was nearly always repairable from *in*side, safe from the weather.

Of course, somebody might have gotten bored with the

91

attractions of the rec room and decided to run a private check on an outside experiment or piece of equipment. Maybe Childs was out checking some machinery, or even a sleepless Norris his seismographs.

If the door had gone tight on one of them, they might be pounding to alert someone inside. And if the others were off in their quarters or the recreation area, well, the wind was loud and it would be tough to hear someone flailing at a door.

Damn. Just when he and Esperanza were about to get it on. Oh well. The lady would just have to wait.

Reentering the shack, he removed the wedge and pushed the door shut. Putting the fresh ice reluctantly aside, he wiggled into his outside clothes and downed a last swallow of warming liquor.

He pulled the door carefully shut behind him. Using the steadying guide ropes he started toward the main building. Snow scudded across the planks of the walkway.

There was the sound again, near the rear of the main structure. He changed direction, then stopped. The noise had vanished and wasn't repeated. He cursed silently. If he'd bundled up and gone outside this time of night for nothing . . .

He turned a slow circle in the darkness. The dim outlines of the two helicopters glimmered in the light of the overhead outside lamps. He had a sudden thought.

Maybe the noise he'd heard hadn't been caused by anyone. The wind was blowing hard now and getting stronger as the anticipated storm rolled in off the Ross Ice Shelf. It was possible that one of the guy wires holding the copters in place had come loose. The end of a cable blowing around in the wind would cause an intermittent metallic banging like the one he'd heard.

Hell. The birds were his responsibility. As long as he was dressed for it he might as well make a quick check and make sure everything was okay. He'd save himself a lot of trouble if something had come loose by fixing it now, before the full winter storm struck the outpost.

Changing direction, he started down another walkway, heading toward the machines. He checked the nearest guy wires first. Everything looked tight, the wires thrumming softly in the wind.

He was slogging around the nearest copter when he noticed that the door to the cockpit was ajar. Now that was odd. Also dangerous. He walked over and opened the door cautiously.

The cockpit was empty (of course it's empty, you idiot). He traced his anxiety to Blair's hysteria that afternoon in the hallway, when he'd been talking with Garry. It was all the biologist's fault, getting everyone on edge the way he had. Garry was right about that. Damn inconsiderate egghead. Ought to keep his crazier speculations to himself.

He fumbled for a flashlight, switched it on and scanned the cockpit interior.

The control board was a mess. Dials were shattered, instrumentation hammered to bits, the console itself cracked in several places. Shards of broken heavy-duty plastic filled the floor of the cockpit like olive-hued snow. The two steering columns were bent. Exposed wires were everywhere, having been snipped and shredded. Their exposed copper tips reminded Macready, unpleasantly, of the tendon things that had bound the two dogs together.

In disbelief he played the beam from the flashlight over the destruction, trying to assess the extent of the damage. Then another unexpected sound interrupted him.

The explosion came from somewhere near the main part of camp. It was soft, muffled by the wind, but he could still recognize the report of a gun.

Oh Christ, he thought wildly, what now? He left the flashlight and the copter, making sure the door was locked tight, and stumbled down the walkway back toward the central compound.

Once inside he followed the voices of confusion, the shouts of men only half awake. Rounding a turn he nearly ran over Palmer and Bennings.

"Mac, you okay?" his assistant shouted at him. Palmer ran past him without waiting for an answer, looking far soberer than normal. Bennings kept pace with him and Macready chased them both.

"Yeah, I'm fine. What the hell's going on? I thought I heard a gun."

"It's Blair," the younger man told him as they raced through the corridor. "He's gone berserk."

"He's in the communications room," Bennings added.

"Got a gun, all right. I hear he beat on Sanders something fierce."

They rounded another turn, Macready shredding outer clothing as he ran.

Nervous men flanked the entrance to the communications room. Macready slowed; he noticed that no one was standing anywhere near the open doorway.

Garry leaned around the corner and peeked inside. A gunshot, startlingly loud in the narrow corridor, forced him back. In its wake came the sound of breaking plastic. The station manager dropped to his knees. This time he was able to peer inside.

Sanders lay on the floor close by. He was groaning and holding his head with both hands. There was some blood. Blair's edgy glances hallward were at eye level and he didn't see the floor-hugging Garry. The biologist was trying to focus a small pistol on the doorway with one hand. The other gripped a fire axe that Blair wielded awkwardly but with considerable effect against the complex telecommunications equipment.

Garry winced at the sight of the damage. Sanders didn't appear badly injured, but the tone of the biologist's voice combined with the crazed expression on his face convinced the station manager it would be prudent not to make any hasty moves.

"Anybody interferes, I'll kill!" the scientist was screaming toward the hall. *Whammm* . . . the high-gain amplifier became scrap. "Nobody's getting in or out of this camp."

Macready addressed his companions. "I heard something funny so I went out to investigate. He smashed one of the choppers up good. Childs, go check the other one and the tractor. Maybe we can do something with the one he smashed up if he got to the other as well."

The big mechanic nodded and sped off down the corridor.

The axe descended on the main radio once more, further reducing its delicate parts to electronic mush. "You think I'm crazy!" Blair shouted at them, his gun hovering over the entrance. "Fine! Think whatever the hell you want. Most of you don't know what's going on, but I'm damned sure some of you do!"

Another vicious crunch echoed through the hallway.

"The back window," Norris suggested softly. "A couple of us could maybe surprise him."

"And maybe not," argued Macready, thinking fast. "Too damn dangerous."

"I hear you whispering out there!" Blair yelled. "Go ahead and whisper, but for God's sake *listen* to me.

"You think this thing wants to become animals? Dogs can't make it a thousand miles to the sea. No skuas to imitate this time of year, no penguins this far inland. Nothing. Except us. Don't you understand? It wanted to become us!" He brought the axe down one more time on something delicate and irreparable.

A gust of cool air preceded Childs's return. He pulled up behind Macready, panting hard. Snow flecked his beard. His report was grim.

"He got both choppers *and* the tractor."

"Not the tractor too?" Bennings said in disbelief.

Childs nodded vigorously. "I don't know how bad yet. The tractor looks like it's in better shape than the chopper. Tougher construction, simpler controls. I didn't stick around to check if he got under the hood. Figured I might be able to help back here." He gestured with a finger. "'Course, in a minute it might not make any difference."

Macready saw the station manager readying his Magnum. "Garry . . . wait a minute." The other man glanced up at him, pistol at the ready.

"You got something in mind, Mac?"

The pilot looked over at Norris. "Fuse box."

The geophysicist glanced toward the station manager. Garry considered briefly, then nodded his assent. Norris took off down the hall, moving fast.

Macready went the other way. The recreation room was deserted. He picked up one of the card tables, folded its legs beneath the top, and double-timed it back to the communications room.

Blair was still babbling, still swinging the axe. "Can't you see?" he was raving at no one in particular. "If one cell of this thing got out in a decent carrier host it could infect every living thing on Earth. Nothing could stop it, nothing! All it needs is any creature with a halfway competent brain. A bird, a mouse, anything.

"Of course, a man would be better. Much better. More

95

efficient." A high giggling came from the distraught biologist. "And this thing, oh, it's *very* efficient."

Macready balanced the table against his belt buckle, moved close to the doorjamb and tried to make his voice sound understanding.

"It's me, Blair. Macready. Look, maybe you're right about all this. Maybe we aren't understanding you. But you've got to remember that we're not trained scientists, most of us. We're hewers of wood and drawers of water for you research boys. So you've got to try and *make* us understand.

"But not like this. We've got to talk it over, face to face, like reasonable men. How can you expect us to act sensibly if you don't?" His grip on the table tightened. "I'm unarmed, Blair, and I'm coming in."

"No you're not!" There was naked panic in the biologist's voice. "Nobody's coming in. I don't trust any of you!"

Macready was counting seconds. Norris ought to have reached the circuit breakers by now. Since the chief still had his Magnum that meant Blair couldn't have anything bigger than one of the little target twenty-twos. The table wouldn't stop a twenty-two short, but it might deflect it or at least slow it down some. And the moving table would make a lousy target.

"If you're right," he said toward the opening, "we've all got to stick together."

"'Stick together,'" Blair repeated. "Ha ha, that's a good one, Mac. That's real funny. Stick together. Sure we do. Like the dogs. Remember the dogs, Mac?" His voice turned threatening. "I'm not going to end up like that."

The lights went out. Macready crouched and charged into the suddenly black room as Blair's pistol roared. In the instant before darkness had descended on the camp Macready had caught a glimpse of the biologist standing defiantly in front of the ruined communications console, gun in one hand and fire axe waving in the other.

Then the table struck something hard but moveable and they went down in a heap. Macready flailed away with his right hand, groping with the other. He struck something yielding and was rewarded with a grunt of pain. His other hand crept up an arm until it reached something metallic.

96

By then there were half a dozen other bodies helping him as the rest of the men piled onto the screaming, deranged biologist.

Macready, Fuchs, and Dr. Copper half-carried, half-escorted the glassy-eyed Blair toward the toolshed, which lay some seventy-five yards from the main compound. Blair stumbled along unresistingly and gave them no trouble.

The clouds had merged into a solid mass that obliterated all the stars from view. It looked as if Bennings's forecast was coming to pass. The wind hadn't picked up much, but the air was definitely colder. Soon they'd have to wear masks in addition to snow goggles if they wanted to go outside.

The shed was larger than Macready's and boasted two windows, triple-paned like those in the compound. Childs had switched on a portable electric heater earlier and the temperature in the shed was comfortable. Its workbench would not be used for a while. Not while Blair was occupying the room.

Fuchs and Macready eased the biologist down onto the single cot. If anything, Blair seemed more stunned by what he'd done than any of his companions.

Copper helped remove his outer clothing. Without parka, gloves, and down vest the biologist wouldn't try to go anywhere. Then Copper rolled up the man's right sleeve and swabbed his arm with disinfectant. There was no protest from the recipient as the sedative entered his bloodstream.

The doctor removed the needle, swabbed the puncture site a second time and slipped the empty hypo back into its holding case. He took hold of Blair's wrist and checked a watch as the biologist blinked up at him.

"Why am I here?"

"It's for your own protection, Blair," Copper told him sternly, still eyeing the watch.

"And mainly for ours," Macready added for good measure. Copper finished checking Blair's pulse, then turned to depart. Fuchs followed him.

Macready paused at the door. "Anything special you want for supper?" There was no reply from the disconsolate figure seated morosely on the cot. Blair didn't look up at the pilot, but continued staring off into the distance.

Macready shrugged, closed the door carefully behind him and double-checked it to make sure the heavy lock was in place. Copper had already started down the walkway toward the compound.

Fuchs joined Macready in the lee of the cabin. He picked up one of the boards they'd brought with them and began nailing it over the first window. A few small tools remained inside the shed. They might be used to break through the glass but they wouldn't get through the one-by-fours the two men were nailing in place. Given the biologist's state of mind, it was conceivable he might try to break out despite the lack of proper clothing. The boards would keep him safely inside.

"Leave a bit of an opening so he can see out," Macready instructed the assistant biologist. "We don't want him to feel too penned up. He's paranoid enough as it is. Besides, he probably didn't know what he was doing."

"Wanna bet?" Fuchs drove a nail crookedly into the thin metal and the wood backing. "Tell that to Sanders."

"You know what I mean," said Macready. Blair's droopy-eyed, heavily drugged features suddenly loomed up against the window. Macready put the hammer down, raised his voice so his words would penetrate the glass.

"How you doin' in there, old boy? No hard feelings. Just doin' my job. I didn't mean to hit you so hard, but you know how it is. Hard to be polite when somebody's got a gun stuck in your face.

"Copper says you'll be all right after a while. He thinks it was all the pressure got to you. Nobody's blaming you for what you did. Leastwise I'm not. Anyone can go snaky out here under normal conditions. Too much poking around with an alien whatsis would send anybody diving off the pier."

Blair's reply barely reached them through the glass. "I don't know who to trust, Mac." He was almost crying.

"I know what you mean, Blair." Macready forced himself to sound convivial. "Trust's a tough thing to come by these days. Just trust in the Lord."

There was a pause. Macready was about to leave the first window and start work on the second when Blair's anxious whisper reached him.

"Watch Clark."

Macready hesitated. "What?"

"Clark. Watch him close." Through the foggy glass Macready could see the biologist's gaze dart furtively from left to right, as though he was afraid something else might be listening. "Ask him why he didn't kennel the dog right away." The face disappeared from view.

"Hey, Blair!" Macready called to him. "What the devil are you talking about? Blair?"

But despite all the pilot's entreaties he could not convince the biologist to say anything more. . . .

8

A large hole in the snow served the camp as a trash dump for nonbiological wastes. It was well off to one side and framed over with a wooden roof to keep anyone from accidentally stumbling into it.

Human by-products were treated differently, out of necessity and experience born of a generation of modern Arctic exploration. They were chemically treated and then stored in drums for burial much farther from camp.

In most hostile-terrain climates simple septic tanks would serve for such material, but not in Antarctica. Not where everything froze solid and steadfastly refused to biodegrade. You had to be careful what you did with your waste or it would hang around and haunt you.

Not much daylight left this far south, Bennings thought as he upended the trash container. It was slung on a handcart mounted on skids instead of wheels. He backed the cart away from the hole and kicked the covering door shut, rubbing his gloved hands as he studied the sky.

Soon winter would take hold of the southern continent and it would really begin to get *cold*. The men would have to retreat permanently into their warren to wait for the return of the sun.

Palmer and Childs slaved over the least mangled of the helicopters. Garry still held out some hope that one of them could be repaired in time to make a run to McMurdo Sound, where its pilot would trade disarming information for reinforcements, supplies, expert advice, and, at the very least, a new radio.

The old one was a pile of sharp-edged plastic flotsam in the telecom room. Any thoughts of repairing an old-style instrument would have been out of the question. But all the camp's electronic equipment was solid-state. So there was a slim chance of fixing up a rudimentary broadcast unit.

Unfortunately, trying to link dozens of chips and other tiny, rainbow-colored components into something resembling a working piece of communications equipment was a task for someone who combined the talents of a Bell labs instructor and a master of jigsaw puzzles.

Sanders was neither. Besides, his head still hurt. He adjusted the large bandage wrapped around his forehead and tried to make some sense of the carnage. From time to time his vision went blurry on him. Matters weren't helped by the minuscule size of some of the requisite components.

Those which had survived Blair's rampage lay in a neat pile on the desk in front of him, looking like pieces of matinee sugar candy. Each had a number stamped on its frontside. Circuit boards were arranged around the heap in a semicircle. The boards also had numbers printed on them. Empty sockets glared from the boards, needing replacements. All you had to do was match the numbers on the replacement modules with those on the boards.

Sure.

"I'll see what I can do," Sanders was telling Norris. "I told Garry I'd give it a try. But most of these units," and he made a sweeping gesture that encompassed the majority of ruined equipment, "are designed for factory repair. I don't have any equipment for fixing microminiature circuits." A magnifying glass lay close by his right hand. Sanders picked it up and halfheartedly began searching for the break where one board was supposed to link with another.

"They didn't teach me much about fixing these things in communications school."

Norris grinned and patted him gently on one shoulder. "That's all right. They didn't teach you much about working them, either."

Sanders responded with something in Spanish, which

Norris couldn't understand. But he thought it sounded nontechnical.

In the lingering darkness of the Antarctic winter, morning was reduced to an abstract remembrance of another world. Your body functioned according to a preset schedule, not badly confused natural urges.

Come breakfast time you had to make do without the comforting arrival of a warming sunrise. Nauls did his best to compensate for its absence with a buffet of eggs, bacon, toast, jellies and butter, country-fried potatoes, and hot or cold cereal.

The feast was necessary as well as welcome. Below sixty degrees latitude, calories vanished as fast as civilization. There were no fat researchers or workers at any of the many international stations scattered around the continent. Even if you'd been overweight all your life, a year's stay in Antarctica would melt away your surplus bulk. It was a phenomenon even the earliest explorers had noticed.

The only ones who could keep weight on in Antarctica were the seals and whales. Most of the men and women who sojourned near the South Pole agreed there were easier ways to lose weight, however.

The mess hall was a long, narrow room, not much wider than the access corridors that connected it to the rest of the camp. At the moment it was filling up with hungry, half-awake men.

Copper intercepted Nauls as the cook was bringing in another load of toast and biscuits. The doctor slipped an innocuous-looking blue capsule onto the tray.

Nauls studied it and smiled at the doc. "Hey, I already took my vitamins today."

"It's not for you," Copper told him quietly. "Put this in Blair's juice before you take him his tray."

"You still think he's dangerous?"

"I hope not. But he needs more than one night to cool down, emotionally as well as physically. This'll help him to relax." He nudged the pill away from the toast.

Nauls shrugged. "You're the doctor."

He was just setting the tray down on the table after having pocketed the pill when Clark burst into the room. Everyone turned to stare at the dog handler. Conversation ceased. He was pale and out of breath.

"The dogs . . ." he gasped Without elaborating or waiting for a response, he whirled and shot back down the hallway.

"Shit, what now?" somebody muttered as eggs and coffee were abandoned.

The kennel was empty. Dry dog food lay untouched in the metal trough. The big water can was full to the brim. There was no sign of any disturbance.

At the far end of the kennel was the ingenious dog door. It led to a narrow ramp that rose to the surface. Clark used it to take the dogs outside when it was time to exercise them, so he wouldn't have to run them through a camp hallway. Wind whistled along the door's edges.

Clark and Garry examined the latch, which normally held the door shut. It was carefully designed so that no dog could accidentally open it.

"It's not broken?" The station manager spoke quietly as he fingered the insulated backing of the metal.

"It's not." Clark tapped the latch. "This was wide open when I came in this morning. I know I latched it. I always check it before going to bed."

Garry's gaze went to the ceiling. "Outside clothes. Let's get topside and have a look around."

Daily duties were momentarily put aside as the men scrambled into heavy outer clothing.

You could see outside, but just barely. Blowing snow obscured the harsh yellow glare that fell from the argon lamps ringing the compound.

The snow was light and the dog tracks were clearly visible on the ground above the kennel. They led from the ramp straight out into the darkness. The men gathered around as Clark bent over them.

"Three sets of paw prints," he announced, tracing them with his glove. "No question about that. All three of them took off together."

Macready stood nearby, writing with a gas-powered pen on a small pad.

Copper was staring northwestward, into the last remnants of daylight, shielding his goggles from the blowing ice particles. "How long do you suppose they've been gone?"

Clark pondered the question. "I haven't seen them since

102

checking the latch last night. Could be as much as ten or twelve hours."

Macready looked up from his list. His face was grim as he followed Copper's gaze. "They couldn't have gotten far in this weather. Probably they had to stop soon after they left and hole up somewhere for the night."

Several of the men turned uncertainly toward the pilot.

"You're not thinking of going after them, are you?" Garry asked him. "I know I've pushed you a little hard about flying in bad weather here lately, Mac, but. . . ."

"Damn right I'm going after them," Macready snapped, putting away the pen.

"What in hell for?" Norris eyed the pilot as though Macready were proposing an unnecessary trip to the seventh level of Dante's Inferno.

Norris continued. "Even if Blair's right and one of them isn't . . . isn't a dog anymore, they'll just die out there. There's no food, not even a solitary penguin. Not even a damn spider. They're over a thousand miles from anything but ice and rock."

"Besides which," Palmer put in with unaccustomed lucidity, "the choppers aren't going to be ready for days, if ever."

Macready ignored them both and handed the list he'd been preparing to Bennings. "Get these things out of supply and meet me over by the snowmobiles."

Garry stared at the pilot in disbelief. "You're not going to catch them in one of those with the head start they've got."

"Like I said, they probably spent most of the night huddled somewhere for warmth. They're not bats, dammit. And we don't *know* that they've been gone the whole ten or twelve hours." He looked sharply at his assistant. "Palmer, how long would it take you to strap those big four-cylinder carburetors onto the bikes?"

"What fo . . . oh, yeah. I get you." He smiled, relishing the opportunity. He'd always wanted to try that with the snowmobiles, but both Garry and Mac had forbidden it. Now he'd have the chance. Not the same as monkeying with a Corvette block, but it'd be fun nonetheless.

"Then get a move on," Macready urged him. The younger man turned and jogged off toward the big mainte-

103

nance barn. "Childs, you come with me. We got work to do."

Macready put his arm around the big mechanic and the two strolled off into the snow, chatting animatedly. Slightly bewildered, the rest of the men watched them go. Ice and snow swirled around them.

Garry shouted after the pilot. "What are you going to do when you catch up to them?"

Bennings was reading the list Macready had handed to him. "Holy shit," he muttered aloud.

The station manager looked over at him, noticing the list. "What's that about?"

Bennings handed it over. "Whatever he's planning to do, he isn't fucking around."

Garry studied the list, then looked up and off to his left. But the two men were already out of sight, swallowed up by the darkness and blowing snow.

Childs worked fast. He was familiar with the equipment Macready had requisitioned, in addition to which he'd used some of it very recently. The adjustments he was making weren't complicated, just highly illegal. But Garry knew about them, and he hadn't raised any objections. Not yet.

Probably figures it's our funeral, the mechanic thought as he tightened a screw. And he's probably right. But as far as Childs was concerned, Macready was more right. The way Childs saw it, they didn't have a choice. If those dogs were *things* now and not dogs, and if they somehow, someway managed to make their way into another unsuspecting camp. . . .

Childs came from a neighborhood where people had died because no one wanted to get involved, because no one wanted to risk themselves to help the fellow across the street. It made him sick, which is why he'd moved away as soon as he was old enough.

He wasn't going to let that sort of thing happen here.

He tightened the screw a last half turn, then put the screwdriver aside and raised the torch. Holding it firmly in his left hand he opened the new valves with the right.

There was a brief sputtering sound. Uncertain flames spurted from the nozzle. He slowly pulled back on the lever fitted to the metal.

A sudden roar erupted in the rear of the workshed and a streak of fire shot fifteen feet across the dark ice.

Childs shut the torch down, frowning as he chose another tool from the chest at his feet. The arc was too wide and he was losing distance. Have to narrow it down some.

Macready strolled out of the shed and came up behind him. The mechanic glanced up from his work. "You see that?"

The pilot was looking out across the ice. "Yeah. Looks pretty good."

"If I narrow the field I can get maybe another five, six feet out of it."

Macready rested a hand on Childs's shoulder. "Forget it. I'd rather have the wider coverage."

"Okay. You're the boss." Childs put back the unused socket wrench and rose. "How's Palmer coming?"

Macready glanced back toward the shed. "Just about through. That kid does better work stoned than most guys do with a clear head."

"If there were any clear heads around here," Childs countered angrily, "we wouldn't have to be doing this."

Macready had no comeback for that one.

Palmer was bent over the snowmobile engine. The cowling was up and you couldn't see his head, but you could hear him working away at the machine's guts. The other snowmobile sat nearby, trimmed and ready to run. Its rear seat had been replaced with a fiberglass storage box.

A wheelbarrow on skids slid into the room. Bennings blew on his gloved hands, a gesture more reflexive than useful, and shut the shed door behind him. He pulled off the gloves and sauntered over to peer past Palmer's arched back.

"How's it coming?"

Palmer glanced up at him. "Almost through." Mechanic's grease darkened his face.

The back door to the shed opened, admitting another blast of frigid air along with Childs and Macready. The big man had disconnected the torch from its tank and carried it gingerly.

Macready noticed the meteorologist immediately. "You get the stuff, Bennings?"

105

"Garry hemmed and hawed a little, but only a little." He indicated the wheelbarrow he'd brought.

"Right." Macready moved toward it, slipping off his parka. Childs was folding up the thick hose attached to the torch and packing it in the storage container mounted on the rear of the waiting snowmobile.

The pilot opened the lid of the wheelbarrow, glanced perfunctorily at the contents, and then moved a tow sled into position behind the other snowmobile. A flexible cable linked the two together.

"Final check," Bennings announced, reading from a list. It was the same list Macready had given him earlier. "Box of dynamite already fused, box of thermite likewise, three shotguns, box of flares, two flare guns, thirty cans gasoline . . . and a case of medicinal alcohol." He put the list in a pocket and looked over at Macready. "Going to get it drunk if you can't blow it up?"

Macready, making sure the trailer hitch was tight, ignored the meteorologist's sally.

"Okay. Let's load 'em."

The sun didn't actually rise this time of year in the southern polar regions. It just peeked hesitantly over the ice and spent a few hours crawling along the horizon until, seemingly exhausted by the effort, it vanished abruptly into the lingering night.

The snowmobiles rumbled smoothly across the twilight landscape, their engines thrumming with unaccustomed extra horsepower thanks to Palmer's ministrations and the addition of the larger carburetors. Bennings piloted the one pulling the trailer while Macready and Childs doubled up on the other.

From time to time they stopped to check the trail. Snow whistled around them, but the flakes were tiny and stayed airborne more often than they settled to the ground.

The dogs had been running hard and fast. Their paw prints were widely spaced. So far the tracks had remained visible. That couldn't last forever, they knew. Soon wind and snow would fill them in. It was a race to see which would give out first: the dogs or their tracks.

Macready took regular sightings through his binoculars, the three men rotating driving shifts. Now something dark and irregular showed against the ice just ahead and slightly to their right.

He tapped Childs on the back, keeping his balance on the passenger seat. "Something over there!" he shouted over the roar of the engine. "Over there!" He pointed several times to indicate direction.

Childs nodded acknowledgment and angled the vehicle slightly to the right. Off to his left, Bennings swerved to match the new course.

Soon you could see it without binoculars. The two snowmobiles slowed as they approached.

It was surrounded by dog tracks. The prints were crowded and repetitive, signs of a short but intense struggle having disturbed the snow.

The dark lump was the half-eaten remains of a husky. Its hind legs and lower body had been picked clean. Torn hide flapped loosely in the wind. The top half of the body, from the sternum up, was missing.

Macready turned a slow circle, searching first with his eyes and then through the binoculars. There was no sign of the missing part of the dog or of its two companions.

"What is it?" Childs muttered, staring distastefully at the mangled husky.

Macready put the binoculars back in their case and walked out into the snow, following the line of still visible tracks. The line was narrower now.

"Maybe dinner," he muttered. The dim horizon showed nothing but faint light and a lowering sky.

"Dogs don't eat each other." Bennings kicked at the frozen body. "I'm no expert like Clark, but I know that much. A dog would rather starve than eat its own kind."

"I know," Macready said softly.

Childs had moved away from the body and was turning a slow half-circle. "Where's the other half?"

"Not around here," Macready told him. "I checked with the binocs. Probably took it along with them."

"For the next meal?" Childs spat into the snow.

"I'd think so. See, that's what Garry wasn't figuring on. One dog couldn't make it a thousand miles. One dog living off one or two others. . . . " He let the obvious go unsaid. "Very convenient, having a steady food supply that travels with you on its own legs."

He went over to the snowmobile trailer, flipped up the lid and removed a two-gallon can of gasoline. He unscrewed the cap, then glanced over at Bennings.

"They're still moving in a straight line. Where are these tracks headed?"

"Nowhere," the meteorologist insisted. "Just straight toward the ocean."

"That's something, anyway." The pilot silently poured the contents of the can over the remains. The men stepped clear. Macready pulled a crumpled piece of paper from a parka pocket and lit it with his lighter, tossing it toward the remains. The bone and skin caught instantly and burned with a steady flame in the steady wind.

"Let's move."

Some of the initial enthusiasm was seeping away from his companions. They'd already traveled a long way from the warmth and comfort of the outpost. Now the gnawed remains of the sled dog had again reminded them of just how deadly an adversary they were pursuing.

"Maybe we ought to think this through again, Mac," Childs murmured half apologetically. He nodded toward the horizon. "They could be hours ahead of us."

Bennings surveyed the feeble sun. "Gonna get dark soon, too. Supposed to be fifty below tonight."

Macready, straddling the snowmobile towing the supply trailer, ignored them both. "Turn back if you want to. I'm going after them."

His companions exchanged an uncertain look, then started toward the machines.

"He's crazy for wanting to go on with this," Childs muttered unhappily.

"Yeah?" Bennings climbed onto the seat behind the mechanic. "Maybe not. Maybe we're the ones who are crazy for thinking of turning back."

"Ah, shut up." Childs gunned the engine.

Only a slight glow came from a sun the color of stale sherbet as the snowmobiles continued to follow the fading dog tracks. Quite unexpectedly, the trail changed direction. Macready slowed to a stop. Childs and Bennings pulled up alongside him, their engines idling roughly.

"What's wrong, Mac?" the mechanic asked.

The pilot broke snow from his beard. The tracks had

turned toward a ridge of low hills and snowcapped bluffs. It was very cold now.

"They turn off that way."

Childs rose in his seat and stared off in the indicated direction. "You think we can get in there?"

"As long as it doesn't get too steep," Macready told him. "You still with me?"

Childs looked back at Bennings. The meteorologist nodded. "Hell, it's too late to turn back tonight anyway. Might as well keep going 'til we stop for sleep. We can argue about what to do tomorrow morning."

"That's fair enough." Macready resumed his seat and veered his machine toward the rocks.

The terrain was more rugged than the pilot had supposed. High cliffs of solid ice rose from the little canyon they were exploring. Pressure ridging had been at work here in ancient times, as well as seismic forces. He felt like an ant crawling up a broken mirror.

They'd been using the snowmobile's headlamps since they'd entered the canyon. The sun hardly supplied enough light to see your own feet. But at least the dog tracks stood out starkly. The shielding cliffs had protected them from the blowing snow.

Bennings was uncomfortable in the maze. Out on the ice flats nothing could spring out at you, catch you by surprise. He wasn't in the mood for surprises. Not here.

What am I doing here, he thought? I should be back in camp, taking anemometer readings, watching the barometer, figuring fronts and lows and plotting percentage drops in temperature gradients against old figures in manuals.

Instead I'm freezing to death while we hunt a couple of dogs that maybe aren't dogs because their DNA has been altered by the invasion of something a hundred millennia old that got buried in the ice and dug up by a bunch of overeager, unsuspecting Norwegians who—

He blinked. The snowmobiles were slowing down. He tried to see around Childs's bulk.

Dead ahead, caught in the light from the snowmobiles headlamps, was a single husky. Bennings didn't know whether to feel frightened or gratified.

The dog could have cared less. It sat in the middle of the little canyon, its back turned unconcernedly toward the approaching men, and munched contentedly on the upper half of the dog carcass they'd encountered out on the plain.

The lack of fear or any other recognizable reaction made Macready doubly cautious. He slowed his own vehicle and raised a hand. Childs and Bennings eased up alongside him.

He pointed at their quarry. It was barely twenty yards away and still gave no sign that it was aware of their presence. "What d'you make of that?"

"That's our runner, no question about that," Childs murmured. "It's finishing up its buddy, just like you said it would."

Macready carefully searched the canyon's rim, first the right side and then the left. Nothing could be seen among the crags. Nothing moved.

"Why the hell's it just sitting there?"

"Who gives a shit." Bennings was too cold for complex thinking. "Let's torch it and move on."

"I'm not sure . . . " Macready began.

Bennings interrupted him. "Don't go clever on me now, Mac. Either we finish this one now or I'm taking one of the mobiles and heading home."

Childs was already unloading the torch and hooking it to the tank. Macready shrugged, arming himself with a thermite bomb. When Childs was ready they started up the sides of the canyon, each hugging the cliff wall. Bennings stood on guard at the snowmobiles in case the dog might try running past them at the last minute.

As Childs and Macready approached, the dog continued to ignore them, seemingly content merely to chew its food. The mechanic's eyes roved the landscape, trying to see into the darkness beyond the animal, into the area out of reach of the snowmobiles' headlights.

"Where's the other one, Mac? Where in hell's the other one?"

Macready shouted back toward the machines. "There's only the one of 'em here, Bennings! Keep a sharp eye out for the other one."

The meteorologist yelled his understanding, took out a flashlight and began playing its beam over the rocks off to his right.

Macready spoke to the dog while trying to look four

110

ways at once. His voice was tense, coaxing. "Where's your buddy, boy? Huh? You can tell us. Dog's best friend, remember? Where'd your friend get to?"

Not only didn't the animal react, it continued to ignore their approach. Macready took out his own flashlight, uneasily playing it over crevices and possible hiding places in the cliff sides. Still nothing.

"Screw this. Childs, let that thing fly. Don't let up until he's ashes. We'll find the other one later."

Childs activated the nozzle. The tip of the torch sprang to life.

Bennings's attention was on the cliff face when something clutched at his ankles. He looked down and barely had time to scream as his body was yanked below the surface. The flashlight went flying. In seconds only his head and shoulders showed above the ice.

Childs and Macready whirled at the sound of the scream, and rushed back toward their companion. Only his head was visible now. Macready stumbled, snow stinging his face as he fell.

Something made a noise behind him, and it wasn't the wind. He'd never heard anything quite like that noise. It was a crackling, a snapping of something that wasn't wood or plastic. It was organic. He thought of fried pigskins being crumbled in a child's hand.

He rolled over. The dog was still facing away from him, but it was no longer eating. Its hair stuck straight up like the quills of a porcupine. As he stared it snarled, a throaty, undoglike sound. It turned to face him. Its skin was splitting, the mouth ripping open as something inside struggled to emerge, like a butterfly bursting from its cocoon.

Only there was nothing in the least attractive about the metamorphosis the husky was undergoing.

"Childs!"

The mechanic halted, his fingers tight on the torch, uncertain who to help first. Bennings was still in sight. In addition to his head he'd managed to get one arm out and was clawing frantically at the slick surface. Each time his shoulders started to emerge, something unseen would yank him back beneath the snow.

Childs took a step back toward Macready, his attention torn between his two companions. The dog continued to change. It had grown larger and darker. Suddenly it leaped, though no dog could possibly jump twenty feet in that clinging snow.

Childs reacted instinctively as the thing attacked the fallen Macready. He opened the flow to the torch. A stream of fire hit the dog-thing in mid-leap. The violence of the blast knocked it head over heels backward, a flaming ball of fur. And something else.

The animal was howling in pain, making a sound no dog ever made, a high-pitched screeching that reminded Macready of fingernails dragging down a blackboard.

He got to his knees and activated the thermite cannister. Aiming as carefully as he could in the confusion and dim light, he heaved it past the snowmobiles. The force of the throw sent him sprawling again.

The cannister landed a foot short of the twisting, flaming dog-thing and exploded. The smaller fire was suddenly enveloped in a blast of white flame.

Childs turned and started toward Bennings. The ice beneath the meteorologist was heaving violently. Macready scrambled to his feet and overtook the mechanic, grabbed him by his parka and tried to pull him back.

"What's the matter?" Childs tried to shake the smaller man off.

The pilot continued to pull at his friend. "Keep away! It'll get you too."

"Damn it!" Childs was half-moaning, half-crying. He repeated the curse over and over.

Suddenly Bennings's head finally vanished beneath the surface, his body jerked out of sight by something still unseen. The ice continued to ripple like boiling water. The activity moved around, coming toward the two men, then drifting away from them.

Part of the unfortunate meteorologist's body popped into view and just as quickly was sucked beneath the surface again. Macready and Childs watched for it to reappear, unable to aid their companion.

"What are we going to *do?*" the frustrated Childs cried. He was trying to trace the course of the subsurface heaving with the tip of the torch.

"How the fuck do I know."

Suddenly Bennings's head and shoulders exploded

through the ice close to the snowmobiles. Something had him in an unbreakable grip, though in the distant glow from the headlamps they couldn't see what. To Childs it looked like the jaws of a dog, except that no dog that ever lived had a mouth that wide.

Bennings's heavy outer clothes began to split, stretched to their limits as the flesh beneath burst its natural boundaries. The clutching jaws writhed, turning the body toward their center. A snake always turns its prey in order to swallow it head first, Macready thought wildly. Bennings face vanished into that fluid, shifting mouth.

He turned and dashed for the snowmobile trailer, shouting back over his shoulder as he ran.

"Torch them!"

"But Bennings . . . !" Childs started to protest.

Macready wouldn't have recognized his own voice. "Can't you see that he's gone? Do it . . . while we've still got the chance to!"

Bennings . . . damn it, Bennings! Childs's teeth ground against one another. Bennings is dead, man. That thing is still alive. He activated the torch.

The powerful stream of fire struck the indistinguishable mass of which Bennings was now a part. The hulking clump of dark flesh burst into flame and ice began to melt around it. A wailing screech filled the night air.

Macready was working like a madman at the snow-mobile trailer, frantically removing can after can of gasoline and tossing them onto the ice.

Something hard as steel thrust out of the ground. It had knobs and sharp projections and things like long, stiff hairs scattered across it. It just missed Macready and went right through the fiberglass body of the trailer.

Macready threw himself to one side. The leg yanked itself clear of the splintered fiberglass and flailed around in search of something to grab.

The pilot scrambled across the snow, uncapped a couple of cans and dumped their contents on that weaving, questing limb. Then he moved away and began pouring the rest onto the larger mass that Childs was melting out of the ice.

The cans went up like small bombs, further immolating the convulsive, twitching abomination beneath the snow.

Behind them, the other dog-thing continued to burn. The continuous screeching and mewling echoed horribly off the walls of the little canyon, deafening the two frantic men.

Macready tossed the last can into the conflagration and clutched at Childs's arm. "That's enough, man."

The mechanic did not seem to hear him. Glassy-eyed, Childs continued to play the fire stream over the already seething mass. Part of Bennings's burning skeleton showed through the flames. If the other thing possessed a skeleton, Macready couldn't make it out. The inferno that filled the canyon was almost too bright to look at.

Macready finally had to step around in front of the mechanic and grab the torch with both hands. "Childs, that's enough! We got it."

The big man looked slowly down at him and blinked. "Yeah. Yeah, okay Mac." He shut off the flow to the torch. They stood there close together, their stunned faces awash with light from the dying flames. As the blaze began to subside, so did that damnable screeching. Soon it sounded far away, weak and unthreatening.

It gave out entirely in a few minutes. The two fires continued to burn. Macready and Childs waited until the last embers had turned dark. Then the pilot emptied a few more gallons of gas over the dark smudges staining the canyon floor and lit them. When they burnt themselves out there was nothing left to burn except ice and rock.

The snowmobile trailer was ruined. That thrusting leg that had come so close to impaling Macready had shattered not only the container but one of the supporting skis. Macready unlatched it and they transferred the remaining supplies to the storage box mounted over the snowmobile's rear seat.

Then they set off the retrace their path, speeding down the canyon back to the glacial plain and the frozen Antarctic night. It would have been more sensible to wait until morning. More sensible, yes, but neither man had any intention of spending a moment longer in that canyon, now occupied only by the ghosts of two gargoyles whose night-shrouded appearance would have put to shame any dozen visages haunting far distant Notre Dame.

Macready and Childs preferred to take the chance of freezing to death out on the clean ice. . . .

9

Only the uppermost sliver of sun revealed itself the following day, signaling the beginning of the vernal equinox. And the beginning of six months of total darkness.

The men had gathered in the recreation room. Clark sat in a chair surrounded by his now suspicious co-workers. The dog handler looked frazzled and sounded defensive.

"I'm telling you," he said for at least the tenth time, "that I don't remember leaving the kennel unlatched."

Childs stood nearby. He was holding the well-used torch, having shortened its range in the event it had to be employed inside. He waved it meaningfully under Clark's nose.

"That's bullshit! You told us after those dogs split that you *always* check it."

"I always do." Clark chewed his lower lip and tried to sound confident. He wasn't. That torch was too damn close. "They must have opened it after I closed up for the night."

"You left it open," Childs said accusingly, "so they could get out."

Clark kept his exasperation in check, along with the sarcastic reply that immediately came to mind. Sarcasm wouldn't be prudent just now, considering the expressions on the faces of the men encircling him. Childs's attitude was that he'd be glad to try out the industrial torch indoors, if Clark would just give him the slightest excuse.

"Would I even have told the rest of you that they had gone if I had anything to hide?" he argued fervently. "Would I have told you that I regularly check the latch after I'd deliberately left it open? Be reasonable!"

"That still doesn't explain why you didn't kennel that stray right away," Garry pointed out.

"I told you that I couldn't find—" He paused, angrily shoving the nozzle of the torch aside. "Keep that thing out of my face, will you?"

115

Childs reached out with one hand, grabbed the handler by the collar, and lifted him out of the chair. The mechanic was right on the edge, had been ever since they'd returned to camp. He was still thinking of Bennings and wondering if they'd managed to kill him while he was still Bennings.

"Don't you be telling me—"

Nauls stepped between them and spoke sharply to the mechanic.

"Lighten your load, sucker. You ain't the judge and executioner around here."

Childs reluctantly let go of the dog handler. Clark slumped back in his chair, keeping a wary eye on the mechanic as he spoke to Nauls.

"Thanks," he said gratefully.

Childs turned his frustration and anger on the peacemaker. "Who you trying to protect, mutherfucker? I'm trying to tell you that this son of a bitch could be one of *them.* You want one of those things that could be anybody messing around in your kitchen, man?"

Garry separated them. No one noticed Macready out in the hallway, watching the confrontation. He'd been outside, rummaging around in the trash dump. He had a bundle tucked under one arm.

"Now hold on, dammit," the station manager told the two combatants. He struggled to keep his voice level. "We're getting nowhere acting like this. Fighting and arguing isn't going to prove anything. If this bit of Blair's theory about this thing taking over cellular structures all the way up to the brain is correct, then that dog could have gotten to anybody. It had enough time. A whole night."

"And if it got to Clark, or anyone else," put in Copper quietly from his seat near the big card table, "then Clark, or anyone else, could have gotten to somebody else."

That's about right, Macready decided. A few eyes turned to him as he stepped into the room. But the attention was still on the speculating doctor.

Copper cleared his throat. "What I'm saying is that, theoretically, any of us could now be whatever the hell this thing was. It learns fast. Too damn fast. It can be subtle when it has to, can bide its time. Like those two changed dogs did."

Norris shook his head, rubbing his chest and grimacing at the slight but persistent pain there.

"It's too much to absorb all at once, Doc. I can buy the business about the dogs. I saw that. But taking over several of us and keeping it a secret from the rest? Hell, we all know each other. If some alien whatsis had gained control of Clark—" the handler stiffened at the sound of his name—"or Childs, or me, or anyone else, wouldn't it give itself away somehow? Wouldn't it make a mistake, do something obviously wrong that the rest of us would pick up on?"

Copper smiled humorlessly. "If it can become enough of a dog to fool another dog, with its acute canine senses, then why *not* a man? This thing arrived here in an extraterrestrial vehicle. It's not an animal. It's highly intelligent as well as extremely adaptable. All it needs to survive is an organic host to take control of. Why not a man instead of a dog?"

"It's just too damn wild," Norris argued weakly. "I can't believe it. Not without stronger evidence than some overcome sled dogs."

Macready pushed back the sombrero he was wearing. "Well, you can believe it now." He dumped the dirty bundle he was carrying onto the card table. It was the shredded pair of long johns that Nauls had found in the kitchen waste bin.

"Nauls found this yesterday. Remember? It's ripped just like the clothing on the Norwegian we brought back. The same thing was happening to Bennings's clothes when Childs and I got to him. Seems these things don't imitate clothes. Just flesh and blood."

"Anything organic," Copper was muttering. He pulled up one leg of his own pants and checked the long underwear beneath it. "Damart. Artificial. Not wool. If it was wool, the thing might be able to imitate that, too."

The men looked from one to another, silent, thinking. Macready picked up the ruined clothing and checked the label on the waistband.

"It's Damart too, Doc, but there's more important information here than that."

"For instance?" said Norris challengingly.

"For instance, the size. Large, in this case." He grinned maliciously and studied the nervous cluster of men. His gaze settled on the one sitting in their midst.

"What size do you wear, Clark?"

The dog handler shifted uncomfortably in his chair. His

lower lip showed blood.

"So what if I do?" he snapped back.

"Yeah," Norris added, "what if he does? I wear a large size, too."

"Extra large," said Childs smugly.

"Large," said Copper.

"And me too." Macready's gaze traveled around the room. "Most of us do." The feeling of unease in the room intensified. Macready let them stew over this new thought a while before continuing.

"I doubt if it got to more than one or two of us. Two at the most. It didn't have enough time for more than that. Besides, if it had I don't think we'd be standing here debating it right now. We'd all be trying to blow each other's heads off, like those poor damn Norwegians. Or else we wouldn't be trying to, which'd be worse.

"But it definitely got to *someone*." He let that sink in before adding, "Somebody in this room ain't who it claims on his driver's license."

Sanders didn't even try to conceal his fright. "Then what are we going to do?"

Norris turned to Copper. Fuchs was standing next to the doctor, looking thoughtful.

"Can there be some kind of test?" the geophysicist asked. "Surely if this things alters cell structure and other biological functions as radically as Blair seems to think it does, there ought to be some way of detecting the changes. Some way of finding out who's what."

"Possibly a serum test," Copper finally whispered. "Yes, that should work."

"Right!" Fuchs's enthusiasm was genuine. "Why not?"

"What's a serum test," the station manager wanted to know, "and how much work's involved?"

"It's a simple blood-typing test," Copper explained. The men crowded around him to listen. "As Blair explained, the thing engenders severe alterations in the cell structure of its hosts. I think that would show up in a check of any basic bodily fluid, such as lymph or blood. Or urine, for that matter. But a blood test would be easier, and harder to 'fix.'

"As to what's involved," he told Garry, "we mix someone's blood with uncontaminated human blood, blood we know to be the real thing. If we don't get the proper serum

118

reaction, it's at least a good indication that the person the blood was drawn from is something other than normal."

"But this thing's takeover is complete down to mustache hairs," Macready argued.

"But not down to follicular cells, if we could analyze one of those hairs properly. I don't see how it could alter its new cell structure enough to fool so basic a test. It's worth a try, anyway. It's simple and fast. If it doesn't work we can always try something else."

"Sounds good to me, Doc, except for one thing," said Childs.

"What's that?"

Childs looked at the assembled, anxious faces. "Whose 'uncontaminated' blood we going to use?"

Copper smiled. "That's where we've got it. We've got whole blood in storage." He sought the station manager's approval. "What about it, Garry? Shall I go ahead and set it up? Fuchs can assist me."

Garry mulled the proposition over, then turned to the eager assistant biologist. "What's your opinion, Fuchs?"

"I think it's a helluva smart idea, chief. Blair would be the first to approve."

The station manager looked slightly uneasy. "Unfortunately, our senior biologist isn't in a position to be making rational evaluations of test procedures or anything else right now. But if you go along with the doc. . . ."

"I certainly do." Fuchs nodded vigorously.

". . . then we'll give it a shot. Like you say, Doc, we can always try something else next if this test turns out inconclusive. How long will it take you to get ready?"

Copper considered, then ventured a conservative estimate. "A couple of hours should be enough. Provided that I'm not . . . interfered with."

"There'll be somebody with the two of you at all times. Get going." He took a key off the ring hanging from his belt and handed it to the doctor. Copper and the young biologist headed for the infirmary.

The rest of the men milled around, chatting amiably. Now that they were going to find out who was real and who was faking it, they relaxed visibly.

"How'd that thing ever get to those three dogs?" Palmer asked Macready. "I thought we stopped it in time."

"Copper isn't sure, but he thinks they may have swallowed functioning pieces of it during the fight in the kennel."

"And that's enough?"

"I don't see why not." The pilot was enjoying his assistant's queasiness. "No reason why it can't take you over from the inside out. I'd think it'd be a lot easier. The tendon-like organs wouldn't have to reach nearly as far, if they began growing inside your stomach instead of—"

Palmer turned away, adding weakly, "Never mind. Sorry I asked. I'll take Copper's word for it."

"At least now maybe we'll find out if those dogs were the last thing it got to," Macready muttered darkly. "Maybe it didn't have time that night to get to anything else."

"*Garry!*" The shout came from down the corridor, faint but imperative. "The rest of you too, come here!"

Macready looked sharply at Palmer. The latter's bilious expression had vanished.

"That's Copper!"

As one man, the crew rushed down the hallway and turned the bend into the infirmary. Fuchs and Copper were there, standing in front of the open storage refrigerator.

The interior was a disaster area. Broken glass and dried blood caked the porcelain. Every bottle and container had been opened, dumped, and then shattered.

Copper was gaping in disbelief at the destruction. His normal composure was gone; his face was pale.

"Somebody got inside, got to the blood. Sabotaged it. There isn't an ounce left that's usable."

"Oh my God," Nauls was muttering. He looked around at his companions. "No dog could do something like this. Opening a kennel latch, that was one thing, sure, but breaking into a locked refrigerator, uh-uh. And that meant that. . . ."

Macready pushed his way through the horrified silence and examined the open door. "How was it broken into?"

"That's just it," Copper told him slowly, "it wasn't. Somebody opened it. Closed it up after they finished their work so's it wouldn't show, and then locked it again. If it had been broken into, I would have noticed it before now."

Sanders had backed away from the refrigerator as though it were a live thing, until he'd come up against the far

120

wall. He kept his back against it, whispering in Spanish and trying to keep space between himself and his nearest neighbor.

Something had to be done, and fast, Macready knew. Maybe this was how it had started at the Norwegian camp. The thing didn't even have to show itself. All it had to do was let you know it was around. Complete paranoia would soon take control of the human survivors and they'd reduce themselves to a manageable level. He wondered if the thing had a sense of irony, of humor, and decided it probably did not.

Talk, he told himself. Say something, say anything, but stay calm. Keep their minds working and their thoughts off shadowy suspicions.

He stepped forward. "Well, let's break this down logically. Who's got access to the lock? The refrigerator's."

Copper thought a moment. "I guess I'm the only one with authorization, outside of Garry."

The station manager nodded his agreement. "And I've got the only key. That's regulations." He indicated the refrigerator. "Drugs kept in there, too."

Eyes began to shift around to focus on the station manager, but no one voiced what their owners were thinking . . . yet.

"Would that serum test really have worked?" Macready asked the doctor.

"I think so. Wouldn't have suggested it if I didn't. I wasn't using it as a ploy to try and force this thing to reveal itself, if that's what you're driving at."

"Somebody else sure as hell thought it would work." Norris glared at his companions as he gestured at the ravaged refrigerator. "If we needed any proof that it would've worked, we've got it now."

Macready was still thinking. "Who else could have used that key, chief?"

"Ahh . . . no one I can think of, offhand," Garry replied slowly. "Like I said, the doc and I are the only ones authorized to unlock that cold storage unit. I give the key to Copper when he needs something inside. It's safer that way."

"I'm beginning to wonder." The pilot glanced at Copper. "Could anyone have gotten it away from you, Doc?"

"I don't see how. When I'm finished with it I return it to Garry right away." He smiled slightly. "I'm always afraid I'll lose it or put it down someplace and forget what I did with it. Since it's the only key, I'm especially careful to see that Garry gets it back."

"When was the last time you used it?"

Copper shuffled his feet, and stared at the floor as he tried to remember. "A day or so ago . . . I guess."

Garry began to notice the inquiring, suspicious eyes turned on him. "I suppose . . . it's possible someone might have lifted it from me."

"That key ring of yours is always hooked to your belt," Childs pointed out accusingly. "Now, how could somebody get to it without you knowing?"

The station manager sounded uncharacteristically flustered. "I suppose that when I was asleep . . . look, I haven't been near that refrigerator."

No one said anything. They continued to stare at the outpost's chief administrator. Sanders edged off into a corner, perspiring heavily.

"Copper's the only one who has any business with it," Garry added.

The men's attention momentarily shifted to the doctor. "Now wait a second, Garry. You've been in the infirmary on several occasions."

Fuchs was trying to be rational amid a rising tide of panic. "I think we can eliminate the doc from suspicion. He's the one who thought of the test."

"Maybe the thing would propose it just so it could reveal this," Norris pointed toward the refrigerator, "and turn suspicion away from itself." He was looking hard at Copper.

Macready sounded doubtful. "Unnecessary. Better not to propose the test at all. Fuchs is right. Would you have thought of it?"

The younger man shook his head. "Human physiology isn't my field."

"So that leaves the doc out. For now, anyway. Because he brought the whole business up."

"So what?" Childs looked like he wanted to torch something. "Is that supposed to leave him in the clear? Bullshit! Maybe Norris is right. Maybe this thing's always

122

going to be two mental steps ahead of us. It'll keep us going around and around in circles until some time late at night it decides to end it all by—"

An inarticulate moan rose from the back of the room. The men turned in time to see Sanders's back disappearing into the hallway. Everyone took off after him.

"Hey, Sanders," Garry shouted after the fleeing radio operator, "don't panic! We have to stay together, get this figured out. It *wants* us separated!"

Sanders didn't stop or slow down. Just then he wasn't thinking too straight. He wished fervently he was back home in Los Angeles, back at the university. Anywhere but where he was, trapped at the bottom of the world with a thing that could be your best friend.

He sped along the corridors, opening doors ahead and slamming them in his wake. Shouts rose from behind.

They were coming for him. The *things*. Maybe they'd all been taken over by now and they'd just been toying with him. *Certimento*, that was it! They'd been feasting on his fear, toying with him until the right moment came.

Then they'd all gather around, all of them, trapping him helplessly in their midst, and as he watched they would change. Thin white ropes would come out of them, like the dog, and they'd enter his hapless body while the men who weren't men any more would smile down at him, smile while something slipped into him and pushed Sanders aside, took over his brain and body cell by cell by cell by—

He was screaming as he burst into the little storage room. The glass case hanging on the near wall contained the guns that were allocated to the station. They'd been provided in case the men felt like doing some recreational shooting or the biologists needed to bring down a specimen.

Among the casually arrayed weapons were the three shotguns Macready, Bennings, and Childs had taken with them on their recent dog hunt. Now they were back in their slots, cleaned and ready for use next summer. Only summer was six long, black months away and Sanders needed a gun *now*.

He tried the case handle, found it locked. The clamor of approaching voices was louder now, accompanied by the pounding of many feet. Sanders looked wildly around the room, and pounced on the heavy duty stapler on the desk.

The glass cracked with the third blow, shattered at the fourth. He fumbled inside the case and extricated one of the shotguns, then a large box of shells.

Frantically he fought to load the single-barreled weapon. It was a twelve-gauge, big-mouthed and lethal. Powerful enough to stop even a thing at close range. His shaking hand yanked back the lid on the box and turned it over. Shells fell into his palm, and bounced all over the floor. Somehow he jammed one after another of the plastic-tipped bullets into the gun.

The men arrived. Garry pulled out his omnipresent Magnum and pointed it squarely at the radio operator.

"Sanders! Put that down. Right . . . now."

Sanders looked up at him, his eyes wide. He was trembling violently. A shell fell from his fingers, bounced on the floor and rolled over to Garry's feet.

"No. I won't."

"I'll put this right through your head." The station manager spoke slowly so that the radio operator would be sure to understand. The tip of the Magnum never wavered.

No one doubted Garry's sincerity.

Sanders' gaze traveled past the station manager to the men grouped behind him in the corridor.

"You guys going to let him give orders? I mean, he could be one of those things. What about the refrigerator lock?" He looked fearfully back at Garry. "How about it, man? How do you explain that away?"

A few heads turned Garry's way, the shotgun momentarily forgotten. None of them were oblivious to the fact that Sanders just might be right.

"Put the gun away," the station manager said again. His tone was soothing. "Just put the gun away, then we'll talk about the refrigerator. But we can't talk as friends if we're all pointing guns at each other, can we? Please put it away, Sanders. I know how you're feeling. We're all confused. But we're also all in this together."

Not all of us, Macready corrected him silently. One of us is feeling very different.

Sanders considered Garry's plea, the motionless Magnum pointed at his head, and the men waiting behind the station manager. He had to do something.

Abruptly he threw the remaining shells he held at the

broken gun case. The men flinched instinctively, but none of the shells went off. Then the radio operator turned and leaned the gun carefully against the wall. He stood there a moment longer, his facial muscles working, and finally burst into tears. Nauls skated over and tried to comfort him.

As the others watched Garry slowly lowered the pistol, put it back in its holster. He inhaled deeply and turned to confront them. His tone was intense.

"I don't know about Copper. But I didn't go near that refrigerator. As you all damn well know, I don't use anything stronger than aspirin."

"But the doc said he'd seen you in the infirmary several times before," Childs reminded him.

Garry turned slightly belligerent as he replied to the big mechanic. "Sure I've been in there. I've also been out in the maintenance shed, even though I'm not a mechanic. I've been in the telecommunications room, though I don't work alongside Sanders. I've been in every corridor and room on this base. So have most of you.

"So what? That doesn't prove a damn thing." No one saw fit to contradict him. "But I guess you'll all rest easier if someone else is in charge for a while." He pulled the gun from the holster and sized up the circle of anxious faces surrounding him. He finally settled on one.

"Can't see anyone objecting to you, Norris."

"Sorry, chief. I respectfully decline." He grinned ruefully and patted his chest. "Don't think I'd be up to it. Haven't been feeling too good lately. You guys know about my heart condition. I think you ought to appoint someone able to take a lot of strain, should the need arise."

Childs reached for the gun. "I'll take it. . . ."

Macready beat him to it. "No offense, Childs, but Norris's point about stability is well taken. Maybe it should be someone a bit more even-tempered."

Childs glared at him, but didn't argue.

Macready inspected his companions. "Any objections?"

Fuchs didn't meet his eyes. Macready prodded him. "Well, you got something to say, say it. This ain't the time to spare anybody's feelings."

Fuchs spoke hesitantly. "First Childs reached for the gun, then you, Mac. Both of you have been out, away from camp. And you had contact with this thing. So did Bennings.

Only, Bennings didn't come back." He looked up, stared at the pilot "How do we know the thing didn't get to both of you?"

"You don't. Nobody knows much of anything right now. Nobody will, until we can find a way to test for this things's presence . . . somehow." He held the gun loosely.

"I'm not gonna insist, though. Anybody got any better suggestions? I'm open."

Uncertain eyes roved through the group, each of them suspicious of his neighbor. Everyone came under scrutiny. There was no such thing as a close friend anymore.

"I guess . . . you're as safe as anyone," Fuchs finally admitted. He ventured a conciliatory smile. "I'm sorry, Mac. I had to say it."

"No hard feelings. I know how you feel."

"Okay, what now?" Norris asked him.

Macready considered. "For one thing we stick together. Let's get back to the rec room and try and talk it out. Everybody. And let's try and keep our emotions under control. Because when we don't—" he glanced meaningfully at the still sobbing Sanders—"that's when we play right into this thing's hands."

Rampant fear of one's friends and neighbors did not make for a very genial atmosphere as they filed back into the recreation room and gathered around the center table. But at least no one was pointing a shotgun or Magnum at someone else.

"From what we know," Macready was declaiming, "this thing likes to go one-on-one. Remember what Blair said about it taking an hour to complete a proper takeover? It likes to get you alone so it can work on you in private."

"Remember what happened to Bennings," Childs reminded the pilot. "He was changing while we watched, and it took minutes, not an hour."

"Yeah, but it was a hurried job and the thing never did break free of him," Macready countered. "It can make a mess in a few minutes, but to do it right takes longer." Childs considered that, nodded slowly in agreement.

"So we stick together," Macready continued, "as much as possible until we're sure it's safe. Nobody goes anywhere to do anything up to and including daily station maintenance

126

unless he's accompanied by someone else. We do everything in twos and threes whenever possible. If we *do* have to split up, it should be for only a short time and the guys involved should at least stay within sight and earshot of each other."

Childs pointed to a corner where Garry, Clark, and the doctor had been isolated. "I'll go along with that, Mac. But what do we do about those three?"

"We got morphine, don't we?" Macready glanced over at Fuchs.

"Again, that's not my department, but I think we do, yes."

"Okay. We keep them loaded. Stash them here in the rec room with the lights on round the clock and watch 'em close."

Palmer was suddenly alert. "Morphine?" He let his upper teeth hang over his lower lip and bugged his eyes. "You know, I was pretty close to that dog, too."

Macready and the rest ignored him.

"We should sleep in shifts," Norris suggested.

"Good idea," agreed the pilot. "Half of us awake at all times. It shouldn't be too hard. It's nighttime outside twenty-four hours a day now anyway. That should keep anybody from crawling into anybody else's bed. Or into anybody."

Thanks to Nauls's reassuring chatter, Sanders had quieted down considerably. "How we going to try and find out who's . . . you know. Who's who?"

"That's the big question." Macready looked over at Fuchs. "You're our remaining link with biology. Can you think of any other tests we could try? Maybe something this thing wouldn't have thought of first, like it did with the serum business?"

Fuchs mulled it over. "I'll give it a try. I could sure use Copper's help, though."

"You can eighty-six that thought right now, man," said Childs sharply. "At least until we figure out who got to that refrigerator." Copper threw his accuser a hurt look.

"Also," Macready went on, "when this thing turns into itself—into its natural form—it turns slowly at first. It takes a while for the metamer . . . matamor . . ."

"Metamorphosis," Fuchs said.

"Thanks. Yeah, when it goes through that process it

takes it a while to finish." He looked over at Childs "Remember when it was trying to become itself and take Bennings at the same time?"

Childs found the constant reminder of the fight in the canyon discomfiting. "Yeah, I remember. It was twisting and jumping all over the place."

"Trying to get back into its own shape," Macready said, nodding. "Which looked to be a damn sight bigger than any human. That ties in with what Blair had to say about the thing's cell structure being flexible, being able to stretch or compact. I've got a hunch from what Childs and I saw that this thing in its natural form is a helluva lot bigger than any dog or man.

"But it takes time to change, just like it does to take someone over. While it's still in the process of reverting, I think we can handle it. Like I said, Childs and I already did."

"Bennings didn't," murmured Norris.

"It surprised us," Macready argued. "We weren't familiar with the surroundings and we didn't expect any kind of radical transformations." He slapped the table. "This is *our* camp. It won't be so easy to surprise us here.

"But if it ever reached full maturity and full power . . . based on what I saw of that Norwegian outpost . . . metal ripped apart, beams busted in half . . . well, I just don't know.

"If Blair's right and it needs an hour to take something else over, it probably needs close to that to achieve maturity. So no matter what anybody's doing, we all return to this room for a check every twenty minutes. Anybody gone longer than that, we kill 'em."

"Kind of an extreme reaction, isn't it?" said Norris.

Macready stared back at him, hard. "There's no reason for anybody who keeps his head to miss that deadline." Even Sanders nodded in agreement, having recovered his equilibrium.

"Better nobody stay in the can too long," he managed to quip. "That'd be a hell of a place to die." There were a few weak laughs.

"Okay then." Macready turned to leave. "We've still got things to do. This outpost ain't going to run itself. No reason why we shouldn't get at it until Fuchs figures out another test. . . ."

128

10

Palmer worked painfully at the engine of the short-haul helicopter. Occasionally he'd glance nervously over his shoulder for movement that went against the wind. Sanders and Macready were dim, distant shapes moving about the trash dump.

He turned back to his work, frowned at the engine and then the pile of parts nearby.

"Well, damn. Where's that magneto? Can't find a thing around here anymore."

Copper, Clark, and Garry sat moodily next to one another on the large rec room couch. Norris had the doctor's bag open on the card table and was awkwardly trying to prepare three injections. He was new at the business, hadn't done any first aid since the Army, and that was a long time ago.

Fuchs couldn't help. The assistant biologist was busy in the lab, trying to think of a new test they could try on each other. That took priority. Not that he would have been of much use. He was used to squirting things out of hypos into cultures and slides, not veins. Norris would have to manage by himself.

Copper shifted his backside on the cushions and smiled pleasantly. "I'll do it, if you like," he told the geophysicist. "You're liable to break the needle in my arm, or miss the vein."

Childs gestured toward him with the torch. "Never you mind, Doc. It'll be all right. He's doing a real fine job." He smiled encouragingly at Norris.

"I'm not sure . . ." the older man began hesitantly.

"Just do your best, man," the mechanic advised him. "You'll manage." He smiled thinly at the three on the couch. Copper glared at him.

The wind whistled around Macready, trying to pry under the warm, insulated rim of his parka hood. The only light came from the flashlights he and Sanders carried. The faint glow of the compound's exterior lamps barely reached the trash dump. They could hear Palmer flailing energetically at the nearby helicopters.

He turned over a heap of damp cardboard, kicked it aside. "Look for shoes, too," he told his companion. "And burned cloth. Any clothing that's more than just worn out."

Having finally succeeded in performing the injections, with a minimum of discomfort to the recipients, Norris had moved into the telecommunications room. He knew more about electronics than medicine and was glad of the opportunity to work on something that wouldn't complain if he made a mistake.

He disconnected the still useless headset and rubbed at his chest. Occasionally Childs would give him a shout and he'd answer back.

He took the small plastic bottle from his shirt pocket and popped a couple of the tiny white pills. The pain in his chest went away. He went back to work on the radio.

Nauls was skating through the labyrinth of corridors, checking out the individual waste bins as well as shelves, lockers, and anyplace else something might have hidden damaging evidence. He checked regularly with Childs or Fuchs.

Macready passed him, coming in from outside. The cook gave him a bored glance.

"That thing's too smart to be throwing away any more of its clothes where we can find 'em, Macready."

"Just keep looking."

"Yeah. What fun."

"Want to trade places? I'll search in here for a while and you can go outside and freeze with the garbage."

"Thanks, but I've got cooking to keep an eye on." He skated off toward the kitchen.

Fuchs sat at the lab desk, pouring over an open book. Several other volumes lay open nearby, stacked like steamed clams. The soft light from the reading lamp illuminated the open pages but not his thoughts, which were filled with confusion and worry.

Macready poked his head into the lab.

"How's it going, Fuchs?"

"Nothing yet." He looked up from the book. "I had one

130

hought, though. If the dogs changed because something hey swallowed took control of them from the inside out, we'd better see to it that everyone prepares his own food and hat we eat out of cans. Not that I don't trust Nauls, but anyone could get to a pot of stew."

"Gotcha. Good idea, Fuchs. Keep at it." He nodded toward the open tomes on the desk. "I don't know how much longer the guys are going to hold together."

"Right." The pilot disappeared and Fuchs turned tiredly back to his work.

The siren howled above the wind outside the compound, signaling the end of a twenty-minute work period. Sanders extricated himself from the trash dump. At least it didn't smell. It was too cold for that.

Palmer joined him and they headed for the entrance together. He was carrying a large piece of engine.

Sanders eyed the machinery curiously. "What's that for, man? You going to work on it inside?"

"No. Just the opposite," Palmer told him. He grunted, trying to shift the heavy metal higher in his arms. "It's Macready's idea. So nobody goes for any unauthorized jaunts."

"Oh." The radio operator nodded sagely.

Macready was waiting for them. He held the door open as the two men staggered into the corridor flanking the main supply rooms. Childs was working nearby, selecting a new tip for the big torch.

Palmer staggered over to the mechanic and dumped the heavy section of engine. "Whew! Heavy mother. Hey, Childs? Where's that magneto from chopper one?"

Childs looked up from his searching, inspecting the new tip he'd chosen. "Ain't it out there?" He closed the storage bin and started up the corridor.

Palmer yelled after him. "No, it ain't out there, wise-ass. Would I be asking if it were?"

A hand touched his shoulder. "Move it, Palmer, or we're going to be late," Macready reminded him.

Norris arrived and dumped radio parts next to the section of engine. Macready locked the door and they all hurried after the mechanic.

"I heard you and Childs talking," Macready said to Palmer. "Something missing?"

131

"Ahhh . . . skip it. Not important." He pushed back the hood of his parka, began unsnapping the coat. "I'm starving. What's for supper?"

"Whatever you feel like."

Palmer frowned at him. "I don't like the sound of that."

"You probably won't think much of the taste, either. It's our new dining policy. Serve yourself and save."

"Save what?"

"Yourself. Canned food only until Fuchs can come up with a foolproof test for thingism. Unless you want to chance ending up like the dogs."

"Oh, yeah, I get it," Palmer replied. But the prospect of living off canned food instead of Nauls's hearty meals for an unknown period of time was just one more development that added to the general misery infecting the outpost.

"Start taking those snowmobiles apart next, okay?" Macready instructed him. They turned a bend in the corridor, leaving the supply room far behind.

"I'm sorry, guys." Nauls skated over to the crowded stove where cans of various colors and sizes were heating. "Macready's orders."

"That's all right, Nauls," Fuchs assured him. "It's for everyone's own good."

"Yeah, I know that. I just hate to see everybody having to down that canned slop instead of my cooking."

Childs made an elaborate display of masticating a spoonful of his own meal, then said thoughtfully, "Actually, I hadn't noticed much difference." He ducked the spoon the cook heaved at him, laughing good-naturedly.

Nauls still had some food to prepare. He checked the tray with more than usual care, since it was all he had to do now other than making certain no one broke the stove or cut himself on a can opener.

Besides which he felt a little guilty about Blair. Most of them were starting to. The biologist might've gone crazy, but even though his head was in the wrong place, his heart wasn't.

Meat loaf, potatoes, English peas, bread and butter . . . all present and accounted for. The others toyed with their cans and watched enviously as he slipped foil over the tray and then slid it into an insulated polyethylene container. Nauls donned his outside gear and skated toward the nearest exit. He paused there to remove his wheels, then opened the door and put his head into the wind.

It was his second tour in Antarctica, but men who'd done three times that assured him you never got used to the polar winter. It was one thing to go to bed while it was still bright and sunshiny outside, in the summertime. That was easy to cope with. But he didn't like waking up to total darkness. It made you think the world had died.

As he neared the toolshed he thought he could make out a new sound over the wind: a distant pounding.

"Take it easy, man," he muttered toward the shed. The need to go outside had killed whatever compassion he'd been feeling for Blair. It was *cold*.

"I got your goodies. Old Nauls wouldn't forget you. Man, you don't know how good you got it, everybody else slopping out of cans. Got your own private chef."

He halted outside the door. The pounding from inside was very loud. He paused uncertainly, then put the tray down and peeked through the tiny window set in the door.

Blair was making the noise, all right, but with a hammer instead of his fists. The hammer was a small, light-duty model. It wasn't heavy enough to break through the thick boards the cook and Macready had installed over the windows.

But Blair wasn't trying to break out. He was nailing new boards over the door from the inside, and though his medical experience was somewhat more than limited, Nauls could tell by the expression on the biologist's face that he was far from cured.

"Hey," he shouted, "what are you doing, man?"

"Nobody's getting in here!" Blair yelled hysterically. "Nobody. You can tell them all that."

Nauls shook his head dolefully and raised the hinged slat that had been cut in the base. He pushed the covered tray through the opening.

"Well, who the hell you think would want to get in there with you? Not me, man."

The tray came shooting back out. It slid across the icy walkway and turned over. Polyethylene and foil split and food came flying out, some of it staining Nauls's coat.

"Now why'd you go and—"

"And I don't want any more food with sedatives in it!" Blair screamed. "I know what you're up to. Don't think I

133

don't. You're all so clever. And if anyone tries to get in here
. . . I've got rope. I'll hang myself before it gets to me."

"Yeah? You promise?" Nauls turned and picked up the
rejected tray. He started back toward the compound
grumbling under his breath.

Time passed, but not slowly. You could feel the tension,
though everyone did his best to conceal it from his neighbor.
Everyday tasks provided welcome relief. They took one's
mind off the horror that might still be lingering over the
camp. Jokes were forced, as was the laughter that greeted
them.

Outwardly, everything seemed normal, but suspicion
and paranoia colored every word, every movement. Suspicion, paranoia, and a desperate fear.

Palmer was working on the second snowmobile. He'd
removed all the spark plugs from both, dismantled the
carburetors, removed and concealed the gas filters.

Now he was taking the engines off their mountings.
They would go into the locked storage room, along with the
vital components of the helicopters and the tractor. The
mounting bolts and screws would be hidden elsewhere.

Macready was taking no chances. He was at work in the
balloon tower with a kitchen knife, methodically slashing
each of the huge, uninflated weather balloons into uninflat-
able strips. There was no telling how long they might have to
remain isolated before Fuchs could come up with a new test.

It was unlikely, but a half-frozen gull or man-o-war bird
just might drop into camp. It would better to take no
chances. Birds could not be pursued.

He finished the last of the balloons, then lingered over
the tanks of hydrogen stored nearby before deciding there
was no need to empty them. There was nothing in camp their
resident thing could surreptitiously combine to make a
suitable envelope out of.

The stereo in the kitchen wailed, its vibrant, undisci-
plined music easing the tension with the unconcern of a
world that seemed a million miles away. Nauls hummed as
he removed the dishes from the washer and stacked them
neatly on their proper shelf.

Childs sighed. One hand scratched at an ear. The other

lipped the pages of a thick magazine. The industrial torch, its new tip gleaming, lay close at hand.

Clark, Copper, and the station manager dozed on the couch nearby. The effects of the morphine would be wearing off soon. Norris would be around to redose the trio, Childs knew.

Clark stirred, rose and mumbled thickly at the guard. "Gotta go to the can, Childs."

Making a face the mechanic put down the magazine. He half-carried the dog handler to the far end of the room and opened the door for him.

"Be quick about it." Clark staggered into the head. A few seconds passed and the lights began to flicker. Childs looked around worriedly.

They went out completely for a second, then came back on. "Oh no," the mechanic muttered. "No . . . not now, man."

When they winked out the second time it was for good. Along with the light something else had vanished: a mechanical breathing so soft and steady you quickly learned to ignore it. The purr of the generator.

"Childs!" That was Nauls, shouting from the kitchen. "That a breaker?"

"No," Childs told him. "Breaker would have gone out instantly. There wouldn't have been any flicker. Listen, don't you hear it?"

"Hear what, man?" came the reply. "I don't hear anything."

"That's what I mean. The generator's gone. You got the controls for the auxiliary there in the hall next to you. They're opposite the door from the kitchen. Get to 'em." He stumbled around in the darkness, cursing as he bumped into the card table. "Where's that damn flashlight?" Something fell from the table and hit the floor. Magazine, probably.

"You fellas okay over there?"

A giggle came from the couch, edgy and fearful.

"Cut that out, Copper." Childs hesitated. The flashlight should be in the corner, on a shelf. He started feeling his way along the wall. "Nauls, what's taking you so long? It's straight out the door."

"I know," came the nervous reply. "I found it. I'm

135

working on it right now, but nothing's happening!"

"That's impossible, man." He reached the shelf and felt among the books and games. No flashlight.

Turning back to the center of the room he shuffled carefully back to the card table. "Okay, Clark. Out of the john right now."

"It's shorted out or something!" Nauls was yelling at him from down the corridor.

Childs ignored the cook's lament. He wanted a response from the bathroom. "Clark. You hear me, Clark? You come on out of there! Now."

When there was still no reply forthcoming, Childs felt around the table until he located the torch. It flared to life with gratifying speed. Blue fire filled the recreation room with ghostly but adequate illumination.

He started toward the john, but something half seen made him pause and turn the torch toward the couch.

"Where . . . where's Garry?" The station manager had disappeared. Copper was staring numbly at the empty cushion next to him. He and Childs were now alone.

"Well, shit." The mechanic groped for the portable siren and switched it on, thankful for the batteries that powered it.

Palmer looked up from the now invisible snowmobile he'd nearly finished dismantling. Macready and Sanders pushed a path out of the trash dump and exchanged a glance with the assistant pilot. Soon all three of them were loping toward the nearest entrance, making their way by flashlight through the long night.

Childs twisted and spun at every little imagined noise, trying to keep the torch between himself and the darkness. "Where are you, Garry? Don't you move an inch, Copper." The doctor giggled again, loudly. It did not improve the mechanic's already shaky state of mind.

"Nauls, bring me a goddamn flashlight!"

The cook abandoned the useless control box and returned to the kitchen, feeling along his familiar cabinets until he reached a particular drawer. His hands moved among the contents, picking up spoons and spatulas and ladles, everything except what he was searching for.

"Somebody's taken mine. I can't find it!"

"Clark!" Childs turned the torch toward the bathroom.

136

"You coming out of there or you want me to come in after you?"

Macready, Sanders, and Palmer stumbled into the hallway, bumping into each other as they fought to get their bearings in the unexpectedly dark corridor. Macready closed the door behind them. Their flashlights provided the only illumination.

"What's happened?" Macready called out. When the outside lights had gone he'd expected some trouble inside, but not this utter, complete blackness. "Anybody know what happened?"

"Macready . . . that you?" It was Norris.

"Yeah! Palmer and Sanders are with me. What the hell's going on?"

"I think it's the generator," the geophysicist replied. "There's no power to anything, the lights included."

"What about the backup?"

"Beats me. All I know is everything's out."

Macready turned to his assistant. "All right, Palmer, let's get down there."

"Macready!"

"That you, Childs?"

"Yeah. I'm still in the rec room."

Macready's thoughts were racing. "You okay?"

"Yeah, I'm fine, man. But Garry's missing."

"Oh shit." The pilot thought a moment. They had other priorities right now. "Well . . . hang on!"

"Gee, thanks." The mechanic's voice was cheerless as it floated down the corridor. "What about power?"

"Palmer and I are getting on it." He started running up the corridor.

The flashlight beam seemed weak and on the verge of failing as the two men stumbled down the short flight of stairs leading to the generator room. At the bottom Macready hesitated, turned and searched the darkness with the light.

"Sanders. Where's Sanders?"

They examined the stairway together, then the floor and walls of the generator room. Sanders was gone.

Palmer took a step back the way they'd come and asked unenthusiastically, "Want me to go look for him?"

"No. Not now," Macready said impatiently. "We've got

137

to get this mother going first, then we can go looking for people."

They approached the silent mass of metal. It squatted like an armored dinosaur in the middle of the floor. The smell of diesel, thick and noxious, was everywhere. But it was fading rapidly.

Palmer used the light, inspecting components. The beam lingered on an open space near the base.

"The fuel pump's gone." Panic cracked his voice. "You've got to get up to Supply and find another unit, Mac. If we don't get this thing started soon it'll freeze up on us and we'll never get it going."

"What about the auxiliary?"

"I know what's been done to this. I don't know about the other."

"You sure about the pump? That's all that's missing?"

The flashlight beam retraced its path across the generator. "I think so. I don't see anything else. This is really Childs's department."

"Childs is busy," Macready reminded his assistant. "Hang on. I'll be back as fast as I can."

"You want my light?"

Macready glanced at his own feeble beam. "No, you keep it. Make sure nothing else has been jimmied." He turned and rushed up the stairs, heedless of tripping in the near dark.

Palmer just waited. It occured to him that he was all alone in the lowest, most isolated area of the compound.

Hell, get your mind on something else, he told himself.

Holding the flashlight tightly in one hand, he lay down on his back and edged under the generator. At least he could make sure everything else was ready to go.

Of course there was always the chance Macready might not return for a while. He might get distracted. Or something might distract him. Palmer furiously began tightening screws, regardless of whether or not they were loose.

Childs paced the rec room floor, swatting his sides to keep warm. The temperature was falling rapidly, the Antarctic night leaching the heat from the compound despite the multiple layers of insulation designed to keep it at bay. The torch lay on the card table, adding a little heat, its blue glow barely reaching to the corners of the room. Copper sat by himself on the couch.

At least he'd stopped that infernal giggling, Childs mused gratefully.

Macready charged out of the supply room, juggling his flashlight and a new solid-state pump unit, and promptly careened off another body.

"Who . . . who's that? Who goes there?"

There was no reply. The dim silhouette hurried off down the hallway.

"Sanders? That you? You flipped out again, man? It's okay . . . it's me, Macready. Hey, who . . .?"

A dim voice drifted up from the other direction. "Mac?" Palmer sounded anxious. "That you, Mac? Where the hell is that pump?"

"Coming!" He threw a last look down the hallway, but saw only darkness. Then he was running for the generator room.

So intent was he on protecting the fuel pump that he nearly fell in his haste to get down the few stairs. Palmer's light beckoned from beneath the generator. Macready dropped to his knees and put the unit close to the other pilot. Palmer backed out and joined him in tearing at the box.

"This going to do it?" Macready asked him. Palmer was studying the exposed unit.

"It's not the same."

"Hell." Macready started to rise. "I'll go look again."

"No, no," Palmer grabbed his arm and held him back. "I mean, it's made by a different manufacturer than the missing unit. It'll fit."

Macready breathed a sigh of relief. "Shit, Palmer, don't do that to me."

"Hold the light for me, will you?" Palmer reached in and grabbed his own flashlight and handed it to Macready. Then he wormed his way back underneath.

"A little higher, Mac." Macready raised the twin beams. Palmer's hands came into view. Their breath was already starting to freeze as the temperature continued to fall.

He held the lights as steady as he could while Palmer worked with increasingly clumsy, numb fingers.

139

"Somebody definitely messed with it." A hose clamp was slipped into place, tightened.

"We going to make it?"

"Hope so. Another fifteen minutes." Palmer was beginning to sound more confident. "Wonder what happened to the auxiliary. What I don't get is—"

He was interrupted by a violent, thunderous screeching. Macready froze. He'd heard that sound twice before now. Once on the tape salvaged from the Norwegian camp, and once far out on the ice. He thought of Bennings as his heart began to hammer against his ribs. . . .

11

Macready had never been so glad to see anything happen in his life as he was to see the lights come back on. Palmer crawled out from beneath the now humming generator, wiping grease off on his pants.

"That should hold it for now, until Childs can get down here and bolt it properly. Where to?"

"Rec room," Macready told him tersely. He was reluctant to abandon the generator room, but had to content himself with slapping a heavy padlock on the door as they exited.

The rec room was crowded by the time they arrived. The congestion, the presence of human bodies, was comforting after the long minutes spent alone with the generator. Neighbor studied neighbor. Palmer, Nauls, and Sanders spread themselves out as far as possible, putting distance between themselves and everyone else.

Norris and Childs were using nylon ropes to tie the doctor, Clark, and Garry to the couch. Macready cursed himself for not ordering it done sooner. Too late now. He forced himself not to think of what might've happened if he hadn't been able to come up with a replacement fuel pump for the generator.

As Norris and Childs worked on the three prisoners

Macready fiddled with the little propane burners he'd scavenged from Supply. They'd be dangerous to operate, but he trusted the makeshift blowtorches more than any of the guns.

"Where were the flashlights?" Sanders was asking him. "What happened to all the flashlights, man?"

"Screw the flashlights," Macready growled at him. "Where the hell were you?"

"I . . . I panicked again, Mac. Just started running, trying to get away. I'm sorry."

"*De nada.* Forget it." He rose, hefted one of the small torches and looked over toward Palmer. "I think these'll work. One of your better ideas."

"Thanks, Mac. But when I was getting the burner tips out of Supply, I noticed something else. It reminded me that I couldn't find the magneto from chopper one. There's tons of stuff missing. Cables, wire, microprocessor chips . . . all kinds of shit. I didn't think it anything of it until I remembered the missing piece from the chopper."

"Now that's funny." Nauls stepped away from the wall. "I've been missing stuff from the kitchen, too. I didn't say anything about it because I didn't think it was important. I mean, what the hell would anybody want with a food processor?"

Macready surveyed the room, counting heads. "Anybody see Fuchs? Or hear him?"

Nobody had. That was clear from their expressions as well as the silence.

Childs was glaring at the station manager as he started to tie the man's arms behind his back. "Where did you go when the lights went out . . . chief?"

Garry was still woozy from the effects of the morphine. "Was dark . . . find a light . . ."

"You lying bastard."

Garry fought the ropes, struggled to his feet. His words were slurred. "I rather don't like your tone. . . ." He reached up a free hand and grabbed Childs by the collar.

"You sit back down." The mechanic whaled the station manager with a powerful right hand. Garry managed to half duck the blow, put his head into the bigger man's chest, and threw his weight to one side. The two of them fell backwards over the couch, almost taking Copper with them.

Macready and Norris dove in immediately, the pilot grabbing Childs and Norris wrestling with the dazed but still dangerous station manager.

"Easy, chief, that's enough. Take it easy!"

Somehow Macready managed to shove Childs to one side. "Stop it, man! You hear me? This is just what *it* wants. Are you fighting for it or against it?"

Childs was holding up a fist the size of a toaster; he stared blankly at the pilot as he digested the latter's words. The fist dropped slowly and the mechanic inhaled deeply. When he spoke again he sounded embarrassed.

"Sorry, Mac. I wasn't thinking." But he continued to glare at the station manager.

They were interrupted by a rumbling sound from above. High wind battered at the roofing. Macready glanced at the ceiling and released Childs.

"You all hear that?" He gazed around the room. "I checked Bennings's charts. That storm's going to start ripping any minute. So we don't have much time."

"Time for what?" Norris wanted to know.

Macready walked over to the card table and began distributing the portable blowtorches. He shoved the first one into Norris's stomach. "We've got to find Fuchs. When we find him, we kill him."

Sanders looked shocked. "Why?"

"If he was still one of us he'd have come back here by now. The lights have been on long enough. He hasn't . . . so that means that he can't, or doesn't want to because he isn't Fuchs anymore. If he *has* become one of those things, we've got to get him before he changes into . . . into whatever it can change into.

"Know what I think? I think it's tired of playing around. It knows we've got it stuck here, so there's no reason for it to keep lying low in hopes of stealing a copter or a snowmobile. The only way it can survive now is by making sure we can't finish it off. That means taking care of us. If it can't do that as a man, it may try doing it as itself.

"Remember, we've got less than an hour. I wish I knew how much less." He looked to his right. "Nauls, you and Childs and I'll check the outside shacks." He tossed torches to Palmer and Sanders.

"You two search the compound. Stay together."

142

Palmer turned a wary gaze on the radio operator. "I ain't going with Sanders."

Sanders's head snapped toward the backup pilot. "Something wrong with me, man?"

Palmer ignored him, avoiding his eyes. "I ain't going with him. I'll go with Childs."

"Well, fuck you, man."

"I ain't going with you!" Palmer's voice was on the edge of hysteria.

"Well who says I want you going with me?" Childs put in gruffly.

Macready stepped between them, angry and out of patience. "Cut the bullshit! We haven't got the time for this. How many times have I got to tell you guys that that's just the way the thing wants us to act. Afraid of each other, paranoid . . . we cut each other's throats and it'll sit back off on the side and laugh itself silly."

Palmer looked like the kid who got caught with his hand in the fudge. "Yeah, I know . . . but I still ain't going with Sanders."

"Okay, okay." Macready made no effort to conceal his disgust. "Sanders, you come with us. Norris, you stay here." He turned to confront the men tied on the couch.

"Any of them move, you fry 'em. And if you hear anything, anything at all that don't sound kosher, you let loose with that siren. We all meet back here in twenty minutes regardless." He lowered his voice meaningfully. "And everybody watches everybody else. Don't get mad, don't fight. Just watch." His eyes met those of close friends. "All clear? Then let's move."

The three men paused above the stairs. The wind blew balefully around them. At least the outside lights were back on, though flashlights were still necessary to illuminate the wooden walkway.

"Okay, watch yourselves now," Macready warned them. A powerful gust of wind gave impetus to his words. "This storm will be on us any minute. I don't want to be stuck out here when it hits.

"Sanders, you check the chemical storage shed." The radio operator nodded and started off to his right across a walkway buried beneath a half inch of slick snow. "Come on, Nauls."

With the cook at his side, the pilot headed up the walkway, leaning into the wind. He'd gone about a yard before he slipped and nearly fell. The flashlight beam was too weak to penetrate the ice-filled night air.

"Light up," he yelled at Nauls. The cook nodded. Each man pulled a flare from his pocket, twisted the head to set it alight. The intense glow brightened their path considerably.

They shuffled onward toward Blair's shed. The guide ropes that flanked the walkway were all that kept them headed in the right direction.

Childs opened the door carefully and peered into the exposed room. Empty. He closed the door quietly, moved a few yards down the hallway and opened the divider. The corridor ahead was also deserted.

"What'd we ever do to these things, anyway?" a voice said close behind him.

The mechanic whirled and glared down at Palmer. The pilot had been mumbling to himself and had fallen a few steps behind his companion.

The abruptness of Childs's move brought Palmer to a startled halt. "What . . .?"

"Don't walk behind me."

"Walk behind . . .?" Realization dawned. Normally Palmer could let his mind drift langorously, but not now. This wasn't the time for idle introspection. "Oh yeah . . . right."

He moved up until he was standing next to the opposite wall, across from the mechanic. "This better?"

"Much better," Childs agreed. He moved past the divider and into the next section of corridor. They continued that way, neither man advancing ahead of or falling far behind his partner. The jerky, awkward mutual lockstep did nothing to lessen the tension between them.

The wind howled around the walls of the shack as Nauls and Macready stopped in front of the door. The pilot glanced around the left side of the building, then the right. None of the boards covering the windows appeared to have been disturbed.

"Let's keep it quiet," Nauls urged him. "Maybe the thing's walking around out here, listening for—"

Macready shook his head and spoke brusquely. "It's got more sense than that, and if it didn't you couldn't hear it anyway. Not over this wind."

Nauls licked his lips, cursing himself when a crust of ice immediately formed over them. He eyed the heavy boards sealing the shed door. "So what do we do? Go on in?"

"Not unless we have to."

The little port set in the door was completely clouded over. Macready squinted at it while Nauls danced behind him, as much from nervousness as a desire to keep warm.

"See anything?"

Macready stared a moment longer, then finally shook his head. "Too steamed up. The side windows should be clearer. Come on."

Huddled close to the wall they moved around the left side. The force of the wind abated slightly in the lee of the shed.

The gap between two of the one-by-fours was also fogged up, but not as badly as the glass in the doorway. Macready peered inside.

Blair was seated at the central table, barely visible in the pale glow from the single weak bulb dangling overhead. He was spooning food out of a can. A hangman's noose hung stark and ready from one of the ceiling beams.

Macready put his mouth close to the glass, careful not to let his lips come in contact with it. "Hey, Blair!"

The biologist jumped up, knocking over his chair and spilling the can of food. His agitated expression belied his seeming serenity. He searched wildly for the source of the shout before his gaze came to rest on the side window.

"Mac, is that you?"

"Yeah. Me and Nauls. Take it easy, Blair." At this reassurance the biologist appeared to relax slightly. He walked over to the window and stared out at the pilot. His eyes were red and lined, his hair unkempt and his clothing disheveled. Macready thought he looked terrible.

"What d'you want, Mac?"

"Has Fuchs been out here?" Macready studied the other man closely, trying to determine if he was likely to go on another mad binge. He couldn't decide, even wished Copper were present. But Copper was under suspicion.

"I've changed my mind," he told Macready. "I'd . . . I'd

145

like to come back inside. I don't want to stay out her anymore. I hear funny things out here."

I'll bet you do, thought Macready silently. The troubl is you were hearing them before you were put out here.

"I asked if you'd seen Fuchs."

Blair made an effort and forced himself to conside Macready's question. "Fuchs? No, it's not Fuchs. You mus let me back in. I won't harm anyone. I promise. You have al the guns hidden away by now, I'm sure. I . . . I can't do an more damage to anything."

"We'll see about it, Blair." Macready turned from th window. "Got a couple of other things to check out first. Nauls followed the pilot away from the shed.

Blair's panicky voice followed them. "I promise! I'n much better now. I'll be good. I'm all right. Don't leave m here. Mac, don't leave me out here . . . !" The win swallowed the rest of his screams as Macready and Naul moved a little faster.

Norris was tired. The past couple of days had beer rough. He wasn't as young as most of the guys. Nor a healthy. He kept his attention split between the sedated tri slumped on the couch and the several entrances to th recreation room. A dull ache throbbed in his chest. H rubbed his sternum reflexively, wincing.

"I'm getting worried about you," Copper said thickl from the couch. "You ought to have an EKG."

Norris self-consciously moved his hand away from hi chest and tried to sound unconcerned. "Let's not worry about anything else just now."

The doctor yawned, not entirely the result of the sedation. He was exhausted too. "Okay. After we get thi mess squared away, then. First thing."

Norris nodded agreeably. Something made a noise outside the kitchen-end doorway and he jerked sharply in its direction. It came again, faint and mechanical. Relay switching over, he decided, relaxing again.

He looked back at the doctor and murmured, "After al this mess. . . ."

The wind outside was no longer merely strong, it had turned decidedly vicious. Macready and Nauls had to use the guide ropes to drag themselves along as they made agonizingly slow progress toward the pilot's shed. The gentle slope seemed like a sixty-degree climb.

They used both flashlight and flares now. The only sign of life was provided by the dull orange glow of the exterior lights impotently trying to penetrate the blowing snow.

A violent gust knocked Macready off his feet. He hung onto the rope with both hands as his legs went out from under him. His boots kicked at the snow. He was on his back, half on the boardwalk and half lying on white oblivion. The wind tore at him, trying to loosen his grip.

Nauls stopped as the pilot's flashlight and flare were blown toward him. He dove for the light, gripping the rope with his other hand, and managed to catch it before the wind carried it out of sight.

Macready fought to get back on his feet. He was painfully aware of his vulnerability, lying there on his back against the slippery ice. Nauls was coming toward him, pulling himself along the ropes. The pilot stared through battered goggles at the younger man, the cook a surreal vision in snow-caked parka and boots.

Then Nauls bent and handed over the flashlight. Trying not to show his relief, Macready finally managed to pull himself upright again.

"Thanks," he shouted above the wind. Nauls just nodded. Together they resumed their hike toward the shed.

Normally the electric cables ran in neat, parallel lines along the lower kitchen wall like so many silver pythons. Now they were twisted and torn as if a small bomb had gone off in their midst. Naked copper gleamed in the fluorescent light.

Childs and Palmer were bent over them, examining the damage.

"Auxiliary power line," Childs muttered angrily as he poked at a particular cable. "That's why the backup never came on, or the storage batteries either."

"Auxiliary cables," Palmer repeated. He leaned closer, feeling betrayed. "Been cut by somebody."

"Cut, bullshit." Childs staightened and stared around

the deserted kitchen. He missed the familiar cooking smells and the friendly cacophony of Nauls's stereo. "Been pulled apart."

"Can we fix them?"

"Probably. Cut off the torn ends and put in clean splices. If we get the time to." He turned to leave. "Come on. I said the reserve batteries were probably all right. I want to make sure." They headed for Supply.

In spite of the intensifying gale Macready and Nauls managed to reach the top of the little hill. The shed provided some protection from the growing storm. It was very dark. The feeble light from the main compound was completely obliterated by blowing snow.

Macready gestured and Nauls took up a ready stance on the far side of the doorway. Reaching out with a gloved hand the pilot flipped up the heavy latch. Then he took a deep breath, shoved the door open and stepped inside, holding a burning flare in front of him.

The first thing he did was trip the light switch just inside the door, but no friendly light flared from the overhead fixture. His gaze turned upward.

There was no light fixture. It was gone, along with most of the roof. A few bent corners showed where the weighted metal had been ripped back.

Aghast, he strode into his room. The wind was nearly as strong inside as out front, now that the roof was gone. Whether from the battering it had already taken from the wind or from something else, the interior was a snow-swept wreck.

He became aware that Nauls was shouting at him. "Where's the roof?" The cook had been standing in the doorway, staring. Now he walked in and turned in a slow circle as he gazed skyward. "This storm do that?"

Macready shook his head. Before they'd forced the door he'd been frightened. Now he was getting angry.

"Possible but not likely," he told his companion. "Must have weighed a ton and a half. I had it weighted against hundred and fifty mile per hour winds. This little blow we're having isn't anywhere near that strong."

They quietly inspected the ruin that had been Macready's home away from home. The oversize chess set was a cracked chunk of red and black plastic. It lay in a corner where it had been thrown. A few of the pieces were visible above the accumulated snow. They lay scattered all over the floor, a pawn here, a broken king there.

Nauls kicked over a chair. As he did so something pale and bloated bounded from beneath. He let out a half scream and instinctively thrust his flare at it.

It caught the inflatable lady in the midsection. There was a sharp report. Macready whirled at the gunshot-like report while Nauls tripped and fell to the floor.

Caught by the gusting wind, the deflated latex soared through the missing roof and disappeared into the night.

"Shit," Macready muttered, though whether because of the loss of his companion or the false alarm Nauls couldn't tell. The cook picked himself off the floor, brushing snow from his rumpled parka.

"Goddamn women," he growled darkly. "Never could tell what they were going to do."

It was cold in the side corridor. The generator was still struggling to replace the heat lost during its temporary shutdown.

Palmer stood by as Childs methodically undid the locks sealing the plant room. It took time. The pilot didn't enjoy waiting. He would greatly have preferred to wait back in the rec room. But orders were orders. At least Mac hadn't forced him to go with the jittery Sanders.

Eventually Childs turned the last dial and pulled the heavy door aside. An unexpected gust of wind-driven snow made the two surprised men step backward. Childs put his head down and moved into it, wedging his body against the doorjamb. Palmer hung close to him.

"My babies," the mechanic murmured, ignoring the cold and the wind as he entered the modified storage closet.

The carefully machined skylight had been smashed. Glass littered the floor, some still attached to the hand-welded metal frames. The plants were dead. Their crowns touched the floor, unable to stand straight under the weight of accumulated ice.

Palmer's eyes widened as he took in first the gap in the

ceiling, then the forest of little green stalagmites. "Somebody broke in," he whispered fearfully, "or out."

Childs didn't seem to hear. "Now who'd go and do a thing like this?" A whole year's off-time cultivation, careful work with the makeshift hydroponics, all shot to hell. He took a step farther into the room.

Fear giving him necessary strength, Palmer reached in and quickly yanked the mechanic back.

"Childs . . . no!"

The bigger man turned on him. "Let go of me, man, before I . . ." He raised a threatening fist.

"No, no." Palmer let go of Childs's shirt and backed off, pleading with him. "Don't stay in there." His gaze went to the hole in the roof. "Don't get near the plants. They look like they're frozen, but we can't be sure. The plants, they're alive. Those things can imitate anything living, remember? Any kind of organic construction."

Childs hesitated, reflexively moved his feet away from the nearest growth. "What's it going to do, being a plant? Grow up my leg?"

"I don't know, but we can't take any chances." Palmer was carrying one of the portable torches Childs and Macready had fashioned. Now he was checking the flow valve as he pointed it toward the storage room.

"We got to burn 'em."

Childs gaze narrowed. "Now hold on just a minute, you dumb—" He took a step toward the pilot.

Palmer dodged around him and activated the torch. A narrow trail of fire sprayed past the mechanic. Ice melted instantly and the plants beneath ignited, burning like thin green candles. A pungent smoke drifted out into the hallway.

Childs gave Palmer a shove, and started dancing on the flames in a frantic attempt to put the fire out.

"You stupid, ignorant son of a—"

Palmer screamed. He'd started to turn away and his gaze had fallen on the door blocking the corridor. The door had swung lazily inward on its hinges, and now stood half closed. Childs stopped stomping and stared past the pilot.

Staring at them from the back of the door was the frozen body of Fuchs. An axe was imbedded in his chest, pinning him to the wood. His eyes were still open. Together with

150

the expression on his face, they effectively mirrored whatever had killed him.

Palmer was still screaming.

Norris heard it and jumped up from his seat in the recreation room. Common sense fought with orders. He looked at the couch. All three of his charges were still tightly bound and sleeping off their drug-induced stupor.

Still, Macready had ordered him not to leave the room. He settled for throwing the alarm.

Sanders had arrived in the storage area after finishing up outside. Now he gazed in fascination at the corpse of the young biologist as the siren continued to wail around them.

He put both hands on the axe and tried to wrench it out. It wouldn't shift, let alone break free. The sharp head was completely buried in Fuchs's chest and into the door beyond.

The radio operator gave up. Stepping back he eyed Childs's hulking frame and said pointedly, "Whoever put this through him is one bad-ass and strong mother."

Childs moved closer, carefully inspecting the gruesome sight. He made a fist and hammered on the handle of the axe. It quivered slightly but didn't loosen. His tone was subdued rather than offended when he turned to the radio operator.

"No one's this strong, boy."

"I just got back in, heard the siren," Sanders told them.

"What about Macready and Nauls?" Palmer was trying hard not to look at the corpse.

"I think they're on their way in. They were just behind me." He shrugged. "*Quien sabe?*"

Childs nodded thoughtfully. "All right. You both remember the orders. That siren goes off, everybody beats it back to the rec room. Wonder what set it off early?"

Palmer looked elsewhere. "Norris probably heard me scream."

"Yeah, and he doesn't know why. Sensible reaction." He clapped the pilot on the shoulder. "Hey, forget it, man. The wonder is that we all aren't running around screaming our damn heads off. Let's get back there. We can do some checking on the way."

They made good time, opening and closing doors to rooms or hallways as they ran, even rechecking those they'd already inspected. But despite the momentary feeling of closeness they'd shared back in the storage area, Palmer still kept his distance from Childs, Childs kept clear of the pilot, and Sanders stayed away from both of them.

"I don't understand," Palmer was saying as they ran, "why didn't it take control of Fuchs? Isn't that it's number . . . to get more recruits?"

Childs considered the question as he opened the door to a closet. It contained several metal buckets full of sand and a large fire extinguisher. That was all. He slammed it shut and moved to the next door.

"I guess it didn't have enough time. The generator was out what, thirty minutes? Twenty? Takes the bastards about an hour or maybe more to take control of somebody, remember?

"Maybe it got started on him and when the lights came back on, it figured it had a choice between trying to hide out and finish the job or splitting and preserving its cover. It could hardly leave Fuchs standing around to tell the rest of us who the mystery guest is. So it offed him."

"Yeah, but why Fuchs?" Sanders wanted to know. The next room held steel cannisters, cold air, and nothing alive. They moved on. "Why not Macready, or you or me? The lights were out all over camp. It could've jumped any one of us."

"Maybe none of the rest of us were as accessible, or alone at the time," Childs suggested. "But I wouldn't bet that was the reason." His thoughts were churning.

"Fuchs was supposed to come up with a new test for this thing, remember? He must have been on to something. These bastards got scared and got rid of him. Maybe they didn't even bother to try taking him over. Probably were more concerned about getting rid of him."

He stopped abruptly in the middle of the corridor, turning to stare back down the passageway. "Hey, where's . . . ?" He glanced over at Sanders. "Didn't you say Nauls and Macready were right behind you?"

Sanders also looked back the way they'd come, sweat standing out on his brow. "Yeah. Yeah, they were. I saw 'em just before I started down the stairs. I could see their lights coming toward me."

"Well then, where the hell are they?" There was a pause

152

nd then they were pounding back down the hallway, houting as they ran.

"Macready!" Palmer yelled.

Childs stopped long enough to bellow up a side orridor. "Nauls! Macready!"

There was no reply. They continued searching and houting for several minutes, until finally they reached the ame outside door Sanders had used. The shouting ceased nd the three men exchanged nervous glances.

"What now?" Palmer whispered, staring at the door.

Childs reached for the latch, his hand hovering over it while conflicting emotions tore through him. Then he pulled is fingers back and spoke resolutely. "The siren's still lowing. You know the orders. Back to the rec room."

Reluctantly, they abandoned the door and whatever night lie just on the other side. As they retraced their steps hey continued to cry out to the two men who'd been outside vith Sanders.

The difference was that now they didn't expect an nswer.

The full-fledged storm rumbled outside, its persistent nowl penetrating even the tightly sealed, heavily insulated ecreation room. It was silent inside. The men looked at :ach other, at the three dozing on the couch, anywhere but oward the thick window that showed only darkness and an occasional flurry of ice particles.

Childs paced back and forth, his fist regularly slam-ning an open palm.

"Quit that," Palmer finally told him. "You're making me nervous." Immediately the irony of his statement struck him and he let out a short, uneasy laugh.

The mechanic spun on a heel and strode up to Norris. "How long they been outside now?"

"Can't be sure," Norris replied carefully. "I sort of half glanced at my watch when they went out." He looked down at the digital readout.

"Take a guess. We need to know."

The geophysicist considered. "Forty . . . forty-five minutes."

"You sure it hasn't been longer? An hour, maybe?"

Norris squirmed. "I told you, I didn't pay much attention. I guess it could be."

The silence was thick in the room as the men regarded each other.

Childs started for the exit. "We'd better start closing off the outside hatchways."

"You sure, Childs?" Palmer asked.

The mechanic stopped and stared across at Norris, who nodded reluctant agreement. "What would Macready do, Palmer?"

The pilot though of his friend and boss. "Yeah, you're right," he said tightly. "I'll start on the north side, you and Sanders take the south and east."

"Aren't you forgetting something?" Childs was giving him a peculiar look.

"I don't . . . oh, yeah. We've got to work together. In that case we'd better get moving." Childs was still staring at him. "Hey, look, I just forgot for a minute, okay?"

"Try not to forget again, huh?" Childs started out of the room.

They were nearly finished with the lockup when Norris's faint shout reached them.

"All of you . . . come here!"

"Shit, now what?" Sanders grumbled. He threw the interior bolt on the door they'd just reached and hurried after his two companions.

When he entered the main hallway he saw Norris and the others bunched up against one of the windows that flanked the door.

"Hey, what's going on?" He pushed toward the window, straining to see around Childs and the rest. Palmer glanced back at him and pointed toward the foggy glass.

A figure was barely visible against the night. It was staggering toward the compound, pulling itself forward by using the guide ropes. Occasionally a particularly powerful gust of wind forced it to halt. It waited until the blast had subsided before stumbling forward again.

"Who is it?" Nauls whispered. "Nauls or Macready?"

"Can't tell for certain yet." Palmer didn't take his eyes from the window. "But we'll know in a minute."

The silhouette came onward, growing larger if not more distinct, until it disappeared. Then a steady pounding

154

ounded from the other side of the door. Childs hefted his orch and took a couple of steps backward, nodding toward Norris. The geophysicist threw the bolts and pulled on the handle.

Sleet and hail and Nauls all came in a single, frozen mass. Norris hastily put his weight against the door and jammed it shut, then rethrew the restraining bolts. Sanders had to help him.

Totally winded, Nauls knelt on the hard floor, head bent, hands resting on his knees. The men gathered around him, watching him closely.

"Where's Macready?" Palmer asked.

The cook's head came up. His expression, beneath the ice melting from his face and the rim of his hood, was grim. He tore off the snow goggles and flung them aside, then dug down inside the bulky front of his parka.

"Cut him loose from the line up by his shack," he mumbled, still fumbling with the parka.

Childs gaped down at him. "Cut him loose?"

"Had to." The cook swallowed. "When we were poking around his place I found this." He pulled a thick wad of clothing from his jacket. It was torn and blackened at the edges, showing clear evidence of having been burned.

He turned out the collar. The name tag inside read clearly: R.J. MACREADY. Norris and the others gathered around, each inspecting the clothing intently.

Nauls let out a long *whoosh* and climbed painfully to his feet. "It was stashed in his old propane furnace. The wind must have dislodged it and knocked it down where I could find it. I don't think he saw me find it. In fact, I know he didn't, or I wouldn't be here showing it to you now."

The men continued to inspect the damning evidence, still finding it hard to believe.

"Made sure I got ahead of him on the towline on the way back, kept my mouth shut . . . cut him loose."

Sanders was incredulous. "I can't believe it. Macready?"

Nauls nodded slowly. "I know it's tough to buy, but it sure as hell explains a lot. He's one of them. No wonder we've been going around in circles for so long. Remember how he took the gun and command from Garry? He's had us chasing our tails for hours, been playing with us. He's one of those things, all right."

155

"When do you think it got to him?" Sanders inquired, badly frightened all over again. He'd finally succeeded in getting himself under control, and now this. Macready had been about the only man in camp the radio operator really trusted.

"Could have been anytime," Palmer murmured disconsolately. "And anywhere."

Childs was frowning at Nauls. Something had been bothering him ever since the exhausted cook had come tumbling into the corridor. "If it did get to him."

Nauls turned on him. "Look, man . . . !"

"When the lights went out," Palmer was muttering.

"Would have been the perfect time," Norris added.

"Right," Palmer agreed. "Garry was missing. And Sanders," he added pointedly.

"Fuck you, Palmer." The radio operator jumped his accuser. Childs and Norris had to separate them.

"Here we go again," said the geophysicist, breathing hard, "acting just like it wants. Can't you two peabrains get that through your skulls? I don't think—"

A new hammering at the door interrupted him and made everyone jump backward. Nauls cowered behind everyone else, staring in terror at the door.

The sound of Macready's voice in between the pounding was unmistakable. "Open up!"

Nobody answered. Norris and Childs raised their blowtorches and pointed them at the door, continuing to back slowly down the corridor.

"Hey, somebody!" the voice continued. "Open up! It's me, Macready." The pounding resumed. "Come on, damn it! The line snapped on me. Been crawling around like a seal out here. Let me in."

Nauls's whisper was harsh in the corridor. "That's bullshit. He's got to know damn well that I cut it. 'Snapped' my ass."

The men kept their voices down as they debated how to proceed.

"Let's open up," Palmer suggested, indicating the torches. "We've got him covered if he tries anything."

Childs glared at him, ignoring the pounding at the door. "Hell, no. I was out on the ice when it took Bennings. You

156

can't believe how fast these suckers can move. The door stays closed, man."

Sanders was shaking and didn't give a damn if anyone noticed. "You think he's changed into one of those things?"

Norris checked his watch. "He hasn't had enough time."

"How do you know, man?" the radio operator asked him.

"Blair said it takes at least an hour."

"Blair don't know nothing. Blair's crazy. Maybe it don't take an hour. Maybe only thirty minutes."

"It's the best estimate we have to work with," Norris argued back. "Hell, it's the *only* estimate we have to work with. I admit I'm not sure about how long he's been outside, but I don't think it's been an hour yet."

Childs was staring at the door, talking to himself. "Nothing human could have made it back here in this weather without a guideline." The wind roared beyond the door, accentuating the mechanic's point.

"Where is everybody?" Macready demanded to know from the other side of the barrier. His voice was weak, tired. "I'm half frostbit."

Palmer took a hesitant step toward the door. "Let's open it. Now."

"Why are you so damn anxious to let him in here?" Childs asked venomously.

Palmer was trembling slightly. "He's so close. If he has changed, this'd be our best chance to blow him away."

Childs vetoed the idea. "No. Why risk it? Just let him freeze out there."

Sanders voice cracked as he spoke. "What if we're wrong about him? What if that's the real Macready out there, trying to get in? He'll freeze to death. What if we're wrong, man?"

"Then we're wrong," Childs told him coldly.

They waited. Several minutes passed. The pounding faded, finally stopped altogether.

"Maybe he's unconscious," Sanders ventured. "We could open the door and give it a fast check."

Norris shook his head. "If you're so damn curious, look out the windows."

Sanders hesitated, then moved forward. He pressed his

157

face against the inner pane and squeezed sideways as he tried to see the doorstep.

"I don't see nothing."

Palmer moved forward and peered out the other window. "Neither do I. If he collapsed against the door, he'd be out of our lines of sight. And it's darker than a witch's bedroom out there."

A muffled noise reached them. Everyone turned at the sound of breaking glass.

Palmer's eyes bulged. "The window to supply room G. It's not a triple pane!"

Sanders pressed back against the wall next to the door. "What are we going to do? What are we going to do?"

"Get a grip on yourself, man," Norris ordered him. "You go off the deep end, nobody's going to have the time to hold your hand." The radio operator nodded slowly, took deep, measured breaths as he fought to comply.

The geophysicist's fingers tightened on the blowtorch. He stared resolutely down the corridor. "All right, we've got no choice now." He and Childs led the way, the others trailing close behind.

It was pitch black inside the supply room. Macready cursed a blue streak as he hunted frantically for a light switch. He was weak and suffereing from mild hypothermia.

Voices sounded outside the door. "What's going on out there?" Macready yelled angrily. "How come nobody let me in? Don't you assholes tell me you didn't hear me, either."

Palmer stood to one side, holding his torch on the door as Childs tried the knob. Locked.

"Dammit," the mechanic murmured, remembering. "He's got the storeroom keys."

"Isn't there another set?"

Childs looked doubtful. "Garry might have another one stashed somewhere, but he's too doped up to think straight. Anyway, we can't afford to wait that long." He looked up the hall, then strode purposefully the other way and ripped a fire axe off the paneling. Norris, Palmer, and the others backed off and gave him plenty of room as he started chopping at the door.

Macready's confused but steady voice echoed from the other side. "Hey! What the blazes are you guys doing?"

158

"You're a dead man, Macready." Childs raised the axe, swung again. "Or a dead whatever the hell you are!"

"Are you guys crazy?"

"No," said the mechanic as he worked, "and we're not going to let you make us that way, either." The axe bit deeply into the yielding wood.

Macready was silent, though they could hear him bumping around inside.

Go outside, Palmer was thinking urgently. Go and freeze outside so we won't have to do it do you.

"We found your clothes," Childs was saying. "The ones you tried to burn."

"What clothes?" Macready demanded to know.

"Forget it, Macready." The mechanic was swinging the axe like a madman. "You been made. It's all over."

"Someone's trying to mark me, you crazy bastard! Trying to frame me." They could hear him messing around with the supplies inside.

Childs cautioned Palmer and Norris as he readied the last couple of blows. "Move in slow now. Watch yourselves. These things are tricky. He might try hanging from the roof or something, so don't look just straight ahead. You ready?" Both men nodded.

With a last swing the wood surrounding the lock and doorknob gave way. Childs gave the freed barrier a solid kick and stepped aside. Palmer moved into the breach, his finger tense on the trigger of the blowtorch. Norris was right behind him.

They froze simultaneously, staring.

Macready stood in front of them, holding a burning flare in his left hand. His hair and beard were white with snow, but his eyes were clear. Frostbite darkened cheeks and nose.

Tucked beneath his right arms was a box labeled "DYNAMITE." The top of the box was missing and the pilot held the sputtering flare dangerously close to the exposed red cylinders. The individual fuses had been cut to quarter-inch lengths.

"Anybody messes with me," he said menacingly, "and the whole camp goes up. . . ."

12

None of the men standing in the hallway was anxious to test Macready's resolve. They stood staring at him, waiting helplessly to see what he'd do next.

"Put those torches on the floor and back off. Very slowly. No fast moves or we'll all warm up in a hurry. For the last time."

Keeping his eyes on Macready, Norris bent and gently put his blowtorch down. Childs laid the axe carefully alongside it, followed by Sanders and Palmer. They backed out into the hall.

Macready moved toward them, forcing them to continue the retreat. "That's it, back way off."

They were all out in the corridor now and moving toward the recreation room. They hadn't gone far when Macready frowned and started to look over a shoulder.

"Hey, where's the rest of—"

Nauls and Norris came barreling out of the supply room into the pilot. They'd rushed outside and returned via the busted supply room window. Hands grabbed for the flare.

Macready spun Nauls off his back and put his shoulder into Norris, sending the older man crashing violently into the wall. Nauls rolled, tackled Macready's legs and brought him to his knees. The others rushed forward.

But Macready still had control of the flare and the dynamite, and started to bring the two together. "So help me," he yelled at them, his voice breaking, "I mean it!"

They skidded to a halt. Nauls quickly let loose of the pilot's legs and rolled to one side.

"It's cool, man," the cook assured him desperately. "We ain't near you, man. Stay cool." He got to his knees, edged over to join the rest of the tense group, making placating motions with both hands.

160

"Yeah, man, really," a frantic Palmer added, his eyes ocked on the crate. "Just relax."

"Anybody touches me again," Macready warned them, is eyes darting from one face to the next, "up we go."

Norris still lay on the floor where he'd fallen after riking the wall. Now he coughed sharply and began to gasp or breath. His whole body gave a little weak quiver and then e was still.

Nauls crawled over to the geophysicist, shook him and ooked back toward his companions. "I don't think he's reathing." He bent his head and put an ear on the older nan's chest.

Macready rose, watching the cook. A little concern rept into his voice. "Go untie the doc and get him in here. Sring the others, too." He grinned menacingly. "From now n no one gets out of my sight."

They all started to move and he gestured threateningly vith the flare. "No. Childs, you and Sanders stay here. You ;o, Palmer. Make it fast."

The assistant pilot nodded once, glad of the oppor- unity to get away from the dynamite, and took off down the corridor.

They waited. Nauls sat next to Norris's motionless orm. He stared accusingly at Macready. "He's not breath- ng. You killed him, man."

"Shut up, Nauls. You talk too much."

Palmer was back in a hurry, supporting the doctor with an arm around his back. Garry and Clark had recovered nough to stagger unsteadily along behind.

Copper glanced once at Macready, took in the pilot's belligerent stance, the flare, the box of dynamite. "Mac, what in . . .?"

"Never mind the cheery greetings, Doc. Save it for later." He gestured toward Norris.

Copper nodded understandingly and knelt over the geophysicist's body. Nauls moved to one side. The doctor checked the recumbent man's eyes, listened to his chest, then looked back up at Macready.

"Get him to the infirmary. Fast. Only chance."

Macready nodded in agreement, looked at the others. "Childs, Sanders, Nauls . . . pick him up and let's go And

161

everyone stay in front of me and in clear view, got it? I don't
want anybody ducking into any open doorways and waiting
for me to come up next to them. I might trip, or get nervous,
or both."

Norris's body was laid out on the examination table.
The refrigerator and its legacy of ruined blood stood mutely
nearby, reminding everyone of the last time they'd gathered
in this room.

Copper turned to reach for something and nearly fell.
He was still woozy from the morphine. Palmer and Sanders
steadied him. Macready stood in a corner with his back
against the wall and watched.

Copper slipped an oxygen mask over Norris's face, then
made a couple of passing grabs at the regulator attached to
the cylinder before finally getting a hand on it. He twisted the
valve control and a hissing sound filled the room. The dial on
the regulator came alive.

Bending over Norris, the doctor ripped the man's shirt
open and yanked apart the stained undershirt. He worked
laboriously, inhibited by the aftereffects of the drug still
coursing through his system. He didn't look up at Macready
when the pilot spoke, instead continued working on his
patient.

"So you sweethearts had yourselves a little trial. I may
just have to kill you on general principles, Nauls." The cook
spat at him.

"You might already have done that to Norris." Behind
him, Copper was swathing the geophysicist's chest with a
gleaming oleaginous substance.

Macready allowed himself a mild sneer. "Did it ever
occur to the jury that anybody could have gotten to some of
my clothes and fixed them up to look nice and incriminating,
like?" His tone was casual but his attitude was not. The flare
still hovered dangerously close to the dynamite.

"We ain't buying that," said the surly Childs.

"Dammit, quit the bickering and give me a hand!"
Copper yelled at them. "Somebody wheel that fibrillator
over here."

"The what?" Childs asked.

"The machine, there, and fast!" Copper replied exasperatedly.

Keeping a cautious eye on the pilot and moving

162

eliberately so as not to alarm him, Sanders grabbed the
andles of the cart and pushed it close to the table. Copper
romptly climbed onto the table and straddled Norris's
hest.

With Copper and the motionless Norris occupying the
able and with Sanders standing close by the fibrillator,
Clark was screened from Macready's sight. Casually he let
is right hand drift toward the tray of surgical instruments
n the second shelf of the cart. He quietly sorted through
hem, discarding shining forceps, a delicate clamp, a pair of
weezers, while keeping a close watch on Macready and the
rama taking place on the table.

No one saw his fingers close around the haft of the
gleaming scalpel. He slowly reversed it, pointing the blade
p his sleeve, the handle hidden in his palm.

Copper spun to his right. "Palmer, turn the oxygen up
nother notch . . . to nine, and hold the mask down over his
ace so he can't throw it off." The assistant pilot hurried to
comply. "Childs, you grab his shoulders."

"Right." The mechanic moved around to the front of
he table, careful not to get too close to Macready. He put
massive hands on either side of Norris's head and leaned
forward, using his weight.

Copper reached toward the cart and grabbed a pair of
palm-sized pads. They were attached to the machine by thick
cords. While Childs waited he took the opportunity to smile
meaningfully at Macready.

"You're going to have to sleep sometime."

Copper glanced over at him. "Quiet down." He nodded
to Sanders. "Turn that thing on."

Sanders's fingers nudged the "on" button forward. A
warning light located just below the switch came to life and a
low hum rose from the machine.

"Now hold him down. Push hard, if you have to,"
Copper instructed the mechanic.

"I'm a real light sleeper, Childs." Macready returned the
smile easily.

"Shut up, Macready!" Busy as he was, Copper still
found the energy to be angry.

Leaning forward, he pressed the two padded contact
plates to the geophysicist's chest. Norris's body heaved
upward as the current shot through him. There was a slight

crackling sound and an odd chirp from behind the oxygen mask.

Copper removed the pads. Norris's chest did not move. The doctor spoke urgently to Sanders. "Again. More current this time." The radio operator stared blankly at the complex instrument.

Copper leaned back and pointed. "There's a dial next to the "on" switch. It's set on three. Turn it up to six." Sanders nodded, and did as directed.

Another buzz from the machine. Copper gave the bare treated skin several jolts. Sanders watched anxiously. So did Clark, the scalpel completely hidden by his hand and shirtsleeve. He started to work his way as inconspicuously as he could around the table. No one paid him any attention.

"And if anyone tries to wake me," Macready was saying easily, "my little alarm here's liable to go off and put everybody back to sleep." He patted the side of the dynamite box with the still-burning flare. Palmer winced.

"Damn you, Macready, that's enough!" Copper berated him. He touched the contacts to Norris's chest again.

And this time there was a reaction. It was as explosive and violent as it was unexpected. Norris's body arched off the table and nearly threw the doctor to the floor. The doctor looked like a bull rider, bouncing crazily on the geophysicist's heaving body.

A new crackling sound filled the room, and it didn't come from the fibrillator. Norris's sternum cracked like a lake bed in the Sahara. The skin peeled back and flaked off in fleshy strips. The oxygen mask was blown toward the ceiling as Palmer back-pedaled to get away from the unnaturally contorting corpse.

A sound came out of Norris's mouth, but it wasn't produced by the man they'd known as Norris. It was a hideous, grating, angry mewing noise.

Copper threw himself off the bucking body and landed hard on the floor. No one moved to give him a hand. They were all mesmerized by the transformation that was coming over the geophysicist's suddenly active form.

Sanders had abandoned the fibrillator and pressed himself back against the nearest wall. *Madre de dios,* what . . .?"

The thing that had been Norris was changing in front of their eyes. This wasn't like that time in the dark kennel, or that horrible night out on the ice sheet. The infirmary lights were bright and efficient. They could clearly see every detail of the noisome metamorphosis.

Clothing tore as organic matter beneath it swelled past restraining polyester bonds. A shoe split like a melon and fell from the table. A single talon became visible inside the expanding, more flexible sock. Other appendages rapidly began to take shape, a gruesome assortment of hooks and bulges and knobby growths that owed their development to no line of earthly evolution.

Macready had put the dynamite and flare on the floor. He charged the table with one of the blowtorches, pushing everyone else aside.

"Get out of the way!"

A stream of fire unloaded on the thing dancing on the infirmary table. The body seemed unable to dodge, whether because it was still incomplete or because the repeated charges from the fibrillator had inhibited its abilities. Macready couldn't tell—not that he gave a damn. The fire spread to the table, which burned merrily.

Belching and hissing, the barely recognizable remnants of Norris's body tumbled to the floor. Macready backed off a step, continued to play the nozzle of the blowtorch across it.

Somehow the flaming, indistinct mass of protoplasm managed to straighten up. It towered over him for a moment, then turned and staggered a couple of feet toward the doorway on things that weren't legs. A black and yellow ooze exploded through the shredded trousers and squirted all over the floor. Macready methodically turned the fire on it.

The monstrosity staggered backward and collapsed onto the fibrillator. It lay there, writhing with horrid, alien life, and burning furiously.

The men watched as it melted into a molten, shapeless mass of burning protoplasm. It smoked intensely. Macready was reminded of a magnesium flare, or the white phosphorus AP bombs the military occasionally used back in 'Nam.

Fire extinguishers were pulled from their holders and brought into play. The fibrillator was a wreck, scorched and blackened, the plastic plates over its readouts melted away. The infirmary table wasn't in much better shape.

While they worked they had to avoid smoking puddles of black goo that still burned on the floor, twitching agitatedly in their tiny agony. Eventually they died, too, their tiny mews fading away into silence.

All eyes traveled to Macready, who'd backed away and was once more standing with the box of dynamite. The flare had finally burnt itself out, but he held the torch ready. That would be slower, but not slow enough.

"Everybody into the rec room," he told them, breaking the stunned silence. "Nobody steps out of anybody else's sight, got that? I've got an idea."

They shuffled out of the room in a body, occasionally turning for a glance back at the smoking surgical table. No one said anything or objected to Macready's order. Their initial anger at the pilot had been replaced by a dull terror that Norris's unmasking did nothing to alleviate.

Macready waited until he was certain that everyone who'd been in the infirmary had moved into the rec room. Then he edged in behind them, always keeping his back against a wall. Putting down the box of dynamite, he used his free hand to draw Garry's Magnum from a jacket pocket.

The rest of the crew milled around on the other side of the room and watched him. He set the dynamite on one of the card tables where everyone could see it clearly.

"What you got in mind, Macready?" Clark wondered aloud. "It better be good."

"Oh, it's nothing elaborate." The pilot grinned at him. "Just a little test I've thought up. Sometimes experience can be more enlightening than a Ph.D."

"What the hell are you raving about, Macready?" Copper muttered disconsolately.

"You'll see, Doc, just like everybody else." He carefully adjusted the aperture of the torch he was holding, setting it for a short, intense throw.

"What kind of test?" Palmer asked. He was subdued after the episode in the infirmary. A kind of dull despair had settled over the men. It wasn't quite hopelessness. Not yet. It was more of a feeling that they'd finally lost all control over their chances for survival, that their destiny lay in the hands of something not human.

166

Only Macready was still defiant and unresigned. Given their present opinion of him, that only left the others feeling more discouraged than ever.

"What kind of test?" he repeated grimly. "I'm sure some of you already know."

There was plenty of rope in the room, cut segments of varying length plus the rest of the large spool they'd been pared from. The rope had been brought in and used to bind Clark, Garry, and Copper. Macready kicked it toward his reluctant assistant. It rolled to a halt at the younger man's feet.

"Palmer, you and Copper tie everyone else down. Real tight. I'll be watching you."

"What for?" Childs had considered taking a leap at the pilot, but the proximity of dynamite and blowtorch restrained him. Someone was going to have to try something pretty soon, though. No telling what Macready was up to.

"For your health," the pilot told him. He didn't sound sarcastic, either.

Garry looked at the others. "Let's rush him. He's not going to blow us up."

"Damned if I won't," Macready said brightly.

Childs took a step forward. "You ain't tying me up."

"Then I'll have to kill you."

Childs glared evenly back at the other man, nodding curtly. "Then kill me."

Macready raised the muzzle of the .44 until it was pointing straight at Childs's forehead. "I mean it." The click of the hammer going back was loud in the room.

"I guess you do," said Childs quietly.

The pilot hesitated, his finger tense on the trigger. There was movement out of the corner of his eye. An instant in which his brain registered several events simultaneously.

Clark—light on metal—scalpel—coming....

He spun and fired twice in rapid succession. The force of the powerful Magnum sent the dog handler spinning backward. He clutched at himself, bounced off a nearby chair, and collapsed to the floor.

Almost as quickly Macready had the gun turned on the rest. The torch hovered dangerously over the dynamite.

"Don't," he warned them. A couple of the men had taken steps toward him. "Palmer, get to work."

167

The assistant pilot dazedly took up the rope and after a disbelieving glance at his boss began securing the others to couches and chairs. It was slow going and he apologized to each of them in turn as he drew the knots tight. Copper worked in silence.

"Finished," both men finally announced.

"Not quite." Macready gestured with the Magnum. "Tie up Copper, and then Clark."

Palmer frowned bemusedly as he looked down at the dog handler. Clark lay where he'd fallen, bleeding and unmoving. "What for? He's dead."

Macready shook his head. "You forget fast, don't you, Palmer? Norris looked pretty dead himself. Bullets don't kill these things, they just inconvenience 'em. Tie him up."

When that final gruesome task was completed he motioned Palmer over to the doorway and smiled at the others. "Don't anybody try anything. I'll be right back. In much less than an hour," he added significantly.

The two men were gone only a few minutes. The returning Palmer put another case of dynamite on the table, then backed away from Macready and awaited further orders.

"Okay, now untie the doc." Palmer complied. The doctor stood, rubbing his wrists where the rope had begun to cut. "Sorry, Doc. I *think* you're okay. You blew Norris's cover, made the thing reveal itself. I don't think you'd have used that fibrillator if you were one of them. But I can't be a hundred percent certain. Not yet."

Copper smiled wanly at him, walked over and peered curiously into the small box the pilot had put down next to the two cases of explosive.

As he watched, Macready removed a Bunsen burner from the box and attached its long rubber tubing to a gas outlet. He used the blowtorch to light the burner. Sanders closed his eyes when the torch came alive. It was still close to the dynamite. Macready seemed not to care.

Putting down the Magnum he used a pocket knife to cut the multiplug fixture off the end of an extension cord. Then he stripped the insulation back to expose the wire. This was done while still keeping the torch under one arm and a careful eye on the rest of them. Finally he instructed Copper to tie up Palmer.

"We should have jumped his ass." Childs was angry at his own timidity.

"Maybe," muttered Sanders. "Too late now."

Macready finished his work. The Bunsen burner hissed steadily.

"What're you up to, Mac?" Palmer looked uncomfortable. Probably the ropes were hurting him.

"We're going to draw a little bit of everybody's blood," the pilot informed him.

Nauls let out a sharp, humorless laugh. "Right. What are you going to do, drink it?"

Macready ignored him. "Watching what happened to Norris back in there," he gestured toward the infirmary, "plus what I remember from the night out on the ice when one of these things killed Bennings gave me the idea that maybe every part of these bastards is a whole. Every piece is self-sufficient and can act independently if the need arises. An animal unto itself.

"When a man bleeds it's just fluid loss, but blood from one of these things doesn't just lie dormant. Remember what Blair said about each cell being taken over independently? Each one becomes a newly activated individual life form, with the usual built-in desire to protect itself from harm.

"Remember those little pieces of Norris, how they squirmed around and gave off that mewling noise? When attacked, it looks like even a fragment of one of these things will try to survive as best it's able. Even a sample of its blood.

"Of course, there's no higher nervous system, no brain to suppress a natural instinct like that if it's in the best interests of the larger whole to do so. The cells have to act instinctively instead of intelligently. Protect themselves from freezing, say. Or from incineration. The kind that might be caused by a hot needle, for instance." He turned to face the doctor.

"Copper, you do the honors."

"You said you thought I was safe because of what had happened in the infirmary," Copper said.

Macready nodded affirmatively. "I said that I *think* you are. I want to be sure."

Copper noted that the nozzle of the blowtorch had been focused on his midsection ever since he'd tied up Palmer, but he chose not to say anything about it. Obviously Macready

169

had no intention of trusting him until he'd run his little test. There was no point in arguing with him.

"All right, I'll do as you ask, Mac." He picked up the scalpel Clark had dropped and moved over to a chair.

"Sorry, Sanders. I've got no choice."

"That's okay, Doc." The radio operator grimaced as Copper pressed gently against one bound finger. Blood beaded up on the skin and dropped into the petri dish the doctor held beneath the cut. The others stared.

"Now the rest," Macready said impatiently. The box he'd carried the Bunsen burner in also contained a dish for everyone in the room.

Copper moved among them, drawing a small quantity of blood from each and returning the dishes to the table where he labeled each with a marking pen.

He finished with Garry, marked the dish and wiped the blade off on a now red-streaked cloth. "That's the last of them."

"Not quite," Macready said, sliding a fresh dish toward the doctor. "Now you."

Copper obligingly nicked his thumb, and watched as the blood dribbled into the glass.

"Slide it back here," Macready directed him. The doctor did as ordered. "Now step back. Way back, over there with the others."

Copper complied. Sweat was beginning to collect on his forehead. He nearly tripped over Childs's feet.

"And lastly, yours truly." Macready used the scalpel on his own thumb, collected the blood in a last dish. Then he put the bare copper wire protruding from the stripped end of the extension cord into the flame from the Bunsen burner.

The men watched intently as the wire began to glow. Macready held it steady in the bluest part of the flame, keeping the torch aimed at the doctor. Both of them were perspiring freely now.

When it was ready the pilot took the wire out of the flame and brought it toward the nearest plate, the one containing the sample of Copper's blood. His eyes were fixed on the staring doctor and a finger was tense on the trigger of the blowtorch.

A soft hiss rose from the petri dish. Macready reheated

the wire and repeated the experiment. Again the hissing, and that was all. The blood in the dish had reacted normally. Both men let out a sigh of relief.

"I guess you're okay, Doc."

Copper's relief was palpable and his reply was only slightly facetious. "Thank you." He was trembling.

"Like I said," Macready reiterated, "I didn't think you'd have used that current on Norris's body if you were one of them." He favored the older man with a weak smile. "It's nice to know for sure again that somebody's nothing more than they're supposed to be.

"Here. Give me a hand." He handed over the torch. "Watch them. And don't forget the dynamite."

Copper nodded, resolutely training the unfamiliar instrument on the bound men while Macready moved his own dish to the edge of the table where everyone could see it clearly.

"Now I'll show you all what I already know and what you can't seem to believe." He heated the wire and stuck the tip into his blood. The same harmless hissing that had risen from Copper's dish now rose from his own. As with Copper, he repeated the action. Same result.

Childs turned away, unable to meet the pilot's gaze. "Doesn't mean anything. Load of bullshit."

"Yeah? We'll see." He studied the dishes, chose another. "Let's try Clark." He heated the wire again, placed it in the handler's dish. More hissing . . . and nothing else.

Childs glanced up at him. "So according to your figuring, that means Clark was human, right?" Macready nodded slowly. "So that makes you a murderer."

Macready ignored him, looked over the group. "Palmer now." He pulled out the proper dish and put the wire into the steady flame from the burner.

Garry was shifting uncomfortably on the couch. His arms were cramping. "Pure nonsense, like Childs says. This won't prove a damn thing."

"That's just what it's supposed to prove." Macready gave the station manager a nasty grin. "I thought you'd feel that way, Garry. You were the only one who could have gotten at the blood in the infirmary refrigerator." He put the wire into Palmer's dish. "We'll do you last."

171

A horrible screech filled the room, sharp and piercing . . . and unexpected.

It came from the red liquid in the petri dish, which was making an amoeba-like attempt to crawl up the vertical walls of the glass. . . .

13

With incredible force Palmer exploded out of his seat straight toward Macready, dragging the couch with Garry and Childs still tied to it along with him. His face was splintering as something fought to get out from behind the fleshy human mask. He barreled into Macready and knocked him clear over the other card table.

"Copper!" the pilot screamed as he went over backward. The room was filled with shouts and curses as bound men fought their restraints. Shouts and curses and a deep, inhuman bellowing.

The doctor tried to fire, but mishandled the unfamiliar controls of the blowtorch. By that time the steadily changing thing that had been Palmer had burst its bonds and jumped on the older man.

Macready dove onto Palmer's back and the three of them went rolling across the floor. He pounded at Palmer's head until a huge, not quite formed arachnid arm split out of the shirt and sent the pilot skidding across the linoleum.

The distraction allowed Copper to regain control of the torch. He swung it around, trying to aim it. There was an awful crackling like the splintering of heavy plastic.

Palmer's mouth split from chin to forehead. A new mouth, dark and vitreous and horrible, moved forward and inhaled the entirety of the doctor's head.

The torch went flying, bouncing off a wall. Climbing to its feet the Palmer-thing wrapped lengthening arms around the dangling, twitching body of the unfortunate doctor. The rest of the men were hysterical. Sanders was crying and praying, refusing to open his eyes, hoping that if he didn't look upon the horror it might go away.

Macready shook the cobwebs out of his brain and scrambled across the floor to grab up the torch. He raised it, aimed and fired.

Nothing happened. The blow against the wall had damaged it. Frustrated, he got behind Palmer and began hammering on the shifting, changing skull.

The shirt on Palmer's back erupted in the pilot's face, exposing not an arm this time but the beginnings of a second set of jaws. Something like a tentacle lunged out of the widening maw, reaching for Macready. He managed to dodge it, throwing himself backward. He bumped into the overloaded table and howled as the Bunsen burner scorched one hand.

Burner . . . he fought for balance, dug at the nearest box of dynamite and pulled out three sticks. He passed the short fuses over the hissing burner. They caught instantly.

Palmer was turning in awkward circles. The body of the doctor hung limply from the contracted mouth, swinging and throwing the thing off balance as it turned to advance on Macready. The second mouth was spitting and snarling as it continued to take shape.

The pilot dodged and ducked, almost knocked sideways by the whirling body of Copper as the thing tried to decide what to do with the doctor while simultaneously focusing on Macready and changing into its natural form. Macready waited until it was barely a yard from him before tossing the lit roll of explosives into the ever-evolving orifice that sought for him.

There was nothing left of the fuse as the pilot turned and flung himself toward the couch, covering Garry and Childs with his body.

There came a muffled *boom*. Parts of limbs and skin and half-formed organs of unknown purpose and peculiar design went flying in all directions. There was surprisingly little blood or any other kind of fluid, for that matter.

But there was a lot of something else.

As they dried out, droplets of cremated flesh continued to slough off the ceiling and rain down on the benumbed men. Macready climbed off his two helpless charges. It took him longer than normal because he was shaking so badly.

"You two okay? Childs? Garry?" Both of them nodded.

After regaining his bearings Macready pulled one of the remaining torches from the box on the table. Then he spent a gratifying if disgusting ten minutes frying every fragment of the thing that still showed signs of life. When that was done, he sat down in a battered chair and waited.

Eventually he'd calmed down enough to resume the testing. Copper wasn't around to help him now. His hand still trembled slightly as he heated the wire in the burner. Thank God, he mused, it hadn't been snuffed out during the fight, or the tubing pulled out of the wall. If that had happened the room would have filled up with gas, which the explosion would have ignited, and all their troubles would have been over. Because all of us would've been all over, he thought.

He checked the dish's identification: Nauls. Copper had written that. Copper was gone now.

Quit thinking about it, he ordered himself. It's not over yet. He looked over toward the cook.

Nauls closed his eyes and tensed as Macready touched the hot wire to the dish. It generated a mild, unthreatening hiss. Macready exhaled slowly and Nauls opened his eyes.

He didn't even bother with the obligatory second try. That didn't seem necessary anymore, not after the way Palmer's blood had reacted. Moving around the table he untied the cook, keeping a torch aimed at the others. Nauls accepted the torch and took up the guard duties while the pilot returned to the burner and reheated the wire.

Sanders next. Macready ran the test, was rewarded with another hissing. The radio operator lost control of himself and sobbed on his knees.

Macready nodded to Nauls, who walked over and untied the distraught Sanders. "Come on, man," he told him, "get yourself together. We ain't got time for this. You're clear, but we ain't finished yet."

Sanders nodded, wiped his face with his freed hands and was given another of the small blowtorches.

Childs looked stoical as the two younger men moved to cover him. His gaze was on Macready.

"Let's do it, man."

The wire dipped into the dish, was followed by the

174

familiar, harmless hissing. The muscles of the mechanic's face melted into a relieved smile.

"Muthafu . . ." He couldn't finish the word. It trailed off into the wheeze of the Bunsen burner.

Suddenly it struck him who or what he might be sitting next to. He started trying to pull away, his eyes wide with the realization.

"Get me . . . get me the hell away from . . . cut me loose, damn it! Somebody, cut me loose! "

Nauls hurried to comply, and began sawing at the ropes with the scalpel as Sanders and Macready stood guard. Garry, ignoring the mechanic's hysteria, didn't move. Childs nearly fell in his haste to get off the couch and away from the station manager.

"Gasoline," Macready said stolidly. Sanders hurried out of the room, returned in minutes with a two-gallon can whose contents he proceeded to dump over Garry's head. Garry continued to sit motionless on the couch, staring straight ahead. The radio operator backed off, raising his torch, his face full of fright but ready nonetheless.

Nobody breathed. Childs had picked up a torch. His finger was tense on the trigger as he stared expectantly at Garry. Macready readied himself as he slowly brought the heated wire down into the last dish.

It produced the comforting hiss of evaporating blood. The pilot frowned and tried it a second time, got the same result. The blood boiled away freely and did nothing to hint that it could be anything except normal human blood.

Everyone let out a sigh of relief. Sanders cracked up again, this time out of happiness. Childs flopped exhaustedly into an empty chair as Macready wiped his face. There was a long silence.

"I know you gentlemen have been through a lot," the station manager finally said quietly, "but when you find the time, I'd rather not spend the rest of the winter tied to this couch."

Childs started to giggle. For the first time in days, the strain began to slip from Macready's face. Nauls scowled at Childs's uncontrollable laughter.

The wind howled overhead, tearing ineffectually at the roof. It had never stopped, but during the past anxious hours it had been completely forgotten. Now it was a familiar, friendly reminder of threats that were quite normal. The men welcomed it.

The cook put aside his torch and walked over to untie the station manager, grumbling at Childs.

"Okay, man, we're all happy. That's enough."

Childs choked back his remaining laughter and wiped tears from his eyes. He sat up and grinned at Macready.

The grin vanished immediately. The pilot was staring, silent and stone-faced, out the window. Snow and ice battered at the triple-paned glass. Childs frowned, connecting the stare with some long-forgotten thoughts. His eyes grew wide as he remembered.

Macready had remembered first. "Blair," he whispered.

The wind roared and clutched at the three men who pulled themselves forward along the guide ropes. Each man carried a flashlight, a flare, and a blowtorch. In addition, Macready's parka was filled with enough dynamite to demolish the entire outpost.

The flares flickered weakly in the gale, but still far outshone the beams from the flashlights. Ice formed on warm beards, stung the men's faces and tried to freeze over their snow goggles.

It wasn't far to the toolshed where they'd imprisoned Blair, but the storm made it seem like ten miles. Icy wind ripped at them, trying to tear their gloved hands away from the life-saving guide ropes so it could send them spinning blindly off into the Antarctic night. Twenty yards from the compound the orange smear provided by its external lights was wiped out by blowing snow. Without the flares and flashlights the trio making their way upslope toward the shed would have been completely blind.

Macready and Childs readied themselves as they neared the shed. Nauls banged into them from behind and the men exchanged irritated looks, but no one said anything.

They could see the shed clearly now. The heavy boards that had sealed off the entrance lay scattered about in the snow. They'd been broken or torn from their nails. The door flapped in the gale, banging against the front wall of the building.

They paused in front of the doorway, trying to steady

themselves against the wind. Macready and Childs had their torches out and the flares held in front of them.

"See anything?" Childs shouted. The wind made his voice seem to come from far away, though they were standing next to each other.

"No." Macready gestured with his flare and Childs nodded his understanding. They entered together.

It was much quieter inside the shed. Unlike at Macready's old shed, the roof was still intact here. They strolled around the single room. Nauls checked the portajohn chamber. The table still stood in the center of the room. Off to one side was the single cot. There were two stacks of canned goods, a neat pile of spare blankets, and a large can full of drinking water. Heat poured from the portable propane radiator.

Everything appeared normal, undisturbed, except . . . the door had been broken open, and there was no sign of Blair.

Childs tumbled in the darkness and uttered a soft curse. He looked down to see what had tripped him, and suddenly he was on his knees.

"Hey Mac, Nauls . . . come here."

They joined him, staring downward. The loose floorboard that had caught his boot came up easily. So did those immediately around it.

Nauls turned his flashlight downward while Childs and Macready held their flares over the opening. Instead of dull ice there was a large hole. The cook moved his light around but was unable to locate a side wall.

There was something in the hole, something large and inorganic. It reflected the light.

Macready's voice was hushed. "Let's get the rest of these boards up." Childs bent to lend a hand.

It didn't take long to remove the rest of the floor. All the boards had been loosened, the nails removed, and then had carefully been laid back in place. Only a loose plank like the one that had tripped up Childs would have warned an observer that something was amiss in the toolshed.

When they finally finished they found themselves standing in the shed's doorway. The excavation occupied the entire interior of the shed. The metallic object nearly filled it.

It was crudely fashioned, but streamlined. Sheets of corrugated steel lay piled in one corner. The corrugations had been smoothed out and the sheets sandwiched together to form thick plates. There was no sign of bolts or welding.

Enough gaps and rough places showed in the object to indicate that it was still incomplete.

"What is it?" Nauls muttered, trying to make sense out of the peculiar angles and ridges.

"Everything that's been missing," Macready told him. "The magnetos, electronic components, other supplies. I'll bet your food processor's in there somewhere, too. The motor, anyway." He nodded at the construction. "All of that missing stuff's been worked into . . . this."

"Spaceship of some kind," Childs whispered in awe.

"I hope to hell not," Macready countered. "If it's that smart maybe we ought to just give ourselves up and let it take over. But I wouldn't bet on it." He leaned into the hole and moved his flare around, illuminating different portions of the incomplete vehicle.

"I'm sure as hell no engineer, but I know a little bit about flying machinery. I don't see how it could make the walls thick enough, or where it would get the compounds to make a powerful enough propellant. Of course, maybe it doesn't need thick walls. Maybe it uses some kind of energy shield instead. Hell, maybe it just climbs aboard and wishes itself elsewhere.

"But I'd bet against the spacecraft theory."

"What then?" Childs asked.

Macready continued to scan it with the flare. "It's some kind of ship, for sure. Since it doesn't need a spaceship, I'd bet on some kind of aircraft. Or a short-range rocket booster. Smart son of a bitch. He put it together piece by piece. And all this time we've been worrying about poor, cooped-up, crazy Blair. I'll bet he hasn't been 'Blair' for some time." He pulled his head out of the hole and nodded back in the direction of the main compound.

"All the others—Palmer and the dogs, they were just decoys to keep us away from here, keep us occupied so the thing could work on this in peace. Almost worked, too. Would have, if we hadn't come up with that new test."

Nauls stared into the hole. "Where was he trying to go?"

178

"Anyplace but here," Macready replied. He unsnapped his parka and searched inside, extricating a bundle of taped dynamite. "But he ain't going to make it."

A screeching. Piercing and far away, smothered by the gale blowing outside, but it made Macready twitch nonetheless.

"Hurry," Childs urged him.

Macready nodded, then used his lighter to ignite the fuse. They backed out of the doorway and he tossed it into the excavation.

They were a minute down the walkway, clutching the guide ropes for support as well as guidance, when the ice heaved behind them. Even in the storm it was satisfyingly loud. Fragments of metal and wood showered past them.

"That's that, then," muttered Nauls.

"Yeah." Childs tapped him on the shoulder. "Watch where you're going." A gust of wind knocked him sideways as he tried to step around the cook. His boots spun on the slick surface and he grabbed the rope with both hands as he went down on his knees, trying to steady himself.

Then the rope was gone, all tension vanished as it gave way somewhere behind them. The end went whistling past the mechanic and the wind sent him tumbling after it.

Macready clung to his own fragment of line as he saw Childs vanish into the darkness. Something bumped into him from behind and he screamed. It yelled back at him as it skittered off into the snow.

Good-bye, Nauls.

The screeching came again, louder this time. It was definitely somewhere behind him.

Frantically, Macready fought to orient himself. The compound had to be there, straight ahead. He thought he could make out the dim glow of the outside lighting, but he wasn't sure. It might be that exhaustion and cold were making him see lights where there weren't any. He struggled forward on hands and knees, hoping he was crawling in the right direction.

That awful, grating wail was growing nearer. Was it coming after him or was he heading toward it? He remembered what had happened to Copper, remembered the half-formed abomination that had come out of that yawning mouth before he'd fed it the dynamite. It might be at his heels now, flicking about over the snow, searching for him, waiting to wrap itself around a leg and draw him down, down into. . . .

He missed the entrance to the dog kennel and its outside doorway, missed seeing Nauls crawl over the rim to tumble down the open ramp to safety.

But he bumped up against the main compound. Desperately he began searching along the wall. The supply room window he'd used to get inside when they'd locked him out earlier ought to be nearby, a little to the right.

And then he was falling. It was a short, unexpected drop. The frozen burned plants he landed on did nothing to cushion his fall. He rolled over, holding a throbbing shoulder. It rotated. Nothing broken, then.

Standing up he took stock of his surroundings, noted the shattered skylight he'd fallen through, and tried to orient himself. Where the hell was he? Couldn't be supp . . . oh yeah. Childs's illegal-but-tolerated "garden." He stumbled forward and rested against the open door as he caught his breath.

Something groaned overhead, followed by a tinkling sound. He looked up at the skylight. Something was bending the steel-support bars outward, widening the opening so it could get inside.

He sprinted for the hallway door. Fuchs's frozen corpse was there to greet him, still pinned to the wood by the deeply imbedded axe. The body was blocking the door handle.

The splintering sound grew suddenly loud behind him. A backward glance showed something black and knobby flailing around inside the garden room.

Unaware that he was moaning softly, Macready finally got Fuchs out of the way long enough to wrench open the door. He slammed it shut behind him and threw the latch.

He rushed up the corridor, skidding around the turns and taking steps two at a time, locking every intervening door behind him. His heart was hammering at his ribs as he raced for the recreation room.

Something slammed into him around the next junction and he screamed.

"Shit, man!" said Nauls, almost crying. "Don't you ever watch where you're going?"

"Christ." Macready eyed the cook up and down. They

180

hadn't been separated very long. Surely not long enough for takeover to have occurred. "Where the hell did you come from?"

"Fell into the doghouse," Nauls told him, fighting for breath. "What about you?"

Macready looked back the way he'd come. The corridor behind them was still quiet, still empty. He knew it wouldn't stay that way for long.

"Came in through Childs's skylight. You know, the one over the little room he and Palmer turned into their private pot patch. The thing was right behind me." The knowledge of how close it had actually been chilled him far more deeply than had the brief sojourn outside.

"What do we do now?" Nauls was pleading for reassurance.

Macready couldn't give him that, but he did have an idea.

"We know it doesn't like the cold. It can tolerate it, but only for a while. We blew up its transportation and that means it can't hang around looking like itself. It's got to find another live body to take over. Come on." He started up the corridor.

They worked quickly and efficiently in the recreation room, pouring gasoline into empty bottles. They'd had three of the small blowtorches left. All three now lay somewhere outside in the snow, lost when the guide rope had been severed. Neither man had any intention of going outside to hunt for them. The Molotov cocktails would have to serve as a substitute.

Garry was busy nearby, stringing a thin wire between two battery-charged generators. Sanders had taken over the task of readying the last of the Molotovs. He held the funnel steady and emptied the last drop of gas from the last can into the glass. The activity gave him back a little courage.

Coke adds life, he thought grimly, noticing the label on the bottle. But not this time.

Macready sat at the nearby card table, fooling with some empty gelatin capsules he'd scrounged from the infirmary. A loaded hypo rested nearby. He'd inject a portion of the syringe's contents into a capsule, carefully set it aside, and move on to the next.

Nauls came skating in with another box of dynamite.

181

Repossession of his wheels boosted his confidence the same way pouring the gas helped Sanders.

He put the crate alongside the others. There was now enough of the explosive in the rec room to blow the compound halfway to Tierra del Fuego.

He looked over at the busy Macready. "What are we going to do about Childs?"

"Forget about Childs. He's gone." Macready spoke without looking up from his work. "If he was still in control of himself he'd have found his way back here an hour ago."

"You don't know that for sure, man." The cook used a small crowbar to pry the lid off the dynamite crate. "Remember how long you were stuck out there before we let you back in?"

"You mean, before I let myself back in," Macready reminded him. He shook his head regretfully, refused to reconsider the matter. "He's been outside too long. That thing out there's had too long to work on him. If it was able to find him. The wind was pushing him along pretty good. He could be halfway to the pole by now."

"But we don't *know* that," Nauls argued. "Why should it bother with him? He's stuck out there in the snow, alone and unarmed. It's got plenty of time to go looking for him. Wouldn't it make more sense to ignore him and take care of us first?"

"Hell, how should I know?" Macready replied gruffly. "I don't think like it does. But I'll bet you're right about one thing."

"Yeah, what's that?"

"It getting ready to take care of us."

Garry spoke softly, separating the two with words. "Make those fuses short, Nauls. They'll go off quicker if we need to use them."

The cook nodded, favored the indifferent Macready with a final scowl, and turned his attention to the linen wicks protruding from each Molotov cocktail.

Garry rose and made sure the wire running across the main entrance to the recreation room was stretched taut. The two generators sat off to either side, out of sight from the hallway. Macready had finished his task with the capsules and was straining to maneuver a storage cabinet into place, blocking one of the other side doorways.

Sanders put the last gas can aside and stared at the main entrance and its almost invisible wire barrier. "What if it doesn't come?"

Macready rammed his shoulder against the unwieldy cabinet. "It'll come. It needs us. We're the only things left to expropriate. Give me a hand with this, will ya?"

Sanders obliged, adding his weight to the pilot's. As soon as the storage cabinet was in place they started wrestling one of the heavy video game consoles toward the second doorway. It took another console to complete the job. One of the games was Space Invaders. No one tried to joke about it.

Macready turned to his helper, gesturing with a thumb toward the last unbarred opening. "You and Nauls got to block off the west side bunks, the mess hall, and the kitchen."

Nauls looked at the pilot as if he'd gone over the edge. "You crazy? It might be inside there already."

"Chance we got to take," replied Macready evenly. "We've got to force him to come down the east side to the door we've got rigged for him."

"Why me?" Nauls wanted to know.

Macready stared at him. "Why not you?"

"Okay, okay. Don't give me that what-are-you-look." He started for the door.

Sanders licked his lips and tried to think of a fault, any fault, with Macready's reasoning. "He might just chose to wait us out."

Macready shook his head. "Uh-uh, I think not. He froze solid here once." He indicated the window and the howling polar storm raging outside. "Maybe it's not as cold here now as it was a hundred thousand years ago, but I'll bet it's cold enough. He could freeze up again, and this time would be the last time. So he's got to come inside."

"All right," countered the radio operator, "so he waits us out from the inside."

Macready smiled. "That's where we've got him. As soon as you and Nauls get back I'm going to blow the generator." He indicated the rectangular metal shapes stacked neatly in one corner. "Garry and I lugged all the portable heaters in here. He'll have to come for us, or freeze." He turned and started pushing a small couch toward the door blockaded by the video consoles.

"We can run the portables off those." He nodded toward the generators linked by the single wire. "We can sit here as long as necessary and outlast him. But I don't think that'll happen. He isn't stupid and he'll figure out his options are limited. Oh, he'll come for us, all right."

Sanders joined Nauls in the doorway.

"Hold it a sec." Macready finished positioning the couch, then went over to the card table where he'd been injecting capsules.

He handed each of them one of the bright red containers. They looked like ordinary cold pills.

"Sodium cyanide," he said quietly. "If it comes down to it, put one between your cheek and gum and bite down hard. This thing can't control anything that's dead. If it could, Fuchs wouldn't be decorating the door in Corridor G." Sanders and Nauls regarded the capsules silently.

"If it gets a hold of you, like it did Copper, use 'em. This stuff's supposed to be fast and painless. They issued me something like it in 'Nam. Never thought I might have to use it here. Now, move it."

They vanished down the hallway. Macready listened until the rumble of Naul's skates faded into the wind. Then he turned to where Sanders had been working and started checking the wicks on the Molotovs.

Garry was running current through the wire blocking the main entrance. The generators hummed, the air crackled, and there was a satisfying amount of smoke and sparks.

"Looks good," Macready complimented him.

"A thousand volts." The station manager checked the reserve level on one of the generators. "That ought to be enough. It's a hell of a lot more than the doc gave the thing that was trying to look like Norris."

Nauls shoved the portable stove around on greased wheels. It squeaked anyway. He managed to wedge it against a locked kitchen door. Across the room Sanders was rolling one of the refrigerators in front of a second door. As soon as it was in position, he bent over and jammed the butcher knives he was carrying into the rollers.

A sudden surge of sound drifted in to them. A purring, bubbling noise. Sanders froze, and turned to face Nauls. "You hear that, man?"

Nauls glanced over at him. "Hear what?"

Suddenly the noise was all around them. Familiar noise, erupting from the stereo speakers flanking both ends of the kitchen. Electric guitar, drums, organ, synthesizer. Someone had the camp-wide system going on maximum volume.

The same thunder swamped the rec room. Macready and Garry stared dumbly at the three speakers fastened to the walls. The pilot shouted at his companion. Garry's lips moved, but all Macready could hear was amplified electronics.

Neither man could hear the other. . . .

14

The music filled the corridors, the empty sleeping rooms, the supply section, and the lavatories. It penetrated the walls and shook the floors.

Except for Childs, who had maintained it, Nauls knew that system better than anyone at the outpost. He shouted over the din and gestured back toward the rec room.

"It's got into the pub!" he screamed at his companion. "It's turned on the stereo!"

Sanders gaped across the room at him, straining to hear. "What say?"

Nauls headed for him. "It's between us and the rec room. How are we going to get back?"

Sanders shook his head, looked frightened and confused. "Can't hear you, man!"

In the recreation room Macready cursed steadily as he ripped first one speaker and then another from their wall brackets.

"What are they doing back there?" he asked the station manager, nodding toward the distant kitchen. The music boomed from only one remaining speaker now, but its pounding ostinato continued to reverberate through the rest of the compound.

Garry stood close by the wire entrance and peered down

the hallway. Nauls's voice reached him as a distorted wail.

"What's he saying?" Macready asked as he tore at the last speaker.

Garry shook his head. "I can't make it out."

"What's that?"

"Macready!" Nauls was howling. "We been cut off!" He leaned cautiously into the corridor. "Hey, can't you guys hear me up there?"

Something went *whump!* against the door at the back of the kitchen. Nauls turned to stare as a large, scythe-like blade poked through the heavy timbers and began sawing downward. Black ooze stained the fringes of the cut. The blade itself was an unrecognizable shade of nonmetallic red. Odd color for a knife. The sound of tearing wood was largely obscured by the blare from the stereo speakers.

Eyes bulging, Sanders pointed a trembling hand at the disintegrating door. A second knife-blade appeared alongside the first, together with more of the lubricating black substance.

Nauls backed away from the splintering barrier as he realized that the dual blades were not knives. They were fingernails.

Sanders had put his back against the third doorway when another pair of talons came crashing through the thinner wood to spread and lock around his neck. He struggled briefly as he was yanked backward. There was a wistful expression on his face as his bit down on the cyanide capsule just before he was wrenched through the broken door.

Nauls wasn't one for futile gestures. Sanders had bought it. The other door was giving way as he took off through the single remaining exit. Crouching low, he shot out into the corridor. His skates sent sparks flying.

In the recreation room a familiar and nerve-tingling screech rose above the music. It was sharp, distinct, louder than ever.

Macready bent under the wire and looked down the hall. There was no movement. Small speakers continued to bellow their indifferent electronic litany from far rooms.

Nauls had skated like this only once before in his life. It had been back in Chicago. The local gang, the Crips, were after him. The mothers were fast, but not as fast as a frightened teenager on skates. It was late, he had no business being out in that neighborhood, and cockiness had overcome common sense.

He'd gone shooting right past their street corner, leaving them furious and startled in his wake, and he'd skated until he'd thought his legs were going to drop off. Around fences, down deserted streets, leaping curbs and gutters, flying through the vacant urban night.

Now he leaned hard into a turn and kicked with his legs as he accelerated down a straight corridor. Not far, he told himself desperately, not far to home. To Delancy Street, to the rec room. His eyes were glazed. He was a bullet, spinning down the barrel of a gun.

Sanders's body came flying out of the hallway wall directly ahead of him. A thick, knob-encrusted arm pinned it like a fly to the paneling opposite.

Nauls skidded and lost his balance as he tried to stop, slid into the nearest wall hard. The cyanide capsule went flying out of his mouth. He ignored it. The rest of whatever had taken the radio operator was starting to crumble through the wall.

He got to his feet and started forward again, leaping over the flexing, massive limb and rolled on the floor just like they'd taught him to do in gym class. Then he was back on his feet and skating like a roller derby jammer for the next turn.

Macready was out in the corridor and running toward the kitchen. He hadn't gotten very far when Nauls came careening around the corner toward him.

"Get back!" the cook screamed at him. Macready slowed but didn't stop.

"The generator. . . ." he started to say.

"Screw the generator!" Nauls shot past the pilot's reaching hand. Hisses and unholy snarls rose above the music. Something like an ambling earthquake was coming up the corridor. Macready turned and rushed after Nauls.

Nauls barely remembered the wire and just did duck under it as he skidded into the rec room. Macready was right behind him chugging like an overheated engine, the cook collapsed on the big couch.

"What happened back there?" Garry asked him quietly.

Nauls looked over at him. His words came in bunches.

187

"Got Sanders . . . he got into his capsule, the poor son of a bitch . . . World War Three wouldn't mess with this fucker . . . can go through walls . . . and it's big, lots bigger than we thought . . . maybe never reached full size before it froze way back when . . . it's like *all over the place.* . . ."

"Calm down and get into your position," Macready told him.

Nauls started off the couch. "Position, my ass. . . ."

Garry worked on the generators, readying them. "I'm going to bump this up as much as I can. We'll have to risk a burnout. It ought to do it."

"Boulder Damn might do it," was Nauls's opinion.

Unexpectedly, the loud music that had been blasting through the compound ceased. Something had turned it off. Or maybe the tape had run out.

Garry whispered to the pilot. "Lights."

Macready nodded and flipped the main wall switch. Each man assumed his predetermined station as the rec room was plunged into darkness. The wind moaned overhead.

Their attention was concentrated on the wired doorway, though after Nauls's description of the way the thing had assaulted the kitchen they didn't neglect to watch the two blocked entrances or the walls.

They waited in the darkness for the thing to come for them. Silence filled the compound.

When some time had gone by and nothing had happened, Garry finally spoke. "How long's it been?"

Macready checked the faint glow of his watch. "Little over two hours, I think."

From behind him Nauls sounded hopeful. "Maybe it ain't coming. Maybe it's going to try and wait us out, like you said earlier. With the generator still on, the rest of the camp'll stay pretty warm."

"Then we have to go after it," Macready told him.

"Bet that's the last place you ever go."

"Shusshhh!" Garry quieted them. "Listen."

In the eerie silence they clearly heard the sound of a far-off door opening, then closing. The action was repeated. It was still far away and accompanied by a rustling noise. Macready and Nauls moved a little farther apart.

A soft bubbling came from outside. It was followed by a

tentative scratching at the door. Garry's fingers tightened on the generator controls. The scratching intensified, then grew louder. Macready's voice was a strained whisper.

"Wait. Wait until it gets through the door." Garry nodded, his palms damp on the main switch.

The scratching had risen to a steady, insistent pounding. The door was heavier than most in the compound. Nauls and Macready quietly lit a pair of Molotovs and concentrated on the entrance.

The door boomed hollowly as something massive threw its weight against it. The room began to shake. Dirt fell from cracks in the quivering ceiling. Macready raised his arm and aimed the slowly flickering Molotov.

Then the roof gave way and *it* dropped into their midst. Instinctively the three stunned men threw themselves away from the dark mass occupying the middle of the room. As he stumbled backward Macready heaved his Molotov and from the other side of the room Nauls did the same.

Both struck close to the thing's right side. For an instant they could see it clearly: a raging, constantly shifting gelatinous form silhouetted by the flames.

Garry bolted for the door. As he jumped something erupted from the center of the humping mound and speared him. The unaffected two-thirds of the enormous body followed its probing tongue or tentacle or whatever it was and engulfed the hapless station manager before he could get the door open.

A chitinous limb lashed out and sent Nauls sprawling. Macready dodged its mate, dove at the generator and threw the switch.

Current ripped through the wired doorway, electrocuting Garry with merciful speed. One of the thing's talons, caught in the door where it had pinned him, twisted away from the crackling pain. The door came away from its hinges and the pinioned talon began pounding it against the floor, trying to shake it loose.

Nauls scrambled frantically through the gap where the door had been. But the seething, screeching horror was between Macready and the exit. Macready's brain screamed at him to do something. The capsule lay against his right cheek. The other two doors were heavily barricaded from the inside, too heavily for him to free one in time.

The window. . . .

He jumped for it and yanked down convulsively on the emergency fire lever. It was tight from lack of use. He put all his weight into a second try and stepped aside as the heavy, triple-paned glass tumbled into the room. Something struck his boot a glancing blow as he scrambled out into the storm.

Battered and bloodied, dragging one leg, Nauls crawled along the corridor. Not only his leg but his mind must be damaged, because he was sure he could hear the sound of a revving motor. It must be the regular shuttle flight, come to carry them away to safety, away from the repellent alien monstrosity that would tear the compound apart in its search for the last humans it could take over.

But the plane wasn't due for months. It only came in winter on rare clear days, and anyone could hear the storm howling outside, howling and screeching and wailing, coming closer and closer.

Terror made him crawl faster, oblivious to the pain in his broken leg. He didn't know that it was broken, only that when he tried to stand fire shot through it and brought him down.

Bathroom stall, close by. He crawled in and locked it. The gurgling that had been pursuing him grew louder. Nauls leaned against the back of the toilet, looking around desperately. He was imprisoned in a tiny wooden box, no windows, only the thin slatted ventilator. A nice little box, all wrapped up for Christmas dinner, a skinny little turkey waiting for big daddy to start carving him up. . . .

The gurgling stopped somewhere on the other side of the door. There came a scratching at the wood. A low moan rose from the depths of Nauls's throat, a sound he couldn't and didn't try to control. He began ripping at the weathered wood forming the back of the stall. Blood started from beneath his nails as he clawed at the reluctant paneling.

A powerful blow struck the door as he wrenched aside one plank. It came away in pieces. Something dark was starting to come through the wood.

Nauls put the jagged end of a large splinter to his throat and gave it a spasmodic shove. . . .

The sound of the motor was loud in the deserted lab. One moment the walls stood firm and the next moment they seemed to explode as the tractor barreled through the wall, its huge shovel tearing half the room to shreds. Glass and wood shattered against each other. The refrigerator and its incriminating load of frozen blood went over on its side like a toy.

Macready was in the driver's seat, his eyes wild, his expression like those usually seen on the faces of inmates in mental institutions. He's made a run for Supply, gone in through the broken window there and gathered up the box of plugs and the breather spring that had been removed from the tractor's engine. Instinct and luck had directed him through the storm to the maintenance shed.

Frostbite formed black warpaint on his exposed cheeks and fingertips. A stick of dynamite was a red slash between his lips. On the seat next to him rode a pair of large metal cylinders marked "HYDROGEN." There were no weather balloons left for them to send soaring into the Antarctic sky. Macready had a different destiny in mind for them.

He let the tractor grind to a halt. Snow swirled around him as he took the stick of dynamite from his lips. He was smiling and no more than half crazy.

"Okay, creep," he shouted toward the interior of the compound, "It's just you and me now! Be on your toes, if you got any. We're going to do a little remodeling. Time to let a little fresh air inside. You like the air around this country, don't you?"

He settled back into the driver's seat and gunned the engine, sending the huge machine ripping through the next wall and into the infirmary. Medical equipment and supplies went flying. The operating table got thrown into the far wall.

The big tractor had been designed to move tons of solid ice and rock. The prefabricated walls crumpled like tinfoil under its heavy treads.

The mess hall was next; tables, chairs, and now-silent speakers splintered beneath the relentless shovel. Macready's voice lifted above the wind. He was singing a ribald Mexican folk tune as he demolished the camp, but his eyes searched every corner and missed nothing.

On through the kitchen. Gas hissed from a broken pipe, the stink of propane momentarily tainting the air before the wind whisked it away. The demented troubador in the driver's seat sang on.

A taloned arm slunk around a corner, for the first time moving away from a human voice instead of toward it. Macready's voice echoed down the hall.

"Chime in if you know the words, old boy. You'd like Mexico. Nice and warm there. No ice to lock you up for a few millenia. You'd like to get there, wouldn't you? Like to hop into my bod and go lie on the beach and pick out a few señoritas to take over? Too bad you'll never get there."

Several more rooms were destroyed before he reached the pub area. He halted the tractor's headlong plunge and backed it up a few yards.

"Medical stopover," he announced to the storm, still whistling his cheery tune into the wind. Somehow a bottle of Jim Beam had survived the chaos unscathed.

"You like whiskey?" he shouted toward the intact remnants of the compound as he pulled the stopper. "Come on, join me for a drink. Be good for you. Put fangs on your chest." He swallowed a substantial slug, felt fire slide down his throat and pool up in his belly. It felt wonderful.

The tractor rammed into the rec room. The engine started to grind. A few intermittent chugs brought it to a halt beneath the hole in the ceiling created by the thing's earlier, unanticipated method of entrance.

"Damn it," the pilot muttered, the smile still on his face, "ran out of gas. Oh well, hi ho, time for a stroll."

As he fiddled absently with the hydrogen tanks his eyes searched the gap overhead, the remaining doorways, the accumulated rubble. Wind-borne ice particles stung his face and hands.

He checked them. The fingertips were as black as if he'd been carrying charcoal, and he winced. Not from any pain: they were too numb for that, but from the knowledge of what might happen to them.

Then he sat back and laughed. Here he was sitting and worrying about his fingertips, like some damn beauty queen. His gaze roved unceasingly over the ruins.

"Sweetheart, it's going to get mighty cold here pretty soon. You better make your move before I die on you, too. Then you'll really be stuck. I mean, I'm only one person, and everybody knows Americans taste better than Norwegians anyway, right?" He upended the bottle and took another swig, keeping his eyes busy. The tractor's headlights still burned, illuminating the wreckage.

"I know you're bugged because we ruined your trip, right? Spiffy little toy you had there. No room for a stewardess, though, and the legroom definitely wasn't first class."

A slight tremor rocked the tractor and he went quiet, listening. He glanced toward the hole in the roof, then around the devastated rec room. Pulling his butane lighter from a pocket he flicked it alight and cupped the flame near the short wick protruding from the single stick of dynamite.

"But your real hang-up," he continued, fighting to keep his voice casual, "is your looks."

The tremor was repeated, slightly stronger this time. Something was pounding away in the darkness, a steady, regular sound that seemed to come from everywhere around him. It took him a moment to realize it was his own heart.

"Atta boy," he murmured encouragingly, "I know you're around. Here's papa. Y'all come visit."

The floor shook slightly beneath the tractor. He stood, searching the dark areas as well as those lit by the machine's headlights. "Come on. Come shake hands, sucker," he whispered tensely.

The tractor rose several inches. Macready lost his balance and tumbled forward, arms windmilling. He found himself staring into the engine at something that might have been a face.

A claw flashed up at him, splitting the steering wheel but missing his face as he threw himself backward.

He kicked at the accelerator and the tractor bounded ten feet. As it rumbled past the gap in the ceiling he jumped and grabbed the edge of the hole.

Ahead of him the thing's face and arms burst through the metal plating of the engine housing. Reaching claws just missed his legs as he scrambled onto the roof. A frustrated hiss echoed through the room below.

Macready steadied himself on the quivering roof. It threatened to collapse any second. He lit the short fuse on the dynamite and tossed it toward the tractor cab.

Half the thing's grotesque body emerged from the opening behind Macready, screeching in fury. Something flexible and tough as a rubber hose whipped out and wrapped itself twice around the pilot's chest, tightening and yanking him backward.

At that instant there was an immense explosion, the leaking hydrogen tanks igniting and sending a white fireball fifty feet into the night sky. Mixed in with the flames were the carbonizing remnants of the thing's body.

The force of the blast smacked Macready from behind and shoved him off the roof. He crashed into the snow below. The severed and now lifeless limb was still wrapped around him, burning along with the back of his jacket. He tore off the limb and flung it aside, then rolled over and over in the snow until the last of the flames eating at his back were smothered. . . .

There wasn't much left of the camp. Half of it was a blackened, smoking ruin and the rest a garbage heap, thanks to Macready's manipulation of the bulldozer. The storm had settled considerably. Still-burning fires illuminated the ruins and the southern lights danced overhead.

Macready stumbled through the devastation, several thick blankets wrapped around him. Whether the spare parkas had gone up in flames or lay buried beneath the rubble or were simply lying around somewhere waiting to be found he didn't yet know. But the multiple layers of blanket kept the wind off and much of the cold away from his abused body.

Pain bent him double. It was hard to limp from one hot spot to the next and wield the fire extinguisher with much accuracy. He mumbled something, though there was no one to hear him, finally gave up and flung the inadequate extinguisher aside. It clanged off something unyielding and metallic: the twisted bulk of Nauls's stove.

The pub area was largely untouched by the fires, a kind providence having apparently decided that now that he'd disposed of the thing's final manifestation he could stay comfortably drunk for the rest of the night. He smiled thinly. He was looking forward to a five-month binge.

He leaned against the handmade bar and lit a cigar from the pub's undamaged stock. His hands were heavily wrapped. No gloves were lying conveniently about, but there'd been plenty of insulated tape in the ruins of the infirmary. What was left of his hands benefited from the bandaging anyway. He puffed on the cigar and poured a double, no soda please, into a glass that was only slightly chipped.

Something grabbed him by the shoulder and spun him around. He was too exhausted to scream.

A face stared back into his own: Childs. White-and-black blotches mottled the exposed skin and icicles decorated the mechanic's woolly beard.

"Did . . . did you kill it? I heard an explosion." Childs's mouth wasn't working too well. His lips were cracked and stained with dried blood. A weak gust of wind caused the powerful frame to stagger. Lack of food and exposure to the elements had severely depleted the mechanic's strength.

"I think so," Macready told him.

"What do you mean, 'you think so'?" Childs stumbled backward a few steps.

They eyed each other suspiciously, the voices guarded. Macready was suddenly alert.

"Yeah, I got it." He gestured with a mummified finger at the mechanic's face. "Pretty mean frostbite."

Childs kept his distance and exhibited a puffy, pale hand.

"It'll turn again soon enough. Then I guess I'll be losing the whole thing." He kicked out first his right foot, then the left. The movements were feeble, shaky. "Think my toes are already gone."

Macready had salvaged one of the card tables and set it up nearby. Carrying bottle and glass he limped over and sat down in the single chair. The back was cracked but the legs were still intact.

A chess set rested on the table, its power wire hanging loosely over the side. By some miracle the box of pieces that had been buried beneath it had survived the cataclysm. Several piles of cards lay nearby. Macready was in the process of combining them to form a single, complete deck.

The two men continued to eye each other warily. "So you're the only one who made it," said Childs.

Macready was setting up the chessboard. Tiny magnets held each piece to the metal board despite the steady wind.

"Not the only one, it looks like."

Childs found a couple of blankets and gratefully wrapped them around his upper body. "The fire's got the
195

temperature way up all over camp. Won't last long, though." He nodded toward the pub's missing wall.

"Neither will we."

"Maybe we should try and fix one of the radios. Try and get some help."

"Maybe we shouldn't."

"Then we'll never make it," the mechanic said calmly.

Macready puffed on the cigar until the tip glowed red, then reached down into the bundle of supplies he'd gathered. From the middle of the pile he pulled a small, cylindrical metal shape.

"Lookee what I found. This one works." He carefully put the blowtorch on the table next to him.

"Maybe we shouldn't make it," he added speculatively.

Childs eyed the blowtorch. "If you're worried about anything, let's take that blood test of yours."

"If we've got any surprises for each other," the pilot replied, "we wouldn't be in any condition to do anything about it. Any testing can wait." He paused, then asked cheerfully, "You don't play chess?"

Childs studied the pilot, then hunted through the wreckage outside the pub. He returned carrying a second chair in reasonably good condition and placed it across the table from Macready.

"I guess I'll be learning."

The pilot grinned and handed the mechanic the bottle. Childs leaned back and drained half of what was left. When he put the bottle down he was smiling.

Around them the persistent fires smoldered on, riding a sea of frozen water. Bright embers levitated by the wind rose lazily into the night sky. The ghostly ribbon of the southern aurora pirouetted overhead, masking many of the stars that had come out in the wake of the storm.

Macready nudged a pawn two squares forward. . . .

ABOUT THE AUTHOR

ALAN DEAN FOSTER, a Scorpio, was born in California where he completed his schooling. After serving a hitch in the U.S. Army, he worked as a copywriter in a public relations-advertising firm. Since then he has taught Motion Picture History and Writing at Los Angeles City College, as well as Literature at U.C.L.A.

A prolific writer, Foster has written very successful novelizations of *Alien, Dark Star, The Black Hole, Outland* and *Clash of the Titans*. He has also had ten novels published including the five Humanx Commonwealth volumes, *Midworld, Cachalot, Icerigger, Mission to Moulokin* and his most recent one, *Spellsinger*.

A red belt in Tang Soo Do (a form of Korean Karate), Foster's hobbies are backpacking, body surfing and basketball. He and his wife recently deserted the Pacific Coast to live in the Arizona desert.

Inside Boston Doctor's Hospital, patients are dying.
No one knows why,
No one but . . .

THE SISTERHOOD

Nurses bound together in mercy. Pledged to end human suffering. Sworn to absolute secrecy. But, within the Sisterhood, evil blooms. Under the white glare of the operating room, patients survive the surgeon's knife. Then, in the dark hollow silence of the nighttime hospital, they die. Suddenly, inexplicably, horribly. No one knows why. No one but the Sisterhood.

One man, a tough, bright doctor, risks his career, his very life, to unmask the terrifying mystery. One woman, a beautiful and dedicated young nurse, unknowingly holds the answer. Together they will discover that no one is safe from . . .

THE SISTERHOOD

A Novel by
MICHAEL PALMER

"Compassion turns to terror . . . Riveting reading, I couldn't put it down."

—V. C. Andrews, author of *Flowers in the Attic*

THRILLERS